WHITE MIST

REGENCY RAKES
BOOK FOUR

JACLYN REDING

OLIVERHEBERBOOKS

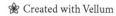 Created with Vellum

PROLOGUE

Cha d'dhùin doras nach d'fhosgail doras
No door ever shut but another opened.

*L*ife as she had known it had ended.

It had happened the morning of the 12th of September 1820—and she had never seen it coming.

Lady Eleanor Wycliffe, heiress of the Westover dukedom—the most illustrious dukedom in all England, no less—had been raised as a good many gently-bred young English ladies are. Her days had been filled with ease and comfort, with nothing more expected of her than to turn a neat stitch, hold an elegant posture, conduct herself in a polite and agreeable manner.

Since before entering the schoolroom at the exalted Miss Effington's Academy for Ladies of Gentle Breeding, Eleanor had been taught that her sole ambition in life was to marry well, to entertain graciously, to do her best to provide that as yet unknown future husband with that as yet unborn, all-important male heir.

Sit up straight, miss. Square your shoulders more.

You need to glide, dear, not stride.

1

You must needs hold your fingers just so when you pour.

Indispensable words whispered to her by an assortment of elder females, words solely intended to send any lady between the ages of twelve and two-and-twenty into a state of abject fear of ending up alone, like So-and-So's sister or Lady Whoever's niece, those social pariahs known to all as—spinsters.

Shudder.

Eleanor, however, had had a marked advantage in it all.

Unlike those poor young girls whose marriages were arranged sometimes without much more than an introduction between the bride and bridegroom, (like her best school chum, Lady Amelia Barrington, who two years before had forever joined her life with that of her father's favorite whist partner), Eleanor had been told since the age of four that she would have the opportunity to choose her lifelong mate.

She had done her part during her first Season in society, searching for and then finding a man with whom she shared common interests, one who treated her kindly, and who could provide her a home and the same comforts to which she was accustomed.

Richard Hartley, the third Earl of Herrick, was handsome, polite, and well-spoken of amongst the best society. He enjoyed books and had an ear for music, as did she. He didn't purposely correct her when she pronounced a word differently than he, and he listened, truly listened to the things she had to say. Had she loved him? They hadn't had nearly enough time together to truly determine that. But it had been a beginning with promise. Eleanor knew they would get on well together, and the best part of it was that Richard's country house, Herrick Manor, was but two miles from the Westover ducal estate in Wiltshire, making him, Eleanor believed, a most sensible choice.

How funny life was, she remembered thinking, that fate had brought them into one another's lives as far away as London when their families had been neighbors for generations. Eleanor had simply taken this as one more reason why they were perhaps meant to spend their lives together.

Her brother, Christian, however, hadn't agreed with her logic.

Christian Wycliffe, Marquess Knighton, was a decade older than Eleanor, and had been family patriarch since the death of their father before Eleanor had been born. Christian had been reluctant about the match with Lord Herrick from the start, but his reluctance, he assured her, was simply due to the fear that she had settled too soon, had chosen too quickly, this only her first Season "out" in society.

"Give yourself time, Nell," he'd said to her when she'd first mentioned Richard to him. "There is no need to rush headlong into something so soon."

But rushing headlong into things was a trait Eleanor seemed to excel in, such as the time she had decided that she did not wish to be left at home with her nursemaid whilst her mother and Christian had gone off to a ball. So with all the foolish bravado of a seven year old, she'd twisted herself into the small compartment hidden behind the seat inside the Knighton landau coach, thinking that once they arrived, her mother would have no choice but to allow her to stay. What Eleanor hadn't considered was the possibility that once she got into the compartment, after having been jostled about during the ride, it might not be so easy getting out. The result was that instead of attending the festivities, Eleanor's mother, Lady Frances, had spent the evening standing alongside, twisting her handkerchief in her gloved hands whilst Christian, the Knighton coachman, and several others had been made to nearly disassemble the carriage to free her.

Still, despite her brother's lack of enthusiasm, Eleanor had remained confident in her choice of Richard. After all, almost all of her acquaintances were already married, and the young man suited her well. They passed a good part of several months earlier that year, dancing, walking in the park (always under her mother's watchful eye, of course), heading toward that inevitable moment when Richard would make the offer for her hand. The society matrons nodded their beturbaned heads in approval, and Eleanor waited patiently while everything had followed its proper course, just as had been prophesized throughout her girlhood—

—until the 12th of September, when Christian had revealed to Eleanor exactly why the marriage with Lord Herrick could never, ever take place.

For a day that would bring about upheaval to rival the trembling of the earth, it had begun with a most deceptive calm.

Eleanor had been visiting at Skynegal, the castle her brother shared with his wife, Grace, in the northwestern Highlands of Scotland. It had been a chill morning, signaling the end to summer with a brisk prelude to the coming autumn.

Eleanor had awoken early, just as the first light was peeking out over the eastern hills, shimmering on an iridescent frost that had dusted the heathery slopes beyond the castle walls. Everything had seemed so *fine.*

She had taken breakfast alone in her room, relishing some quiet time by the glowing warmth of the peat fire, tucked beneath the folds of a woolen blanket while reading and even sewing a bit. She had thought to pass the whole of the day in similarly peaceful pursuits, until shortly before midday, when a letter had arrived for her bearing the distinctive heraldic seal of the Earl of Herrick.

Richard had written to her from a property his family held in Yorkshire, and in the letter, just as Eleanor had longingly anticipated, he had proposed their marriage, following up with information about his London solicitor, Mr. Jeremiah Swire, who, if she accepted, would see to the signing of the marital contracts and other legal details.

Though not the romantic, bent-on-his-knee, moonlight-cast sort of declaration both she and Amelia B. had whispered about as young girls, Eleanor had been teeming with excitement as she had gone immediately to search out Christian.

She had found him alone in his study.

After reading Richard's letter—twice—Christian sat quietly behind his desk, listening while Eleanor diligently attended to every argument she expected he'd bring forth, and even some he had not thought of. She reminded her brother how his own marriage to Grace earlier that same year and even that of their parents had been arranged by their grandfather, the Duke of Westover. She contended that hers would have a far firmer foundation since she and Richard had spent time in each other's company, had chosen one another instead of having one another chosen for them.

Eleanor had been confident of her position, countering each reason Christian found against the match with another reason for it. When Christian finally fell silent, Eleanor had begun to think she'd won him over.

She couldn't have been more mistaken.

"I'm sorry, Nell. A marriage to Herrick is simply impossible. There is nothing more to be said about it."

The Christian she'd faced at that singular moment had looked so suddenly different from the beloved brother she had always known. He had the same chestnut hair, a shade or two darker than her own, and their mother's striking blue eyes, but the brow above them had been creased deeply and the smile he'd always shown her was no more.

It wasn't until that moment that Eleanor had begun to truly worry.

"But why, Christian? Please just tell me why you are set so decidedly against Lord Herrick? Is it that you think him dishonorable? Is there something you have learned about him that I should be made aware of?"

"No," he replied on a bitter frown. "From everything I have

seen and heard of him, Herrick is the gentleman he presents himself to be."

Eleanor tried a different approach. "Richard told me you didn't get on together as boys. He thought perhaps that might color him unfavorably in your eyes, but I would have thought—"

Christian shook his head. "This has nothing to do with any schoolyard scuffle, Nell."

"Then why, Christian? If I am telling you Lord Herrick is the man I wish to marry, why can you not give your blessing to it? Wasn't it you who always said I'd have my choice? Didn't you promise me that? Well, I've done my part. I've made my choice, and it is Richard."

Christian didn't answer her. He only stared at her, unmoving as well as, it would seem, unmoved.

Frustrated at his stoicism in the face of her future happiness, Eleanor then challenged her brother as she had never done before. She sat upright in the chair, her hands gripping tightly to its arms, and said, "Then you leave me no choice, Christian. Since you cannot think beyond your own feelings to mine, I must tell you that I am prepared to meet Richard at Gretna Green if need be."

"No!"

At no time in her twenty years could Eleanor ever remember Christian raising his voice to her. Not even when she'd ruined his favorite pair of riding boots by tromping about the hedge maze in the rain with them had he spoken so sharply. Christian had always indulged her, often shamelessly, giving her virtually anything she'd ever asked, even filching three of her favorite lemon tarts from the kitchen when she was five years old, despite the fact that it had ruined her appetite for supper.

Thus his sudden outburst that morning had alarmed her. The words he spoke next, uttered in quiet contrast, had utterly gutted her.

"The reason you cannot marry Herrick has nothing to do

with my personal feelings about him, Nell. You could not possibly understand. Faith, you weren't yet born when..."

Eleanor spent the next quarter hour sitting stone still as Christian then poured out a grim tale that began by revealing that their father, Christopher Wycliffe, had not died of the sickness she had been told he had since she'd been old enough to ask. There had been no fever, no last gasp of breath uttered one chilling night so long ago when she was yet a babe tucked away inside their mother's womb.

Instead, Christian went on, telling her their father had died fighting for their mother's honor in a duel against the man with whom she had been having an illicit affair, the same man who quite possibly, nay, probably, was Eleanor's own true blood sire— the former Earl of Herrick, William Hartley.

Richard's father.

Even now, Eleanor could remember the horrible and utter helplessness of feeling that moment as if the very walls had been closing in around her. Her throat had grown tight, choking off any response she might have spoken, her eyes had burned with impending tears. Her breath soon came in gulps as she'd shaken her head against her brother's terrible insinuations, as if by doing so, she could somehow make them go away.

"This is not true, Christian," she sobbed. "I refuse to believe it. Richard told me his father died from a fall off a cliff when he'd been out riding early one morning. No one saw him, only his horse returned to the stable alone. His body was never found. And Mother, how could you make such a terrible accusation against her? Why are you doing this, Christian? Why are you making this up?"

Christian closed his eyes then, battling with his emotions. "I am not making this up, Nell. God, how I wish I was, for I have spent most of my life trying to keep you from ever having to hear these words." He looked at her, visibly torn. "I was there that night along with the duke. (Christian had never called their grandfather anything but by his title.) I watched Lord Herrick fire upon our father. I saw him fall. I knelt beside him while he died. His pistol was lying there in the grass, yet cocked. I picked it up. I didn't know what I was doing. I only saw Lord Herrick walking away. I aimed for him. I—"

Christian stopped, shaking his head, unable to bring himself to speak the next words.

He didn't have to.

"You...you killed him?"

"I swear to you, I don't even remember firing. I only saw him drop into the grass before everything fell into a blur. The next two weeks were the most hellish nightmare. The duke concealed everything of that night, disposing of Lord Herrick's body, bribing the physician to attest that Father had died from an illness. He wanted to banish our mother, too, denounce her publicly as an adulteress, but I begged him not to. I promised him that if he would spare her, and the child she carried, if he would set aside the question of your paternity and go on as things had been, I would do whatever he asked of me. I would give him my life to direct as his heir. And I did."

Eleanor just stared at her brother, as she struggled to keep hold of her every breath. Her ears hummed. Her hands trembled.

A moment later, her consciousness cleared on a single realization.

"This? This is why you agreed to marry Grace almost without ever having seen her first? All those years I wondered why you were so adamant about allowing me to choose when you yourself seemed so unconcerned about who you'd take to wife. All along it was because you had sacrificed your life to protect Mother, to keep anyone, including me, from knowing that I am a really nothing more than a *bastard*?"

Christian just stared at her, his expression frozen with the obvious pain of his regret.

But was it regret that he had had to hurt her? Or regret that he had had to tell her the truth now after all these many years?

If Eleanor had never met Richard, had never thought of becoming his wife, she would have likely spent the rest of her life oblivious to the truth, never knowing that she was not, in fact, the person she had always thought, Lady Eleanor Wycliffe, daughter to one of the most illustrious families in England. She would have never known she was instead a by-blow of an adulterous affair that had resulted in the murder of two men, one very likely her father in blood, the other her father on paper.

When her mother had arrived at Christian's study a short while after, and had confirmed what she'd been told, the shame of it darkening her blue eyes, Eleanor had finally surrendered to her new reality.

Everything she had ever known of her life had been a terrible charade. She had grown up believing that her mother and father had lived a fairytale together before her father had been unjustly snatched away by death. She had believed it because it was what she had been told by the very people she should have been most able to trust.

She remembered thinking of a quote from Euripides' *Phrixus* about the gods visiting the sins of the fathers upon their children, and wondered if the gods punished *doubly* those children whose fathers and mothers had transgressed. If so, then she was surely damned for eternity, for what crueler fate than to have lived the whole of one's life in the role of someone who had never existed?

That night, while everyone else in the castle had been asleep, Eleanor had gone, stealing away under the protective cover of a moonless Highland night. She didn't think to tell anyone where she was going. In truth, she didn't really know herself.

She'd taken fifty pounds she'd found in Christian's study and had used it to traverse the Highlands, making it as far south as the tiny seaside hamlet of Oban. It was there she sat now, sipping blackberry tea in the back parlor of a thatched-roof inn, set along the main street that faced the harbor. She was utterly exhausted, her feet cramped in her slippers from the days of riding and then, after she'd sold the horse, the walking she had done. Nearly all the money she'd had was now gone. She could but think it laughable that once she settled her bill with the innkeeper, she would have just enough left to buy her a place on a packet boat that would take her right back up the coast to Skynegal.

Back to the lies.

Back to the betrayal.

Perhaps it was a sign. Perhaps she should have simply gone on with her life as she always had, blissfully ignorant, pouring tea with her fingers poised just so while pretending not to know the terrible truth of the past. Perhaps that was the person she was meant to be, the secretly illegitimate, blissfully naïve, *false* Westover heiress.

It was just as Eleanor was on the verge of asking the innkeeper's wife for direction to that north-going packet boat, that she happened to spot a notice hanging crookedly on the wall.

Governess needed for a lass of noble birth, aged eight years. Inquire at Dunevin, Isle of Trelay.

She read it again. And then a third time.

What followed was one of those occasions that come along once, maybe twice, in a person's lifetime. Some called it a crossroads, others a deciding moment. Whatever it was, Eleanor knew she suddenly had a choice. She could board that northbound packet boat and go back the way she'd come. She knew what awaited her should she go back. She would spend her life living out a lie, trying every day to conceal the truth of her bastardy while facing daily the pity in the eyes of those who knew.

Or she could follow the leeward path, The untried one, precarious and perhaps even frightening, but on it, she just might find a journey to the truth...

...the truth of just who Lady Eleanor Wycliffe really was.

1

ISLE OF TRELAY IN THE SCOTTISH HEBRIDES

The Prince of Darkness is a gentleman.

— WILLIAM SHAKESPEARE (KING LEAR, ACT
III, SCENE IV)

*H*e heard the ghillie's lumbering approach a full minute before he appeared, huffing and puffing up the steep hillside slope after having made the nearly quarter-mile trek from the castle to get there.

"There's a visitor, laird," the man paused, bending at the waist in order to catch his breath. "A visitor come t' castle t' see you."

Gabriel MacFeagh, Viscount Dunevin, barely lifted a brow at the arrival. Instead, he stood kneeling before what was once a plump peahen, now naught but a mess of feathers and bloody remains partially hidden beneath a covering of thick heath.

"Winter's nearing," he said more to himself than to the man beside him. "The creatures of the isle are on the hunt for the food stores they'll need to keep them through the icy months to come."

The smaller bite marks and telltale lingering odor of musk

told him this work had been done by a polecat, a weasel-like varmint distinguished by a thieving dark mask of fur across its eyes. It was a nuisance they could not afford to ignore. Known to kill merely for the sake of killing, a hungry jill with a litter of kittens had been known to raid her way through an entire henhouse without ever being seen. Even small lambs had been known to fall victim to these nocturnal trespassers. From the looks of the peahen, or rather what remained of it, this jill would soon be coming back.

Gabriel rose up to his full six foot and inches of height, shaking his dark head as he dropped the hen carcass into a sack he'd brought with him in order to keep from attracting other predators this close to the castle.

"Looks as if that polecat was at the hens again last night, Fergus. This is the second one we've lost this week. Better tell MacNeill we'll be needing to set some traps."

As squat as his lord was tall, Fergus MacIan had been the viscount's personal manservant since his becoming laird some ten years earlier. Before that, he had served both Gabriel's brother and their father, having lived on the distant isle nearly all his life. Standing beside Gabriel now, conspicuous in his tartan suit and trews, Fergus scratched his grizzled head beneath his Kilmarnock bonnet and nodded in agreement.

"Aye, we'd best be seeing to it afore much longer, laird. Tha' last time the beast took off four o' the chicks and still we couldna catch it, the filthy *messan*."

Gabriel turned, the hem of his kilt dragging over the knee-deep blanket of heather and sedge that covered the hillside. He whistled for Cudu, his black beast of a deerhound, who was poking his snout among the hollows and marram at the foot of the hill, searching for a rabbit to make sport of.

"Thig a-nall an seo," Gabriel called to him in Gaelic for it was the language the beast best responded to. He watched as the dog

lifted its slender head in response and began loping up the hillside to join him.

Above, Gabriel caught sight of a fulmar in the distance, soaring gracefully over the surface of the churning Atlantic. The bird's narrow wings were a poetic silhouette against the afternoon sun, one that at this time of year offered very little light and even less warmth. A bit off the shore, several herring boats had just started coming in for the night, bearing the silvery fish that would be salted and cured, the staple of the crofter's winter diet. Beyond that to the south-west, he could just make out the hazy hills of Donegal in Ireland, rising like distant islets on the outlying horizon.

Trelay had been home to the MacFeaghs for nearly four hundred years, but the clan had put down roots in the isles long, long before that; just when they had first come to the Hebrides, however, was a story lost to the drifting mists of time.

Ancient legend held that Trelay, "the Isle of the Exiled" as it was called, and its neighboring isles of Colonsay and Oronsay, had been the first landing place of St. Columba after he'd been banished from his native Ireland. The saint had thought to settle there, to continue his good works, but upon climbing one of its hillsides—perhaps even the same one Gabriel now stood upon— and seeing his beloved Irish homeland outlined in the mists, he took himself off for the more northerly Iona, having vowed never to dwell within eyesight of his native soil. Before leaving, he'd established an ancient priory, the rocky ruins of which were still visible on the isle's western shore, a last remnant of a more sacrosanct age for this now ill-fated isle.

"Who is it that awaits, Fergus?" Gabriel finally asked, scratching Cudu's wiry head as he ambled to a halt before him. Even standing on all fours, the dog's head hit Fergus at mid-chest. "Certainly it isn't Clyne, my steward, come early to collect the rents? We've more than another fortnight afore Michaelmas."

Fergus shook his head, kicking a brogued foot through the heath. "Och, no, laird. 'Tis a lass it is who seeks to speak wit' ye."

"A lass?" Gabriel stopped. "Is she mad?"

Cudu whined at the suggestion.

Fergus simply grinned beneath his bushy beard.

"Nae, laird, she looks as if her mind is quite sound. Says she's come from Oban in answer to your notice for a governess for Miss Juliana."

A governess. Gabriel had all but forgotten about the advertisements he'd papered the mainland with nearly a year earlier when the last governess, Miss Bates, had unfortunately left his employ. She had been merely one in a steady stream of others, although he had managed to keep her a sixmonth, longer than most.

It was a series of events that had fast become routine. While he might finally find someone willing to travel to the distant isle, one of the most remote of Scotland, within months, sometimes weeks of their arrival, they would come to him with some sad tale of a sick aunt or helpless grandmother who suddenly needed their attention, requiring that they leave Trelay—immediately.

While in the beginning Gabriel had believed them, even paying one's transport all the way back to Edinburgh, he soon began to notice that with each successive departure, they all of them had that same look in their eyes.

By the time Miss Bates had taken her leave the year before, Gabriel had come to recognize that look...as fear.

After Miss Bates, and despite inquiries made as far away as London and even France, his efforts to secure his daughter a proper governess had not received a single response. Word of the isle's tainted history had, it seemed, apparently traversed international boundaries. He'd just about given up, resigning himself to the inevitable probability that his daughter would never know a world other than this foreboding place, when, now, a stranger seemingly appears out of the very mists, offering a renewed glimmer of hope.

It was on that auspicious thought that Gabriel happened to glance down at his hands, stained with blood from the carcass of the peahen. An image of that same horrified expression his departed governesses had left him with flashed to his mind's eye. He turned to regard Fergus yet standing beside him.

"Ask Màiri to fix our guest some tea whilst I clean up. It wouldn't do for the lady to meet the Devil of Dunevin Castle even afore she's had the chance to unpack her baggage."

She was utterly surrounded by them.

Eleanor could feel their frozen gazes on her at all sides, watching her in silent study as she sat with her hands folded, gloved fingers laced together in her lap. No matter where she looked, no matter how she tried to avoid them, they were *there*. If she closed her eyes, she could almost hear them, their voices whispering to her on the flurry of the island wind—

Run...

Get out now...

Before it is too late...

Eleanor's eyes shot open.

A medley of assorted deer, wildcat, and furry pine marten met her gaze, stuffed and mounted on gray stone walls that were unfinished and rose a good twenty feet above her head. Nearby, a fierce-looking claymore whose scratched and pitted blade had no doubt contended with more than its share of severed heads hung alongside a dagger that looked quite able to gut an ox.

Oh dear, she thought to herself. What in heaven had she just done?

Eleanor sat alone, back lamppost straight, knees pressed tightly together, wondering not for the first time what could have possessed her to come there.

Perhaps she should have listened to the warnings of Mrs.

MacIver, the innkeeper's wife in Oban, cautioning Eleanor not to leave the safety of the Scottish mainland for the remote and perpetually mist-shrouded isle of Trelay.

'Twas the place haunted by lost souls, home of the Dark Viscount, Lord Dunevin—or as Mrs. MacIver had called him— *The Devil of Dunevin Castle.*

"He's the last of the MacFeagh and may they die wi' him," the woman had said in a hushed and secretive voice, crossing herself as if she truly feared the man could somehow hear all the way to the Scottish mainland. "They are a clan branded by generations of unexplained deaths and rumors of otherworldly worship. 'Twas said their kind held mystic powers. Sprung from a seal-woman, they were. Even the name, MacFeagh, had roots itself in the Gaelic *MacDhuibh-shith,* 'son of the dark fairy.'"

As if to lend credence to the woman's dire admonitions, when first within sight of the island as her boat had approached, a sudden white mist had swelled thickly around them. The notion of Charon's mythical ferry approaching the gates of Hades had come upon Eleanor so suddenly so that she half expected to see the dog, Cerberus, with his three ferocious heads and snake-like tail, standing guard at the bleak shore. Even the boatman Eleanor had hired with the last of her money to take her across the choppy waters of the Firth of Lorne had shaken his head when she'd stepped foot from his small smack, his brow tilted sadly as if he truly believed once she disembarked, she would never be heard from again.

"Watch yerself there, lassie," he said, his eyes hinting that he meant more than just the step off the boat onto shore.

But then Highlanders were a superstitious lot, she knew, and Lady Eleanor Wycliffe was not.

Even as she sat now amongst the draft and must of this most ancient keep, Eleanor assured herself that the room didn't really have the looks of the den of Satan. In fact, there wasn't a pitchfork or puff of hellish smoke to be found. There were books tucked neatly in tall shelves, a worn carpet stretched across the stone floor, a broad and battered desk with papers piled properly in one corner.

Behind her, a fire burned happily in the stone hearth. No smell of brimstone filled the air, only salt and mustiness and age, and the earthy scent of the peat that the locals were even now drying on the moor to prepare for the coming winter. The wind didn't howl with the yawning terror of the underworld, but instead whistled through the battlements at the top of the castle's central tower, tugging playfully at the tartan curtains through the narrow window beside her.

Indeed, the place presented itself as just what it was, a very ancient-looking tower fortress on a most remote Hebridean island off the Scottish western coast, and if she put aside all those many things she'd been told about the castle's owner, she could even begin to believe there was nothing for her to be nervous about.

Until a sound came from outside the door then, like an approaching footstep, bringing Eleanor instantly more upright.

He is coming, she thought, and her bravado turned to instant ether as she wrapped her fingers around the carved arms of the chair.

What would she say when he arrived? *Good afternoon, my lord. Yes, I've come to apply for the position of governess to your spawn— pardon me—child. And if you please, I would be ever so grateful if you would not sacrifice me to the nether reaches while I am in residence...*

What if he was truly as terrifying as everyone said? Mrs. MacIver had told her the child couldn't speak, that her voice had been stolen away by her father in effort to keep her from revealing the truth of his evil deeds. And what exactly, Eleanor wondered suddenly, had happened to the previous governess?

With a quick glance away from the dagger on the wall, she

looked to the window, wondering how far was the drop should she need to flee.

"I've brung ya tae."

Eleanor gasped at the voice that came suddenly from behind her. She turned and drew a steady breath to calm herself when she found not the devilish viscount she had expected, but the wizened codger who had answered the castle door at her arrival. She hadn't heard anyone come in.

The man could have stepped straight out of the pages of history, dressed as he was in colorful trews, his head covered by a feathered blue bonnet. His face was blanketed from nose to chin by a grizzled beard. He was shorter than she, with the sort of permanently fierce expression brought on by squinting against sharp winds. He reminded her of the engravings she'd once seen of battling Highland warriors, only instead of a claymore clasped in his hands, he bore a silver tea tray.

"His lairdship bids me to beg yer pardon. He'll be occupied a wee bit longer."

Without bothering to wait for her reply, the man dumped the tea tray unceremoniously upon the table beside her and turned away, leaving just as abruptly as he had come.

The ladies at Miss Effington's Academy would have been appalled.

Eleanor waited until he had closed the door behind him, and then a moment more, before she lifted the lid from the china teapot to peer cautiously inside. It certainly had the looks of tea, she thought, then sniffed the flowery brew, for she had read once that arsenic carried a particularly almond-like scent. She eyed the small plate of biscuits beside the pot, giving the dusting of cinnamon and sugar atop them a most speculative study.

Her first thought, of course, was to leave the tray untouched, but then her stomach thought the better of it, undertaking a decisive rumble. It had been hours in making the crossing from the mainland; it was now nearing the close of day and she hadn't had a bite to eat since breakfast. Perhaps a few sips of tea and a nibble of biscuit would serve to quell the nervousness she felt. Besides, if she was to serve as governess here, she couldn't very well avoid taking meals in the household.

Throwing caution to the wind, Eleanor took up a biscuit and sank her teeth into it.

It was delicious, of course, as much as a biscuit could be delicious, and she finished that one and then another before the clock had passed another quarter hour. She left the third biscuit on the plate and, having finished her cup of tea, stood from the chair to poke about the room in hopes of easing her niggling apprehension.

Eleanor stopped to peer at one object or another that was set about the room—a globe that showed the placement of the constellations, a single-handed lantern clock engraved with dolphins—trying to glean something, anything about what sort of man the viscount might be.

She glanced thoughtfully at the titles that lined the bookshelves, more than a little impressed by the collection. Was he a well-read man, interested in a collection of topics? Or were these many volumes simply an assortment that had been accumulated throughout generations? The angling rod and pair of well-worn boots in the corner might lead her to think he enjoyed a pastime more suited to one blessed with patience. The size of the boots, however, hinted he was no small figure of a man.

Eleanor came to the window and paused a moment there, gazing onto the dramatic panorama below. It was a most beautiful place. In contrast to the bleakness of the rocky shore, the isle's midlands were stunningly lush even at this late time of year, splashed with hues running one into the other like a kaleidoscope of watercolor paints.

Cattle of the darkest black she'd ever seen grazed lazily on the verdant grassy machair overlooking the crude stone jetty that served as the isle's landing point, where she had first arrived not an hour before. Fleecy, black-faced sheep peppered the rolling hillside behind them, while along the distant coast, she spied several small crofter's cottages, motley structures that resembled lopsided stacks of stone topped by roofs made of thatch or green turf.

A dog barked a sudden deep baritone from below and she turned her attention, catching sight not of the dog, but of a lone figure seated upon a boulder that faced out onto the sea. Something about the image, the feeling of isolation on that wind-swept bluff, drew Eleanor's notice. A small brass telescope stood on the table beside her. Curious, she took a moment to bow her head to the eyepiece for a closer look.

The figure of a child, a girl, came slowly into focus through the glass. Dark hair, the color of a raven's wing, lifted on the wind, gusting about her face and eyes like tangled cobwebs. The child seemed not to notice it. Nor did she seem to notice the small lamb standing beside her making a meal of the ribbon sash of her dress. She simply sat there, still as any standing stone, the feeling of loneliness about her so strong, so overpowering, it was as evident as the mist that clung to the isle's shoreline.

There could be no doubt she was the viscount's daughter, Eleanor's potential charge.

"I am sorry to have kept you waiting so long."

Eleanor jerked away from the eyepiece, nearly upsetting the object in the process. She had been so fixed on watching the child, she hadn't heard him come in. This time, though, there was no doubting who he was.

No small figure of a man indeed; he was the most imposing person Eleanor had ever faced. Taller even than her brother, and broad through the shoulders, just his arrival made the room seem inimitably smaller. Eleanor watched as he headed toward the desk, noting his height, well over six feet, the blackness of his hair that swept just below his coat collar.

He wore a belted plaid in shades of dark red, white, and green, with a length of it draped carelessly over the shoulder of his coat. The collar of his shirt was open underneath and his face was darkened by the slight growth of a beard, as if he hadn't shaved in days. His eyes were so dark, she couldn't tell their color, his mouth held no hint of a smile. With his rough looks and presence, Eleanor couldn't help the thought that the title "Devil of Dunevin" suited him aptly.

Her pulse, she noticed then, was drumming.

"I'm Dunevin," he said, "laird of the castle and this isle. I'm the one who posted the notice you saw in Oban." He motioned to the chair she had previously occupied. "Please, won't you sit down?"

He spoke as someone who'd been educated in the south with only the slightest hint of a burr. His voice was deeply timbred, quietly compelling like the distant roll of thunder one heard before a storm. It was the sort of voice that brought gooseflesh to running up the arms of young maidens.

And Eleanor was one such maiden.

Dunevin said without preamble, "Fergus didn't tell me you were so young."

Still struck by the sight of him, the sound of him, the presence of him, it took Eleanor a moment to respond. "I'm sorry?"

"What are you, miss, all of eighteen?"

His direct, almost blunt manner of speaking broke her from her bemusement of him and she answered after first clearing her throat, "I am one-and-twenty, my lord."

He raised a brow. "Indeed? One-and-twenty?"

"Well, nearly." She shifted beneath his unblinking stare. "In any case, I assure you I am quite able to manage."

The viscount watched her, mentally measuring her, she knew. He wondered what a seemingly genteel young lady was doing in a place like his remote island, alone. His silence was beyond unnerving.

"I'm afraid Fergus didn't tell me your name, Miss...?"

"Harte," she responded without thinking, saying the first name that sprang to mind. "Miss Nell Harte."

It was as good a name as any other, she supposed, for it wouldn't have done to tell him her real one, not when the names of Wycliffe and Westover were nearly as renowned as that of Hanover across the kingdom.

"Well, *Miss Nell Harte*," he said, repeating the fictitious name in a way that made her wonder if he were mocking her, "from whence do you hail?"

"Surrey," she lied.

"Surrey?" he repeated.

"Yes."

"The seat of my wife's family is located very near there in a small parish called Abinger. Do you know it?"

Eleanor swallowed, caught with indecision as to whether she should stretch her false tale and tell him she did know it, or admit that she didn't and quite possibly alert him to the fact that she knew nothing really of Surrey other than that it was located in the south of England.

"Abinger...," she answered quickly on a nod, "Yes. Yes, I do."

"Indeed, then you must have shared the acquaintance of the curate there, Mr. Pevensley. It was he who married me to my wife."

Eleanor nodded on a cautious smile, saying even as her brain screamed at her to shut up, "Indeed I saw him shortly before I departed. He was doing quite well."

What in Heaven's name had just possessed her to say that?

"Indeed..."

The viscount fell silent, staring at her again with that same penetrating look that made her want to pull the edges of her cloak more closely about her. Eleanor prayed he wouldn't question her further about the curate. A moment passed. The wind whistled through the window. Eleanor adjusted the cuff of her jacket sleeve.

"References?"

She had been afraid of this, of course, but hadn't been totally caught off guard by it. "I'm afraid I haven't any, my lord."

Dunevin looked at her. "No references?"

She shook her head and simply smiled, folding her hands neatly on her lap before her. She offered no further explanation. She didn't have one.

The viscount leveled her a stare. "Miss Harte, forgive me for being, well, *blunt*, but from what I can see you are barely out of the schoolroom yourself, you have appeared from out of nowhere, from Lord-Knows-Where, certainly not anywhere near Abinger since the curate, Mr. Pevensley, has been dead nearly these five years past—"

Eleanor felt an embarrassed flush rise to her cheeks.

"—You are applying for the position of governess to my only child, yet you have no references to show that you are at all qualified for the position. Quite obviously, given these initial observations, I must assume you have something to hide. Your name probably isn't even Harte. So tell me what makes you think I would hire somebody under these circumstances to see to the care and education of my only daughter?"

Eleanor straightened in her seat, refusing to shrink under his censure. She said in a voice that was surprisingly clear, "Because, if you'll pardon my frankness, my lord, there is no one else *willing* to take the position."

Dunevin stared at her, silent, rigid, quite obviously displeased.

Eleanor opened her reticule and unfolded the notice she had taken from the wall of the inn on the desk before him. "I'm told I am the only one to have shown any interest in the position in some time."

The viscount didn't even bother to glance at it. Instead he stared at her, hard, his mouth turned in a decided frown.

Eleanor pressed on. "I know that the last governess you managed to employ left her position nearly a twelve-month ago. I also know that you have been unable to secure another for the position since, despite numerous inquiries made across the land."

She sat forward in her chair. "Lord Dunevin, while I cannot go into the details of my background, I can assure you I was raised among polite society all my life, not in Surrey, no, but elsewhere. You are right in assuming I have never served as a governess before, which is the reason for my lack of references. My upbringing, however, I believe, more than qualifies me for the job. I can speak both French and Latin, as well as some Italian. I was instructed at the best of ladies' establishments in England. I have poured literally hundreds of cups of tea, have arranged countless dinner menus, and although it doesn't quite look it now," she went on, looking down at her travel-worn gown, "I do know the proper way to dress. I can dance the allemande, the quadrille, the waltz, and dozens of others. I can sew a variety of stitches neatly and evenly. I can cipher. I am accomplished musically. I can recite poetry and quote philosophers. I daresay you'll not find another more qualified for this position in your lifetime—" she took a breath, "—so as I see it, you can allow your daughter to languish without an education for yet another year, perhaps more—or you can give me a chance. That is all I'm asking for, the opportunity to show you that I can teach your daughter the accomplishments she needs to move in society. I assume that is what you are hoping for?"

The viscount stared at her, his expression frozen.

Eleanor sat, returning his stare, half expecting him to turn her out when next he opened his mouth. She had no idea what she would do if he did, where she would go. One thing was certain, if he did turn her out, she was going to have a long swim back to the mainland. She hadn't two shillings left to rub together to keep her.

But, remarkably, Dunevin did not turn her out, at least not immediately. Instead the viscount stood and crossed the room to the window, his hands clasped loosely behind his back. As he stood there, she noticed the way his hair swept just below the collar of his coat, the pensive set of his shoulders. He remained there for several minutes, not speaking, just watching his daughter from the window as Eleanor had from that same vantage moments earlier.

From where she sat, Eleanor could still see that the child had not moved despite the fact that a soft rain had begun to fall. A moment passed. Two. The rain fell harder, driven by the rising wind. Still she sat. Still the viscount stood watching.

Finally, when Eleanor was on the verge of running out to fetch the child herself, she spotted a maidservant making her way from inside the castle toward her. She quickly wrapped a cloak around the child's shoulders and drew her up from her sitting place, walking her back toward the shelter of the castle walls.

Still the viscount did not move.

"What is your daughter's name?" Eleanor asked softly, unable to bear the silence any longer.

"Juliana."

Dunevin turned, his face as clouded as the sky outside. "She does not speak."

Eleanor nodded. "Yes, I know."

He looked at her. And then he shook his head. "The locals have already begun to bend your ear with their gruesome tales, I see, no doubt leaving nothing out in their descriptions. They likely tried everything to dissuade you from making the crossing —" he paused—"and yet you came seeking the position of governess despite their warnings. Why?"

"Fantastic tales about the misfortunes of others do not interest me, my lord. I have always found that idle gossip is naught but the work of th—" Eleanor stopped herself, hoping he didn't realize what she had begun to say.

"—of the devil," he finished, "or so they say. Tell me, Miss Harte, does the same hold true if it is gossip *about* the devil?"

His look to her was suddenly so intense, Eleanor could not think of a single thing to say in response.

The viscount left his place at the window and returned to the desk to open the top drawer with an annoyed tug. "It seems both of us are in need of each other then. You have made a good argument, Miss Harte. You are hired. Anyone who has sense enough to discount the superstitious stuff and nonsense of the mainlanders most certainly deserves at least a chance. The salary is one hundred pounds per annum. Your room and board, meals, are provided. Are those terms acceptable?"

Not six months earlier, Eleanor had spent a hundred pounds and more just on the wardrobe for her coming-out into society and without giving it more than a second thought. But that had been Westover money, money that she now knew was intended to hide the truth of the past behind a mask of propriety.

The money she would have now would be earned on her own. The sense of independence that one hundred pounds per annum gave her was worth more than all of the Westover riches.

Eleanor nodded.

The viscount removed some coins from the desk drawer and dropped them into a small drawstring pouch. He then placed the pouch on the desk before her.

"Consider this an advance on your salary. You might do well to use some of it to purchase a pair of sturdy shoes and a more serviceable overcoat. Winter comes fast to the isles, Miss Harte, and you won't find much use for kid slippers here. My ghillie, Fergus, can make arrangements for you with the cobbler in Oban."

He crossed to the door and opened it on where the very man stood waiting outside. "Fergus, please show Miss Harte to the nursery floor." He turned to her. "You will find my daughter there now. Dinner is at half past six, we keep country hours here. If you have need of anything else, Fergus will see to it for you."

Eleanor stood to leave, wondering at his sudden urgency to be rid of her. "Should I not speak with Lady Dunevin first before going to meet your daughter, my lord?"

Dunevin's face lost all expression. He stood there, for a short time frozen by her words. "I'm afraid that won't be possible, Miss Harte. Apparently the mainlanders neglected to tell you. Lady Dunevin is dead."

And with that, the Devil of Dunevin Castle swept from the room just as suddenly as he had come.

2

_____

Is cruaidh an leònar a bhreugadh
nach urrainn a ghearan a dhèanamh.
'This hard to soothe the child that cannot tell his ailment.

— GAELIC PROVERB

The Dunevin nursery was comprised of three rooms perched at the topmost floor of the castle's donjon, its main tower. Accessed by a succession of turnpike stairs nestled in each of the keep's corner turrets, the task alone of getting there was no easy undertaking.

The first flight of stairs took them to the floor above the main hall, where they then crossed an upper gallery to the adjacent turret. No sooner had they reached the next highest floor than the stairs had come to an end once again, and they were made to cross to the third turret in order to continue on to the next flight of stairs. It went on this way for five floors, necessitating a confused sort of zigzagging pattern through the place until, by the time they reached the nursery at the top level, Eleanor had very little confidence in her ability to find her way back unassisted.

The viscount's manservant, Fergus, whose task it was to direct her through this tangled skein of stairs and towers, explained that the ancient keep had been constructed specifically in that manner as a means of defense. "It would allow the Dunevin laird the opportunity to escape in times of invasion," he'd said, "through a secret passageway that only the laird and his most trusted servant knew about."

Having traversed the complex labyrinth herself, Eleanor could only agree. If she'd had to find her way alone, she'd not have made it past the third floor. In fact, on more than one occasion as they'd made the climb, she'd half expected to turn a corner onto the crumbling bones of some long departed intruder who'd wasted away centuries earlier, still clutching his claymore after getting lost laying siege to the place.

The governess's bedchamber, to which Eleanor was directed first and which would be her own retreat in the days to come, was modest in both size and furnishing, holding a plaided box bed, one side table, a small chest of drawers, and a simple washstand in the far corner. The walls, lime-washed over bare stone, had no decoration save a crude hook that Fergus demonstrated would hold the "cruisie" lamp he'd brought, an iron ladle-shaped fixture that burned by way of a rush pith stuck in a shallow depth of fishy smelling oil.

The room was what was called in earlier days "a mural chamber," built into the very thickness of the keep's walls, and a twin to the one the viscount's daughter occupied one door further down the passageway. It was the schoolroom that took up the better part of the tower's top floor, stretching at great length across the hall.

In contrast to the bedchambers, the walls there were finished in plasterwork and there was a hearth framed in carved stone, indicating to Eleanor that the room had originally served as a bedchamber with the two smaller chambers used perhaps as an adjoining garderobe or servants' quarters. For all its space, though, the schoolroom contained but a single window, the only window on the entire floor.

Eleanor stood now, unnoticed in the doorway, contemplating the play of the waning daylight through that one small window against Juliana MacFeagh's inscrutable profile as she sat across the room. There were just the two of them, Fergus having returned belowstairs shortly after delivering her there, leaving Eleanor to acquaint herself with the silent young girl whose care was now hers.

She was a pretty child, slender, with hair that was the same endless black as her father's. Still damp from the rain, it curled softly below her shoulders, the length of pale ribbon that tied it back from her face hanging limply over one ear. She wore a light blue frock sashed at the waist over white pantaloons that peeked out from under layers of tartan skirts. Her mouth was small, pursed into something resembling a frown but not quite, and her eyes, large on her delicate face, were, like her father's, of a dark, indistinguishable color.

From the outside, she appeared to be a perfectly ordinary-looking nine year old girl, the sort who would spend her days dressing up for imaginary tea parties and arranging her hair in elaborate coiffures. It was only when one looked closer that there was something else about her, something deep inside that kept her distant, somehow untouchable. It reminded Eleanor of a bisque Dressel doll she had once seen in a shop window on Bond Street in London, lovely to look at, but so fragile, it could only be displayed and never played with.

Eleanor entered the room quietly, crossing the lengthening afternoon shadows as she came to stand beside her young charge. Juliana remained where she was, sitting on one of the recessed seats that had been cut into the stone wall beneath the window.

She didn't move. If she at all realized Eleanor was there, she gave her arrival no notice whatsoever.

"Hello, Juliana," Eleanor said, smiling at her in greeting. "I am Miss Harte. I'm to be your new governess."

She held out a hand, but the child did not move to take it. She did, however, glance at Eleanor briefly, allowing a slight wrinkling of her forehead, indicating that although she might not speak, Juliana could indeed hear.

A moment passed. Juliana went back to staring out the window, shifting slightly away from where Eleanor yet stood. Behind her, the rain trickled spiritlessly down the window pane, the wind soughing across the courtyard below like a plaintive moan. Time ticked by. Eleanor searched for something, anything to breach the interminable silence between them.

"We have a little time to us before the dinner hour," she said. "The rain will keep us from going outside, but I thought perhaps we might find something here to occupy us."

There came no response.

Eleanor said to the back of Juliana's head, "Do you read?"

Again, nothing, so she turned to look about the room for a book or a plaything or anything that might engage the little girl's interest.

The place, she decided immediately, was as bleak and as characterless as a book filled with nothing but empty pages. Except for a single faded map of Scotland that looked as if it had been drawn two centuries before, the walls were bare and painted in a pale nothing of a color that wasn't quite green, wasn't quite beige, but something hideously in between. The furnishings, stiff and unappealing, had been covered in the same lackluster color, a finishing touch to the aura of cheerlessness that pervaded the place. Narrow iron bars flanked the outside of the window, and although likely intended as a measure of safety, it only lent to the impression more of a tollbooth than a haven for learning.

The only other ornament, Eleanor found with dismay, was a slender, well-worn birch rod propped menacingly near the door.

It was no wonder the child spent her time looking out the window.

On the shelves, Eleanor noted a few examples of the typical children's literature, Aesop's *Fables* and the tales of the Grimms alongside Wedderburn's more rudimentary *Institutiones Grammaticae*. Sparse toys that looked as if they'd never been touched by a child's hand stood beside others that had endured through generations of play. One in particular, a wooden doll with painted black eyes and curled flaxen hair, caught Eleanor's eye.

She was a fashion doll, one used by dressmakers in France to display their latest designs in miniature to their English patrons. She was fully dressed in quilted petticoats and linen shift under a gown with hooped skirts such as those popular in the previous century. But it wasn't the elaborate costume that drew Eleanor to it. There was something in the doll's expression, a twin to Juliana's same faraway look, that brought her to reaching for the small figurine.

Juliana sprang to her feet, moving from her window seat to pull the doll quickly away from Eleanor's grasp. She stared at Eleanor with silent, narrow-eyed suspicion.

"Oh, I wouldn't have harmed her," Eleanor said softly. "I was just going to look at her."

Juliana said nothing. Instead, she returned to her seat to once again face the horizon through the window bars. She held tightly to the doll, sitting in that same way a rabbit would when cornered, rigid and unmoving, as if hoping to disappear into its surroundings.

Eleanor approached Juliana again, slowly this time, lowering onto the window seat beside her. She leaned forward and rested her arms on her upraised knees as she watched, and waited. "She's a very pretty doll, Juliana."

Juliana kept her eyes fixed staunchly on the window, making

no effort to respond. Her only movement was the soft breathing rise and fall of her chest.

"You know," Eleanor persisted, "when I was a girl, I had a doll quite like her. She was called a 'Queen Anne' doll but I named her 'Frances' for my mother because she looked just like—"

Eleanor forgot her next words. Juliana had abandoned the window and turned suddenly to look at her. Her mouth may have said nothing, but her dark eyes were filled with such stark longing, Eleanor was taken by a chill that had nothing to do with the inclement weather.

Like her own childhood toy, this doll was obviously a connection for Juliana to the mother she had lost; considering its age, perhaps even a remnant from Lady Dunevin's own childhood that had been passed on to her only daughter. As she sat looking on the torment that filled the child's eyes, for a fleeting moment, thoughts of Eleanor's own mother surfaced, thoughts she had spent the past weeks since leaving Skynegal stubbornly refusing to acknowledge.

How very much she missed her mother. For as far back as Eleanor could remember, Frances, Lady Knighton, had been more than a mother to her only daughter; she had been her closest friend. From telling her stories at night to teaching her the intricate steps of a dozen different dances, Frances had shared everything with Eleanor. Even now, if she closed her eyes, Eleanor could almost feel the familiar gentle touch of her mother's hand when she had brushed out Eleanor's hair after her bath, a task she had continued even after Eleanor had grown into womanhood.

She remembered fondly her mother's love of wildflowers and the hours she had spent with Eleanor walking through countless country fields, relating little anecdotes about every one they encountered. She remembered the conversations they had shared together, talks of grand balls and the magnificent parties Eleanor would attend when it was finally her time to "come out" into society.

They had planned for that first Season for so long, discussing every detail down to the color of each pair of slippers—even, Eleanor remembered wistfully, what it would be like to be kissed that first time by the handsome young swain who would one day make her his wife.

"It will feel as if the earth has stopped spinning and everything around you has vanished into a shimmering white cloud," Frances had told her when Eleanor had asked one long ago spring day. They had been walking in Hyde Park, a daily outing for mother and daughter. The daffodils and crocuses had been in brilliant bloom, and Frances had turned to face her daughter with a tender, knowing smile.

"The first time you kiss the man you love, for that one moment in time, somehow you will have forgotten even how to breathe. Imagine standing in the very midst of a rainbow, my darling girl. Your heart will have wings and for the rest of your life, nothing will ever be the same."

Eleanor looked now on the innocent face of this child who could never again see her own mother, talk to her, share with her, and felt the urge to reach out to Juliana, offer her some small comfort against so great a loss. "Juliana, I—"

But the moment was shattered nearly before it had begun when Fergus appeared at the door.

"'Tis time for you to come doun to sup," he said, throwing a sidewise glance at Juliana, who sat before Eleanor yet gripping the doll in her arms.

Eleanor let go her breath, nodded to him. "Thank you, Fergus."

She waited until he had gone before turning back to the window, but that rare chance, that brief moment's possibility had already gone. Juliana had retreated, her dark eyes sadly distant once again.

Not wishing to press her, Eleanor stood.

"It sounds as if we are expected belowstairs, Juliana. I'm not quite certain I can find my way back down, though. I wonder if you wouldn't mind perhaps leading the way?"

Juliana simply stared at her. After a moment, however, the child stood and started for the door.

Eleanor followed Juliana quietly as they walked the gamut of upper corridors and towers with only the sound of their skirts rustling against the stone floor and the distant patter of the rain yet falling on the courtyard outside. She tried to think of something to say, some magical phrase that would reach behind that wall of silence to the troubled little girl hiding beyond, but decided to leave Juliana to her thoughts. She had only just arrived and Juliana would need to adjust to this new change in her life. They would have days ahead of them to get to know one another.

The rain had brought on the dusk's darkness early and Eleanor had taken a candle with them to light their way. Its small flame danced and flickered as they walked, throwing silvery shadows against the beautifully woven arras hung from the stone walls.

When Eleanor and Juliana arrived at the dining room, Lord Dunevin was already seated down the length of the dining table. The room was large and brilliantly decorated but it wasn't the silver that gleamed in the candlelight or even the beautiful carved marble fireplace that caught her attention. What Eleanor noticed first upon entering the room was that the table was only set for one other person.

"Good evening, my lord," Eleanor said cheerfully, pretending not to notice as they came in. She bowed her head in greeting. "My apologies for our tardiness. Juliana and I were just getting acquainted in the nursery and lost track of the time."

The viscount looked up from the burgundy in his wineglass. "My daughter does not take meals in the dining room, Miss Harte."

The cut of his words brought an immediate chill to the place that even the fire blazing in the hearth could not chase away. Eleanor shook it off, looked from the viscount to where Juliana stood beside her. The child had bowed her head and was staring at the toes of her shoes sticking out from under her pantaloons, as if she had just been reprimanded for a misdeed. After a moment of absolute silence, she started to turn for the door, to leave, but Eleanor set her hand on her shoulder, stopping her.

"Indeed, my lord," she said, keeping her voice pleasant. "If I may ask then, where does Juliana take her meals?"

The viscount frowned at her. "She sups in the nursery."

Eleanor wasn't surprised by the viscount's pronouncement; a good many members of the nobility chose to live wholly separate lives from their children, only seeing them at scheduled intervals each week and on special occasions, leaving their care to others the rest of the time. But given the isolation of both their home and her muteness, Eleanor would have thought Juliana better served by the company of others.

"My lord, begging your pardon, but beyond the obvious fact that by the time her meal makes it up all those stairs and towers to her it must be quite cold, however can you be certain she is getting the proper nourishment?"

"My servants see to it."

Eleanor frowned at his indifference. "With all due respect, sir, I know of households where the servants would just as soon keep the meat and pastry for themselves while serving the children gruel. Do you think that wise?"

The look that came over the viscount's face then told Eleanor that he wasn't a man accustomed to having his word questioned by anyone, most especially not by someone who had so recently entered into his employ. His eyes caught hers and held them.

"My servants, Miss Harte, have all proven themselves loyal to me through years of service. That same loyalty extends to the members of my family. And need I remind you that you can now be counted among the same servants you have just so gratu-itously accused?"

Meant to intimidate, his words didn't have their desired effect, for though he tried very hard to cloak it in callousness, Eleanor saw something else entirely.

Lord Dunevin was hiding—but hiding from what?

Juliana's muteness? Did that make her somehow flawed in his eyes? Eleanor knew many families in society who would think so. The slightest blemish, the faintest lisp were easily cause for alarm when perfection was the only ideal. Those who were perfect flaunted it, while those who weren't strove to conceal whatever made them unique for fear of society's censure.

"My lord, if Juliana is to make her way among polite society, she will need to learn proper dining decorum. By taking meals at opposite ends of the house, you cannot possibly know if she has learned the correct holding of her fork, let alone the quietest way in which to sip her soup. In a society where one's every move is under constant scrutiny, many a lady's reputation has been damaged by poor table manners. The only way Juliana can learn and accustom herself to the society of others is to practice on a daily basis."

It took Gabriel several moments to realize that he was staring at his new governess without a word to offer in response. This woman, who had appeared virtually from out of nowhere, who stood only to his chin with flashing green eyes and hair the color of the richest sable, had just blithely challenged him as even most men had never done.

Did she truly not realize who he was? That most would quail at the prospect of simply standing before him, the Devil of Dunevin Castle?

He gave her his fiercest scowl, the one that was known to have sent many a fainthearted housemaid fleeing for the main-land, but she merely smiled, yet waiting for his response. He didn't want to relent, to allow Juliana to stay, but at the same time he was unable to argue against what Miss Harte was saying. Juliana did need to learn how to conduct herself in social situations, for there would come a day when she might no longer have the safety of this isle to hide behind.

Wasn't that the very reason he had hired this governess in the first place? To prepare Juliana for the world beyond these shores? Surely he could manage to sit in the same room with his daughter through the course of a meal.

"Very well," was all he said before turning his attention to his soup which Fergus had just begun ladling out. Juliana remained standing, staring from her father to Eleanor.

"There, Juliana," the governess said, smiling and pointing to the chair at Gabriel's right, where the place had already been set. She then lowered into the chair across at his left. Fergus, ever at ready, hastily brought a service to place before her.

From the moment their soup was served, the meal was seized by a silence far more deafening than the tempest that was making its bluster known against the window panes across the room. The storm had moved in suddenly off the firth and Gabriel wondered fleetingly if its unexpected appearance could be attributed in any way to the arrival of their new governess. She was certainly proving to be as unpredictable, as enigmatic as the ever-changing Hebridean skies.

Who was this woman? he wondered, stealing a glance at her as he refilled his wine glass from the decanter. Lowered lashes cast demure shadows against her cheeks in the muted candlelight as she looked down at her plate. What was she doing there? Why was she hiding on his isle—or, more importantly, from whom?

He watched as she lifted up her soup spoon, making sure that Juliana followed her example, and sipped lightly at the steaming broth, a partan bree that was as smooth as it was tasty, a specialty of the Dunevin cook. He watched the tip of her tongue as it ran along the fullness of her bottom lip. The room seemed to grow instantly warmer.

Gabriel knew the governess's name wasn't any more Miss Nell Harte than his was Napoleon Bonaparte, but he also knew that whoever she was, she was a lady of good breeding, certainly naïve to have come to his isle alone, but refined and educated, and since that was exactly what he needed just then for Juliana, she was nothing short of a godsend.

He needed her. He needed Juliana to be taught the social accomplishments that would quickly help her to appear as normal as possible. His time, he knew all too well, was running dangerously short.

Gabriel didn't realize he was still staring openly at the mysterious Miss Harte until she asked, "Is there something you wanted, my lord? The salt cellar perhaps?"

Gabriel quickly looked away and focused his attention straight ahead down the length of the table at the shadows. "No, thank you, Miss Harte."

Silence followed through four courses that felt rather like ten until Miss Harte finally set down her dessert fork and said, "I noticed your stables upon my arrival on the island, my lord. If the weather will permit, I thought perhaps to acquaint myself with the isle's surroundings tomorrow. Does Juliana like to ride?"

Gabriel looked at her as if she'd just spoken in a foreign tongue. While it would be a completely reasonable question to anyone else, she could never realize that to him, it was as impossible to answer as if she'd just questioned why the March hare was mad. In the past three years, Gabriel could count on his fingers the number of times he had spent in his daughter's company. He no more knew if she could ride than if she could turn a proper curtsey. But the governess was looking at him, awaiting his response, and so, after a moment, Gabriel spoke, directing his words to the wall paneling at the other end of the room.

"I cannot say with any certainty whether she likes to ride or not, Miss Harte."

"I see..." She knit her brow over her cup of tea a moment then said, "I was considering Juliana's curriculum earlier in the nursery and thought perhaps to begin our studies with literature. Does Juliana know how to read?"

"I believe she has a rudimentary understanding, but I am not certain."

"Do you know whether she has been introduced to the classics, if she is at all acquainted with Virgil or Homer?"

"I do not."

"Can she cipher? Has she had any musical training?"

This time Gabriel didn't even bother to respond, just shook his head at the wainscoting. Couldn't she understand he wasn't purposely being obtuse—he just truly did not know anything about his own child?

"Can you say with any certainty the date of your daughter's birth, my lord?"

The question had been intended to give him a turn, he knew, to pull his attention away from the opposite wall.

And it had succeeded.

Finally, he looked at her. "February the twentieth, Miss Harte."

Having made her point, the governess simply smiled. "Thank you, my lord. I shall make note of its approach."

The tall case clock standing behind them chose that moment to strike the eighth hour of the evening. Over an hour had passed that seemed more like several. Gabriel suddenly wanted to be anywhere but there, in that room, facing the evidence of the daughter he had neglected these three years past.

He stood, wiping his mouth before setting his napkin beside his dessert plate. "It grows late and I've business to attend to. If you'll excuse me."

The viscount turned from the table before Eleanor could frame any response and without, she noted sourly, bidding his daughter a good night.

He was angry, Eleanor knew, angry at the recrimination of her last question to him, and she probably shouldn't have asked it, but his detachment from the concerns of his daughter had been beyond frustrating. In any case, she had succeeded in reminding him that he did indeed have a daughter, a daughter who very much needed his attention. Why he refused to give it was something Eleanor was determined to discover.

Eleanor looked beside her to where Juliana was staring at her pudding which had remained untouched. Like most everything else that went on around her, the child gave the leaving of her father no notice, at least not outwardly. But inwardly, who could know?

Eleanor stood from the table. "Come, Juliana, shall we see if we cannot find something of interest to do in the nursery for the remainder of the evening?"

She waited while Juliana rose from her seat, pushed in her chair, and headed slowly from the room. As she followed behind the curious and silent child, Eleanor thought to herself that before coming to the island, she had believed there could be no one in the world more lost than she.

She saw now that she had been wrong in that assumption...

...Twice.

3

"**G**ood night, Juliana."

The small ormolu clock on the table down the hall struck its tenth dulcet chime as Eleanor closed the door to Juliana's bedchamber softly behind her. It had finally come, the close to a most uncertain day, one fraught with anxiousness, the beginning of a new life in a most unfamiliar place.

Eleanor started down the passageway but paused outside her bedchamber. She knew if she retired just then, she would only lie awake in the darkness. Even now, her head was brimming with flurried thoughts and unsettled questions, so rather than retire, she decided she would go down to the kitchen instead to see about making herself a relaxing cup of tea.

Everyone else in the castle, it seemed, had retired for the night, for the halls were dark, vacant and silent—not even the rain made any sound. Eleanor took the candlestick with her that she had used to read Juliana a story and made her way slowly along each successive flight of tower stairs down to the lower castle floors. She lost her way only once, taking the left instead of the right tower at the last floor, and found herself somehow standing outside the closed door to the viscount's study, where she had first anxiously awaited him earlier that day. The coppery flickering light of the hearth burned from underneath.

Apparently, not everyone had retired, after all.

Eleanor stood for a moment outside the door, contemplating the mysterious Lord Dunevin. She remembered the direful warnings she'd received of him before coming to the island that day. The people on the mainland had called him a demon, painting him as a grim villain who had committed countless atrocities against any number of hapless victims. Thus far, however, Eleanor had seen nothing to lend credence to those plaintive accusations. Instead of frightening her, the viscount intrigued her, a curious contradiction, a man at odds with himself even in appearance. He was certainly rugged and imposing in stature, but he spoke with such a quiet depth, the voice of a man who sought rather to occupy a place on the periphery instead of the glare of society's censure.

Even with the brief amount of time she had spent in his company, Eleanor had already determined that he carried a dreadful burden. It was in his eyes, so dark and remote, shadowed, and it brought Eleanor to wondering how long he had been without his wife. Had the viscountess died giving birth to Juliana? It might explain why Lord Dunevin seemed so uncomfortable in the presence of his daughter, why he avoided taking so much as a meal with her. Or, perhaps, did he blame Juliana somehow for the loss of his wife?

It had been Eleanor's experience that when somebody lost a loved one, the others in their life were drawn yet closer because of them. The viscount hadn't wanted to be anywhere near his daughter that evening, yet during their interview earlier in the day, he had been so very concerned about the education and care she should receive.

Why, Eleanor wondered, why hadn't he simply sent Juliana off to one of the schools for young ladies that so many members of the nobility were fond of, like her own Miss Effington's Academy? It would have been an easy solution, yet somehow Eleanor knew there was something more to it, some other reason that would remain a mystery, at least for this particular night, anyway, as she turned from the study door and continued on her way.

The kitchen, she'd been told by Fergus earlier that evening, was situated outside the great hall through a covered arcade, and was accessed by a small turning stair in the corner tower. As she made her way there, Eleanor had half-expected to find a place cramped and musty and ridden with smoke. Instead, she came into a large spacious chamber with several other smaller rooms that branched off of it to serve as pantry, scullery, wine cellar.

The moment she entered, the warmth of the great arched cooking hearth wrapped itself around her, drawing Eleanor in like a welcoming embrace. The air was touched by the mingling scents of the peat that fueled the fire and the bunches of drying herbs that hung from hooks in the low beamed ceiling. Iron cooking pots of various sizes and other assorted utensils lined the pristine lime-washed walls in neat rows, and a huge trestle table took up the center of the room on which she found, happily, a small kettle.

She took it and filled it from an earthenware pitcher of fresh water she found standing nearby, then stirred the glowing embers in the hearth, dropping on a fresh brick of peat before she set the kettle on the iron hook that hung down from the blackened chimney.

While she waited for the water to boil, Eleanor searched for the tea, which she soon found in a small caddy chest tucked in a hutch where there were also several porcelain teapots and cups. She set out the things she needed and then took up the boiling kettle to prepare the tea, measuring in the fragrant leaves before she set the brew aside to steep.

Wondering if there might be something in the kitchen she could nibble on with her tea, Eleanor turned. She nearly let out a gasp when she found a woman standing in the doorway behind her, silently watching her.

"Goodness," Eleanor said. "I didn't hear you come in."

The woman simply shrugged. "I thought I heard someone messing about in my kitchen."

She was a stocky figure of a woman, middling age, dressed in a simple linen nightshift that tied at her chin and fell to her ankles. Her hair was a pale wheaten brown streaked through with gray and it hung down the middle of her back in a single thick plait.

"I'm sorry to have awakened you. I—"

"You must be the new governess," the woman said, crossing into the room on bare feet. She took up the water pitcher from where Eleanor had left it and put it back in its original spot, sweeping a hand over the tabletop as if to whisk away a scattering of imaginary crumbs. "I'm Màiri Mórag Macaphee—cook, housekeeper, and resident tyrant."

She turned then and regarded Eleanor, who must have appeared panic-stricken at having been caught invading what was so obviously this woman's lair. The woman smiled broadly, revealing a healthy, easy grin. "But if you'll share a wee cuppa with me, you can call me Màiri."

Eleanor immediately relaxed. "I am El—, Nell, and yes, that would be wonderful."

The woman looked at her, one brow rising slightly. "Nell, it is then."

Màiri took a second cup down from the hutch while Eleanor strained off the tea leaves and poured, taking both cups to a small table with two chairs that stood in a cozy corner. It sat in the glow of the moonlight coming from a window set high on the wall. Màiri followed, stopping first to fetch a small tin of what was revealed to be a buttery shortbread, setting it on the table between them.

"You're a wee bit young to be a governess," Màiri proclaimed

46

over a small bite as she studied Eleanor closely in the moonlight. "Have you no care to take you a husband, lass?"

Eleanor stiffened at the unexpected reminder of Richard, Lord Herrick, and the betrayal of her family, a thing she just then realized she hadn't thought about all day. It was the first time she hadn't since leaving Skynegal.

She answered with a vague, "I have no wish to marry."

"Hmm," Màiri nodded. "That's quite a decision to be making at your tender age. Did he break your heart then? What was it? Take himself off with another lass, did he?"

"No, nothing like that." Eleanor stared down at the table as she feigned at ministering to her tea cup, saying simply, "In the end, we just didn't suit."

"I see." Màiri studied her skeptically over a bite of shortbread. "Well, then, 'tis a good thing you found out afore the vows were said, else you might have ended up like Alys, my youngest daughter, who wed herself to a right lazy sort because she couldn't see naught beyond the bonny blue o' his eyes."

Màiri took a sip of her steaming tea, closed her eyes, and smiled. "*Och*, lass, but that is a fine brew you've made. Finer than any I could make. Wherever did you learn to make such a fine cuppa?"

"Miss Eff—" Eleanor stopped herself before finishing.

Màiri's soft eyes twinkled in the moonlight. "Well, whoever this Miss F. is, she certainly knows her way around a teapot."

Eleanor couldn't help but smile at the woman's easy humor; she already liked her. "The secret is to swirl some of the boiling water inside the pot first to heat it before steeping."

Màiri stared at her. "Is that so?"

But it wasn't the tea she was interested in discussing, or Miss F. "So, Miss Harte, where is it you're from then? My guess would be somewhere around Londontown?"

"I, uh—" Eleanor was prevented from answering when Màiri

suddenly took up both her hands, peering at them in the moonlight.

"Well, wherever it is you're from, it wasna a working life you led there, that much is certain. Not a bit of rough skin on those hands. The only other leddy I ever saw with hands that soft and pure was the laird's sweet wife, Leddy Georgiana. With your polite talk and pretty hands, I'd almost guess you were one o' the quality." She peered at Eleanor closely then. "But what would a leddy o' quality be doing working here in a place like this now?"

The woman's questioning stare searched for more than Eleanor was willing to reveal. She quickly pulled away on the pretense of taking up her teacup. "My mother insisted that I wear gloves when I was young. It was a matter of great import to her."

Màiri gave a slow nod of understanding. She would press Eleanor no more. Instead, she said, "Well 'tis a brave lass you are to come all the way to Trelay to run from your ill-suited beau, but I'm verra glad you did, I am. Miss Juliana needs someone now, poor wee lost lassie. 'Tis a good thing, your coming. So alone she is without her dear mother. What a blessing it would be to hear her child's laughter once again through these lonely halls."

Eleanor was taken aback by Màiri's words. She had assumed Juliana had been mute since birth. "Do you mean to say that Juliana once spoke?"

"*Och*, aye, lass. Spoke, and sang even. She would come in 'ere to this kitchen ever'aday chattering for hours whilst I baked. Even when she would be helping me t' roll out the oatcakes, she would be asking questions, that one, curious as a dormouse she was. Been only since she lost her mother that she hasna spoken. Not a word." Màiri shook her head regretfully over a sip of tea.

Eleanor looked at her, curious now. "Màiri, when did Lady Dunevin die?"

Màiri gave a rueful sigh before answering. "'Twas nigh on three years ago now and afore you ask what happened, I'll tell you nae'abody knows. She simply vanished while walking about the isle one day and hasna been seen since. Whether it were a terrible accident or whether Lady Dunevin took her own life, no one can say." She paused. "No one except Miss Juliana, that is, who willna talk to us about it."

"Do you mean to say that Juliana knows what happened to Lady Dunevin?"

"We dinna know for certain, but she was with her mother when she disappeared."

Eleanor remembered the words of Mrs. MacIver, the innkeeper's wife in Oban. *He stole his sweet daughter's voice to keep her from telling the truth of his dark deeds...*

"Is it possible, perhaps, that Juliana is afraid to speak?"

Màiri knew immediately what Eleanor meant. She shook her head sternly. "*Och,* lass, dinna believe those meddlesome mainlanders who will say 'twas his lairdship that killed his leddy. The laird, he was devastated to lose her, he was. Both he and Miss Juliana, they neither of them have been the same since."

She finished the last of her tea and set the cup down with a decided nod. "But now you have come to the isle to set things to rights." She looked at Eleanor directly. "I feel it in my own bones, I do. 'Tis you who must heal Miss Juliana's broken heart."

"Me? I am but her governess and likely a temporary one at that. She doesn't even look at me when I speak to her. I wonder that she even hears me."

Màiri smiled. "Aye, she hears you, lass. That she does. That child hears ever'athing. It might not seem like it, but Miss Juliana is there, the girl she used to be, just lost somewhere behind her silence. I have seen it, 'tis in her eyes. She tries hard to hide it, but 'tis there. She just needs someone to unlock the words, miss. And tha' someone is you."

Eleanor peered at her. "But you don't even know me."

"I dinna have to ken you, lass. 'Twas three nights afore this one that I prayed to St. Columba, patron of this isle, to bring the wee lassie an angel to save her." She finished on a hopeful smile,

"And you are here now. It canna be more destined than that. 'Tis a beginning, your coming here. Aye, a new beginning and a new hope for us all."

∼

IT WAS NEARLY AN HOUR LATER WHEN ELEANOR FINALLY LEFT THE comfort of the kitchen fire to make the winding climb to her bedchamber for the night.

Màiri, she had decided very soon after meeting her, was a woman of inherent warmth and earthly wisdom and her generous manner had put at ease many of Eleanor's misgivings of the day. After those first innocently curious questions, Màiri had accepted Eleanor's reluctance to discuss herself and had turned the conversation to more social topics, telling Eleanor about the manner of life at Dunevin, the sheltered isolation of the isle, the unpredictability of the Hebridean weather, and most importantly, where she hid that tin of shortbread should Eleanor find herself plagued by what Màiri called "the nibblies" in the middle of the night.

By the time she had returned abovestairs, it was nearing midnight. The light that had shone beneath the door of the viscount's study earlier was nearly gone; but a sparse flicker of ebbing firelight remained.

Eleanor headed for her chamber at the nursery floor, but stopped outside of it, eyeing the door to Juliana's bedchamber down the hall. She remembered how as a young girl she had always found a sense of security in waking each morning to see the break of day through an open chamber door, even imagining it as the lamplight of her own mythological Argus standing sentinel for her with his hundred eyes. Perhaps that same gesture would offer comfort to Juliana come the dawn. With that thought in mind, Eleanor started down the hall for Juliana's door.

She turned the handle quietly so as not to awaken her. Inside was total darkness, but she had left her candle burning on the table in the hall, so she moved a bit to where its light could fall on Juliana's bed across the room. And when the shape of the room finally came clear, Eleanor froze.

The bed was empty.

Eleanor walked across the room, tugging back the vacant covers. "Juliana?"

There came no response.

Eleanor turned for the hall to retrieve the candle and looked all around the room, in the corner chair, inside the wardrobe even, but Juliana was nowhere to be found. She called to her again before realizing the futility of waiting for a response from a mute child. Her heart began to thud in her chest. She had been a governess but a matter of hours and already she had lost her charge.

Eleanor looked under the bed once more on a hapless whim before retreating to the hall. She stopped herself there for a moment to take hold of her scattered senses.

Juliana was *not* lost, she told herself. She was in her own home, a safe place several stories above the ground. No harm could come to her. These weren't the Dark Ages when warring clansmen would come in the midst of the night to raid and pillage and steal. This was the nineteenth century. Blood feuds and the like were a thing of the past. Juliana was inside the castle —somewhere. All Eleanor had to do was find her.

Before heading for the stairs, Eleanor checked in her own bedchamber and then the schoolroom but to no avail. Juliana was nowhere to be found.

Eleanor retraced her steps and took the first flight down to the next floor below and the other bedchambers. She wasn't certain which of them belonged to the viscount, nor did she relish the idea of waking him to tell him his daughter was missing, but she was unfamiliar with the lay of the castle and so conceded she would have no choice but to alert him.

The first two doors she went to were locked, no answer coming to her soft knocking. At the end of the hall there were two doors remaining. Eleanor headed for the one on the left and raised her hand before she noticed that it was slightly ajar. Without knocking, Eleanor pushed the door softly inward to peer inside.

The bedchamber she found on the other side was decidedly feminine in décor. A good many of the furnishings were shrouded by dustcloths and a quick glance at the hearth in the moonlight revealed it hadn't been used at all recently.

The light bed hangings, the finely spindled bed, the lingering soft scents that filled the air—Eleanor need not have looked any further to know that this had been the viscountess's bedchamber. It was a place that spoke of gentleness and sanctuary, and as she made directly for the bed that stood across the room, she wasn't at all surprised to find someone there.

Juliana was lying asleep in the middle of the bed, curved into a tight ball of childish innocence beneath the rumpled bedclothes. The doll Eleanor had remarked on earlier that day in the nursery was tucked safely in her arms. In the light from the candle, the child's face was peaceful, angelic, untroubled, the dullness that had marked her eyes in daylight hidden behind the shelter of her slumber.

Juliana had obviously come here to find the peace she was unable to find elsewhere. Looking on her as she slept so serenely, Eleanor didn't have the heart to wake her, much less direct her back abovestairs. Nor could she leave her there alone, so instead, Eleanor put out the candle, setting the smoking taper on the bedside table, and slid quietly onto the mattress beside her.

4

Bu dual da sin.
That was his birthright

— GAELIC
PROVERB

*G*abriel sat staring silently into the peat fire that burned in the hearth at his feet, watching as it danced molten amber through the brandy in his glass. It was nearing midnight and he was alone in the near darkness of his study, elbows at rest on the carved arms of his chair, his legs stretched at full length before him.

To anyone looking, he would appear the noble lord at ease, his cravat untied and loose around his neck, the sleeves of his cambric rolled over his forearms—except that his mouth wore a frown and his mood a cloak of disquietude heavier than the weight of any boulder.

He'd spent the past hours since supper at his desk going over some of the estate papers, then later, to this chair, listening to the sounds of the castle retiring for the night, the closing of the doors, the banking of the rush lights, the checking of the window latches that could snap open at a sudden gust blowing in off the firth. The rain had slowed some time before, and it had been well over an hour since he had heard the last footstep, no doubt that of his ghillie, Fergus, shuffling out of the great hall for his chamber in the castle's opposite tower.

It had been a long and disconcerting day and Gabriel knew he should have already taken himself off to bed. There was a harvest to prepare for and the winter beyond that. Plans needed to be made for the stock and the plenishing of the isle for the bleak months to come. Sleep, however, would not come easy for the Dark Lord of Dunevin.

All night, even as he'd been going through his paperwork, Gabriel's thoughts had been occupied by the events of the day. The unwelcome image of Juliana's dark absent stare at supper that night, the memory of what had once been, haunted him still.

Could it really be that just three years before laughter had spilled from that sweet child's lips like the first dappled sunlight breaking through the clouds after a storm?

It seemed almost impossible to believe that his daughter had once sung with the voice of an angel. Just to hear her calling him "Da" had been each day's utmost reward. A light had shone within her more brilliant than the brightest star. Each day had been a new and glorious adventure...

...until Fate had come along to remind Gabriel that there was a terrible consequence to be paid for his foolish bid for happiness —one that had stolen both his daughter's sweet voice—and his young wife's life.

Lady Georgiana Alvington had been all of seventeen years when Gabriel had first seen her, standing like a fragile golden daffodil across a crowded London ballroom. It had been spring, he remembered, the beginning of another mad London season, and he had just returned from the Peninsula after having received the news of his brother Malcolm's untimely death.

Gabriel hadn't planned to attend any festivities that evening; he was in London only long enough to see to the legalities of the estate and the transfer of the title of Dunevin to him. It was his colonel, Barrett, who had requested he go to the ball that night; the hostess, after all, was his colonel's wife.

"You'll have time on your hands in town before you can depart for the Highlands," Barrett had said with a pat to Gabriel's shoulder. "With the boys all gone to the Peninsula, the dancing partners are scarce, and my wife despairs of having her soirée dubbed a disaster."

Colonel Bernard Barrett had been the closest thing to a father Gabriel had ever known, despite the fact that his own sire, Alexander MacFeagh, had lived to see Gabriel's twentieth year. It had been Colonel Barrett who had urged Gabriel to secure his commission into the 105th Dragoons, and then again the colonel who had helped him to sell that commission to a fellow officer when he'd received word calling him back to Scotland.

During the years he had served under him, the colonel had taught Gabriel such things as how to defend himself against enemy attack and how best to determine an opponent's weakness. He had taught him courage, prudence, and gallantry, but most vital of them all was the true definition of honor.

If the colonel had known the dark truth of Gabriel's family history, he had never revealed it. All those many months they had spent traversing Portugal and Spain chasing after Napoleon, Colonel Barrett had always treated Gabriel with the utmost fairness and respect at a time when many English soldiers had shown a great deal of disdain for their Scottish comrades. Even three quarters of a century couldn't erase the bitterness of the ill-fated rebellion of '45.

Yet Barrett had given Gabriel the chance to prove himself,

both as a soldier on the field of battle and as a man in charge of a company of others, and because of that, Gabriel had gone to Mrs. Barrett's ball, vowing, however, to stay no longer than an hour.

It was at that same ball he had first spotted Georgiana.

She had been standing against the far wall, trying very hard to blend in to Mrs. Barrett's woodwork, alongside a bevy of other young ladies fresh from the country, all dressed in the latest fashion, smiling and fluttering their decorated fans in order to catch a young buck's eye.

Something about Georgiana had caught his attention, and not only that she'd looked quite lovely that evening, her blonde hair curled high upon her head, showing off the curve of her neck and shoulder. The eloquence of her fan, even the smartness of her sleeveless silk spencerette, none of it had kept him looking time and again to that same place against the wall. What had drawn his attention in the midst of that crowded ballroom had been nothing else but Georgiana's eyes.

They had been the palest silver gray, like shimmering rain-drops on a moonlit night, and they had held more sadness than he had ever thought possible.

Having been born with a family history as dark and as isolating as his own, Gabriel had easily recognized a fellow victim of unhappiness. He had watched Georgiana on and off that night as she had stood rooted to that same spot on the far wall, dance after dance, while the others had hied off and the merriment had gone on around her.

He remembered thinking what a pity that so pretty a lass should be so obviously miserable. What a pity, too, that no one else in that busy place had noticed.

As he was readying to leave, his promised hour ended, Gabriel happened to catch a remark hissed sharply to Georgiana under her mother's breath, chastising her for a lack of effort in attracting male attention. Something in Georgiana's eyes as she stood frozen by her mother's displeasure had told Gabriel that she'd be facing far worse than sharp words after the ball.

He never knew what came over him; he only knew he would have done almost anything at that moment to dispel that petrified look from her eyes—

—even ask Georgiana to dance.

That single impulsive moment had led to a courtship that resulted in their marriage barely three months later. When he returned to his childhood home on Trelay to take up residence as the isle's new laird, it was with Georgiana as his wife.

It was only when they were in Scotland, a safe distance away from London and its haunting memories, that Gabriel learned the true depth of his new wife's melancholy, a melancholy seated in years of mental abuse at the hands of her mother—and the very worst sort of physical abuse at the hands of her father.

No matter how gentle, how understanding Gabriel tried to be with her, Georgiana could never prevent herself from stiffening against him whenever he moved to touch her. She would apologize to him over and over and finally ease enough to share his bed, but after weeks of dutiful lovemaking that culminated each time in her tears, Gabriel had given up altogether any attempt at intimacy with his wife.

By then, however, Georgiana had been expecting their child.

Throughout her pregnancy, Georgiana had openly declared that she was carrying Gabriel's son, almost as if by saying it often enough, she could somehow make it true. He would be called Gabriel for his father, she'd said, ignoring the direful warnings of the women of the island who told her it was bad luck to christen a child while it yet lay within the womb.

Even after Juliana had been born a daughter, Georgiana had refused to believe it—not until she had seen the babe for herself. Gabriel had watched as she had looked upon their child that day, not with the wondrous joy of a new mother, but with that same terrible fear that had so caught him the first time he'd seen her in that crowded London ballroom.

Gabriel assured Georgiana over and over that she had nothing to fear any longer, that the life she had led before wedding him was locked away to the past, but Georgiana still made Gabriel promise her that he would never allow her family the opportunity to abuse Juliana as they had her. They would stop at nothing, Georgiana had said, to get what they wanted.

Wishing only to ease those terrible anxieties, Gabriel had given Georgiana his word, never knowing just how significant keeping it would someday become.

Time had passed quickly and Georgiana had soon eased into her new role of mother. She saw to every aspect of Juliana's care herself, feeding her at her own breast, delighting in the mess of a finicky eater, the thunder of a two-year-old's tantrum. Gabriel had believed Georgiana happy, truly happy for the first time in her life, free from the dark memory of her own wretched childhood.

He couldn't have been more mistaken.

He knew so very little of what had happened that cheerless winter morning three years before. It had been a day much like any other with no indication of the events that would take place.

That day had dawned frosty, but the sun had broken through the clouds, showering the isle with its radiant light. After breakfast, Georgiana had dressed herself and then six-year-old Juliana for a walk along the heights above the isle's westerly shore, a jaunt they had made often together. She had asked Gabriel to go with them, but he had declined, having a pile of papers to go through for his steward, Clyne.

Instead, he had watched the two of them go, waving from his study window in the tower as they made their way across the frost-dusted machair to disappear over the distant hilltop. The wind had been icy and Georgiana had promised Gabriel they wouldn't stay out too long.

Still, somehow, Gabriel had felt a niggling sense of unease.

If only he had heeded it.

When they hadn't returned after two hours later, Gabriel had gone out after them, only to find his daughter alone, wet and shivering above the farthest shore, struck suddenly dumb, unable to tell him where her mother had gone.

One of Georgiana's shoes had washed up on the shore a week later; her body, however, was never found, almost as if she had been carried away by the rolling white mist of the morning. It didn't matter whether it had been a dreadful accident or whether Georgiana had for some reason taken her own life. Standing on that beach, clutching her water-soaked slipper in his trembling hand, Gabriel had felt the full weight of the responsibility for her death as keenly as if he had taken her life himself.

He knew he should have seen it coming. It was a terrible history that had been written nearly three hundred years before, revisiting itself time and again through generations of the *cursed* MacFeaghs.

Gabriel downed the last of his brandy and moved from his place by the fire, crossing the darkened room to where a large trunk that looked every bit as ancient as the castle itself stood in an inconspicuous spot in the far corner. Flipping back the worn and faded tapestry cloth that covered its lid, he smoothed a hand against the dark oak underneath, pitted and scarred through many centuries past.

Gabriel slid a length of silver chain that hung around his neck from inside the covering of his shirt. On its end, glinting in the muted firelight, hung the tiny, timeless key that had hung about the necks of every MacFeagh chief who had come before him.

The crude iron lock upon the trunk was as much a mystery as the origins of the trunk itself. Scarred where various intruders had tried over time to force it open, the lock had been fashioned in a manner most mysterious so that only the single key that fitted it would release it, a sort of Excaliburesque relic. Even with the key in hand, only the MacFeagh chief could open the trunk's lock. To anyone else who dared try, the key would prove both useless—and fatal—for death surely followed for those who had tried, as if the very metal it had been forged from was somehow enchanted.

It was the only lock worthy to protect the Clan MacFeagh's most prized possession.

Fitting the key into its place, Gabriel released the catch that allowed him to lift the lid on a trunk that now lay conspicuously empty, barren of the relic that had once lain protected inside centuries earlier.

The ancient ensign-staff of the MacFeagh had been a symbol of the clan for as long as history had been recorded, passed down generation after generation since the clan's very beginnings. Because of the MacFeagh's connection to the bishops of the priory at Trelay founded by St. Columba all those many centuries before, many said the staff had been fashioned from the wood of the very *curragh* in which the holy saint had sailed from Ireland and was therefore certainly blessed. Legend described the staff as both long and sturdy, magically indestructible, made of a gleaming white wood of unknown origin. History dictated that for as long as the MacFeagh chief held the ancient relic, the clan would prosper—and prosper they had for several hundred years.

Led by the great Murchardus Maca'phi, the clan had reigned unchallenged over not only Trelay, but several of the neighboring isles during the earlier centuries. Once honored as the hereditary keepers of the records for the ancient Lords of the Isles, the clan's present misfortune's began early in the sixteenth century when, legend says, a descendant of Murchardus, a Murdoch MacFeagh, the chief at the time, fell under the curse of a witch from the nearby isle of Jura.

History recorded that Murdoch, a great bear of a man with the trademark dark MacFeagh hair and eyes, had been sailing in his *bhirlinn* when a fierce squall had suddenly risen up against him, tossing him and his crew helplessly into the icy waters of the firth. He had fought the treacherous swells valiantly, listening to the dying cries as each of the others had perished, until exhausted himself, he'd finally lost consciousness.

When next he awoke, he found himself lying beneath the warmth of a pile of furs in a sea cave by a crackling fire. The haggard old witch who tended the blaze told MacFeagh she had saved him from drowning by means of a magic spell, bringing him to the safety of her cave home on Jura.

MacFeagh had been so grateful to her, he'd promised to reward her with one of his many prized possessions. He remained with the witch to mend for several weeks, but when his strength returned and the time came that he thought to go back to his own home which he could see through the mist on the adjacent isle, the witch stubbornly refused to give him up, drawing his boat back time and again by means of a magical tethering thread. She had lived a lonely existence on Jura, and found she quite liked having him to keep her company. MacFeagh had no choice but to remain her unwilling guest, tortured by the sight of his beloved home so near, yet so far from reach.

Until he managed to gain the witch's trust enough to learn of a hatchet she had that could sever the enchanted thread she held him prisoner with. Late one moonless night, MacFeagh stole the hatchet and cleaved the thread to escape from her, arriving home to the relief and joy of his worried family while the betrayed wail of the witch carried behind him on the sea wind.

The following day, the witch presented herself at MacFeagh's door, demanding that he fulfill his promise of the gift of his most prized possession. But when he offered her a marvelous jeweled brooch, she refused, saying she would only accept the ancient and renowned staff of the MacFeagh in exchange for her having saved his life.

Murdoch refused, offering her goods and riches beyond all imagination, but still she demanded the cherished staff. Unwilling to part with his hereditary relic and unsettled by her dark presence, MacFeagh had the witch carried away back to Jura and warned her never to return.

By the time the next morning dawned, three of the chief's five children had mysteriously perished, found lying in their beds, their faces peaceful in sleep, as if their very breath had been stolen from them. Grief-stricken, MacFeagh went immediately to the trunk, only to find that the ancient staff was missing, removed somehow through a means by which the lock hadn't been opened.

In its place lay a scrap of crude parchment. Written upon it were these words in ancient Gaelic:

> *For nine hundred years, and then one hundred more,*
> *any creature or beast you allow past your heart's door,*
> *will soon slip away and suffer death's most telling stone,*
> *while helpless you watch on, forsaken and alone.*
> *Only here on this misty isle might the truth be found,*
> *St. Colomb's staff will loose the curse by which you are bound.*
> *One of pure heart and eye will right the wrongs of the past,*
> *to bring about an end to the suffering at last!*

From then on, and over the next three centuries, the loved ones of every MacFeagh chief would often perish suddenly and under extreme circumstances—drowning, fire, even accidental falls. It seemed that whenever a MacFeagh made the mistake of allowing someone close to his heart, the curse would return with its fatal Midas touch, just as the witch had prophesized that long ago day.

Because of this, the enduring MacFeagh chiefs had become a clan of distant, untouchable men, watching helplessly while without warning those around them fell victim to the witch's bitter curse. As a boy, Gabriel had rarely seen his father, the great Alexander MacFeagh. His care and well-being had been seen to by his mother, Lillidh, while his father had spent his time grooming his elder brother, Malcolm, for the reclusive role of MacFeagh chief.

Malcolm had been a diligent student, carrying on the dreaded legacy well, growing into a fierce man as cold and callous as their father. Everyone had predicted that he would serve well as laird, for he allowed nobody to matter to him, not even their mother.

But no one had foreseen Malcolm's untimely demise, a freakish accident that had occurred after he had mistakenly eaten the poisonous monkshood instead of the horseradish root he'd intended. Thus no one could have predicted the sudden inheritance of Gabriel, the second son.

Gabriel had been ill-prepared to assume the damned role of MacFeagh chief. Unlike Malcolm, he hadn't been raised to bury his emotions behind an impenetrable wall of cool indifference, eschewing all feeling, all compassion. As such, Gabriel made the fatal mistake of caring for Georgiana, of trying to help her—and, ultimately, it had led to her death, perpetuating the common belief that the MacFeaghs murdered their own, and proving to Gabriel that he had to do whatever he could to protect his daughter from a similar fate.

During the course of the three years since Georgiana's death, Gabriel had done everything he could to avoid spending anything more than a few moments in the company of his daughter on any given occasion. He made certain she was cared for, seeing to it that she was properly clothed and fed and that her every physical comfort was looked after by the handful of servants who had proven themselves loyal and trustworthy to him and his family.

But it was as close to her as he could allow himself to get.

To talk to her, care for her, know her at all would put Juliana's life too much at risk—and he had already made that mistake once. It wasn't a mistake he had any intention of repeating.

Thus Gabriel would do everything in his power to keep from loving his daughter.

If only so that he could spare her life.

5

*E*leanor opened her eyes onto the new light of the morning—and onto the unexpected sight of Juliana standing at the side of the bed. Her hair was still tucked beneath her frilled night cap as she stared at Eleanor in stony silence.

The window behind her revealed that the hour was yet early, the sun's light barely beginning to climb in a dappled morning sky.

For the first few moments, Eleanor wondered what it was that had awakened her. She couldn't recall having felt Juliana rise from the bed or even nudge her to wake. But something had indeed awakened her.

Searching her memory, Eleanor remembered a sound then, like the thumping of a foot against the floor—the foot of someone standing very close to the side of the bed.

"What is it, Juliana?" she said, sitting up on the bed. Her neck twinged from the uncomfortable position she'd been in all night, poised at the edge of the mattress beside Juliana. "Is something the matter?"

Juliana didn't respond, not even with a nod or shake of her head. Instead, she turned and walked across the room to the door, that same ambiguous expression on her face as she opened it quietly and then stood beside it, waiting.

Waiting for Eleanor to leave the room.

Was she angry, Eleanor wondered, that she had awoken to find someone, this new stranger, with her in her mother's bed? Perhaps she considered it an intrusion on a last sacred connection between mother and daughter. Eleanor hadn't considered that the night before when she had decided to remain with Juliana. Her only thought had been to keep watch over her, to make certain she didn't go wandering elsewhere through the castle in the dark of the night.

Deciding that it would be best to go along with the child's wishes, Eleanor got up from the bed and crossed the room to leave. She hadn't dressed in her nightclothes the night before after finding Juliana missing, so she still wore the pale muslin gown, now hopelessly wrinkled, that she had worn to supper. Her hair was mussed, drooping from its pins. A bath and a fresh gown would certainly be in order before breakfast.

Eleanor started for the hall to leave, until she noticed that Juliana hadn't followed her. She turned to see that the little girl was at the bed again, pulling up the rumpled bedclothes. She smoothed out the wrinkles in the coverlet. She set the pillows to rights. In moments, there remained no indication that anyone might have slept there at all.

The ritual ease and practice of her movements told Eleanor that the child had done this many a time before. How long had Juliana been coming there to her mother's bedchamber to sleep? Since Lady Dunevin had died? Did no one else in the castle know of her nightly visits there?

When she was finished making up the bed, Juliana turned, snatched up her doll from where she had set it on the chair beside the bed, and walked quietly from the room, closing the door behind them. As Eleanor fell into place behind her, walking down the shadowed hall, she decided that Màiri had been right in what she'd said to her in the kitchen the previous night.

There was something there behind Juliana's silent stare after all.

～

THE RAIN THAT HAD DAMPENED THE PREVIOUS EVENING RETURNED that morning, although waning to a drizzle by midday. The temperature in the isles proved a good deal colder than that on the mainland, spurred by a biting sea wind that blew in fiercely off the channel to the west with such constancy that the stark trees along the coast were forever bowed in an easterly direction.

Rather than trouble someone to haul buckets of water to her chamber in the tower, Eleanor had taken a quick bath in a small antechamber off the kitchen in a wooden laundry tub with water Màiri heated over the fire. The shock of stepping out of the water's warmth onto the cold stone floor with bare feet had stripped away the last of her fatigue. Eleanor quickly realized that the thin silks and decorative muslins that made up the whole of her wardrobe would provide very little comfort against the bitter island chill.

Her fingers prickled even now as she struggled to fasten the tiny buttons that lined the front of her lilac-colored daygown. Thank goodness she had sleeves, narrow and reaching to her wrists. Still, she would have to see about getting herself some of the warmer woolens that were the staple costume of the isles. Until she could, Màiri had loaned her one of her own heavy pairs of woolen stockings and a thickly woven tartan shawl with which to keep warm.

After taking a breakfast of tea and bannocks, and Màiri's hot porridge with fresh cream, Eleanor and Juliana retreated abovestairs to the confines of the nursery and the heat of the small hearth there, where she kept a kettle of tea simmering throughout the day to warm them. Eleanor had left word with Fergus that his lordship was invited to call on them there to discuss Juliana's curriculum. Hours later, however, Lord Dunevin still had not shown any indication of showing up.

Eleanor spent a good part of the morning sorting through the numerous books and maps and other printed material she'd found in the schoolroom. She scribbled notes to herself about them on a parchment she had discovered in the drawer of the corner desk while Juliana merely sat at the window as she had the day before, watching as the rain moved off into the sea and the sun pushed its way back through the autumn clouds.

Other than the thumping of her foot early that morning, Juliana had made no further effort to communicate with Eleanor, taking her breakfast in silence while Màiri had chatted over tea with Eleanor.

Eleanor had set out a children's storybook earlier that morning, hoping she might glean something of Juliana's likes and dislikes from it, but Juliana had barely given it notice. It sat, yet untouched and unread where she had placed it on the schoolroom table.

Setting aside the dwindling pile of books she had left to go through, Eleanor suddenly sparked upon an idea. She crossed the room and took down a box of small painted alphabet tiles she had found earlier that morning, returning to the table near to where Juliana sat. Sitting in one of the two small chairs, Eleanor spread the ivory tiles out upon the tabletop with the painted letters facing upward. Some of the tiles had one letter, others two-letter combinations of consonant and vowel. When she was finished placing them all, nearly filling the tabletop with them, Eleanor turned to regard her silent young charge.

"Juliana, I thought perhaps we'd try a little game together..."

She might as well have been in another room or even on another isle, for all the notice Juliana gave her. Without affording the slightest indication that she had heard her, Juliana remained sitting as she was, curled upon the window seat, the back of her head facing the room, as she stared out at the dim horizon, oblivious to anything and everything else around her.

What was it, Eleanor wondered, that so drew the child's attention to the sea?

"Juliana, please. I would very much like to teach you, but I cannot do this alone."

Eleanor knit her brow in frustration at Juliana's continued unresponsiveness, but she would not give up on this child, not like everybody else clearly had.

She tried again. "I do not know what your other governesses were like, but I promise you I only want to help you. Won't you please help me to help you?"

There passed a silent moment before somehow, blessedly, Eleanor's words seemed to break through to her. Juliana finally turned from the window to look at her. Her expression spoke more loudly than any words could. Her eyes were dark, alert, and filled with a subtle interest.

This little girl wanted to be saved. But from what?

Somehow, Eleanor determined, she would find out.

She motioned toward the opposite chair. "Won't you come and join me for a moment?"

Juliana slid slowly from her window seat and approached the small table. She lowered into the chair, her eyes moving about at the scattered letter tiles before she turned her attention to Eleanor, waiting.

Eleanor smiled, the spark of hope seizing her inside. "I want you to know that I will never try to make you speak. If you do not wish to, then you needn't ever utter another word. I understand. But if there is ever anything you should wish to communicate to me, if you are cold and would like a shawl, or if you are hungry, there are ways other than speaking to do so."

Juliana stared at her, listening—oh, thank heavens, yes, listening. Eleanor drew an expectant breath.

"First, I thought perhaps we'd try something with these tiles."

Eleanor reached for the storybook she had given Juliana to read earlier that morning. Picking up several of the tiles, she spelled out *B-O-O-K* with them. Then she looked to Juliana, who studied the tiles before looking up at her again.

Eleanor would have sworn she saw a flicker of something there, the smallest indication that she wouldn't shut Eleanor away. Anything was better than the distant and obscure silence.

"Now it is your turn," Eleanor said with a quick nod of encouragement. "Choose anything you wish."

Juliana watched her a moment, then turned to peer about the room. Her gaze fell immediately upon a small wooden horse, painted in red with worn wheels and a frayed string by which it could be pulled. She got up slowly to retrieve it from where it sat on a shelf and brought it over to the table. Looking through the scattered tiles, she tentatively picked up one and then another and another until she had spelled out a single word with them.

H-O-R-S-E.

Eleanor smiled, a thrill rushing through her that left her feeling quite as if the sunshine had indeed broken through the lowering clouds.

They were communicating.

She tempered her excitement, nodded, and said, "Very good, Juliana," as she looked about the room. "Okay, now it is my turn again."

On they went through several more—

B-A-L-L

M-A-P

S-O-L-D-I-E-R

C-A-N-D-L-E

—labeling various objects about the room, until it fell to Eleanor's turn once again. But this time she didn't go searching through the shelves for some other item to place on the table.

Instead, she pushed aside some of the tiles that were yet scattered about the table top. Then, taking her time, she set down her next batch of letters neatly in front of where Juliana was sitting.

F-R-I-E-N-D.

Eleanor watched, breath held with anticipation, as Juliana read the word, her head bowed. She could see her chew her lip for a moment before she slowly raised her gaze. Their eyes caught, and held.

Eleanor waited, feeling suddenly as if she were standing before a long locked doorway, waiting to see if she would be allowed inside. She could see the uncertainty play across Juliana's face, this child who had hidden herself away from the world for so long. Silently, she hoped against all hope that Juliana would give her this one small chance.

"I would very much like to be your friend, Juliana," Eleanor said softly to her.

She didn't press her to respond, but instead waited. They sat there, just the two of them, listening as the clock ticked away the minutes. Outside, a dog barked on the courtyard below the window. A few moments later, Juliana reached with one hand slowly forward, forming a word with some of the tiles that yet remained on the table.

Y-E-S.

Juliana looked up from the tiles. Their eyes met again and Eleanor smiled, her throat tightening as she blinked back the rush of emotions she felt.

"Juliana, I—"

The door across the room suddenly came open, without a warning knock. The wonder of the special moment between them was abruptly shattered.

Fergus stood there, staring at them from across the room.

"His lairdship will see you in his study now, miss."

The man certainly had a proclivity for poor timing. Just like the night before, he had come at the very moment when Eleanor had finally been making progress with Juliana.

Juliana turned so quickly from the table that she swept the few remaining tiles, skittering some of them to the floorboards. In a flash, she was back at her place on the window seat, her back to the room once again, staring out at the dusky expanse of sky and stormy sea.

Eleanor frowned as she bent to retrieve the tiles from the floor. "You may tell his lordship I shall be down directly."

Fergus didn't respond, but remained at the door, watching as she deposited the tiles into their box. His arrival there had brought a marked chill to the room. His expression as he looked on the room seemed almost irritated, as if he believed Juliana had scattered the tiles purposely off the table.

"Thank you, Fergus," Eleanor said, dismissing him. In a hapless effort to bring back the warmth of the special moments before his arrival, Eleanor took up the hearth tongs and dropped a fresh peat brick onto the fire, stirring it to flame. When Fergus didn't immediately move to leave, she added, "Was there something else?"

The older man stared at her in a manner that almost seemed meant to intimidate her. "No, miss."

He turned then, and vanished down the hall.

Eleanor stood and brushed her hands over her skirts to smooth them, wishing she could brush away the chill of that man's presence with it. Not everyone, it seemed, would be as welcoming to her new place in the Dunevin household as Màiri had been.

"Well, I shouldn't keep your father waiting," she said. "Will you be comfortable here alone while I am gone, or would you like me to ask Màiri to join you till I return?"

Eleanor's spirits dropped when Juliana didn't respond. Hoping that she hadn't lost what little ground she had gained by the morning's exercise, Eleanor came up behind her and placed a hand gently on her shoulder. "I shall be right back then."

Juliana remained fixed on the window.

Disheartened, Eleanor turned and left the room. But she would not lose hope. She had reached Juliana once, broken through her silence. And she would do it again.

Minutes later, Eleanor was standing at the open doorway to the viscount's study. He was seated inside behind his great desk and a large deerhound—probably the one she'd heard barking earlier—lay stretched out like a furry carpet before the hearth. The dog picked up its head at her arrival, watchful as she knocked softly on the doorjamb.

"My lord?"

The viscount looked up at her from the parchment he was reading. He wore a pair of spectacles which softened the intensity of his gaze, making him appear more scholar than Highlander.

"Miss Harte," he said, motioning her forward. "Good day to you. Please come inside."

Eleanor crossed the room to sit on one of the two tartan-covered chairs that sat at cross-angles before the desk. The dog, curious about the new stranger, rose from the hearth and slunk across the length of the carpet to nose at her feet. Sitting as she was beside the lanky height of him, they were very nearly eye-to-eye.

The viscount scowled at the dog in Gaelic, "Cudu, a-sìos. Sit down."

"Oh, no, 'tis all right."

Eleanor held out her fingers to the stately hound, who glanced once at his master before he sniffed at her outstretched hand with his narrow snout. After a moment, he lowered his head in hopes of a scratch behind his grizzled ears. Eleanor willingly obliged and from that moment, her feet had the welcome warmth of a furry companion.

Lord Dunevin folded his hands before him on the desktop and looked at her. "Fergus left word that you wished a moment to discuss Juliana's curriculum with me."

Eleanor cleared her throat on a nod. "Yes, my lord, although I had rather hoped to discuss this with you *in* the schoolroom."

The viscount stared at her, incredulous, and Eleanor was reminded once again that she was no longer his social equal, Lady Eleanor Wycliffe, heiress to the Westover fortune, but his employee, Miss Nell Harte. She decided she should soften her tone.

"My apologies, my lord. I didn't mean to speak disrespectfully."

He shook his head. "Not at all. I was rather occupied this morning," he offered by way of an explanation.

Eleanor caught herself studying the line of his beard-shadowed chin and the few strands of dark hair that fell over his forehead. She wondered if the line that creased his brow ever ceased. She wondered if he ever smiled. When she realized he was staring at her, she quickly broke away and turned her attention to the notes that she had made earlier that morning.

"Yes, well, the materials I found in the schoolroom are, on the whole, adequate, but I noted several fields of study that weren't represented that I would recommend be included in Juliana's education."

"Indeed?"

"Yes." She handed him her notes, sitting forward in her chair. "I took the liberty of listing some additional subjects I thought might prove beneficial."

The viscount took up the page. At first it appeared as if he might only give it a cursory glance, but something she had written caught his attention and he gave it a second, more thorough study.

He glanced up at her. "Astronomy? Botany? And this last one, do I read it right? Anatomy?"

Eleanor nodded.

"Miss Harte, I'm not of the mind to turn my daughter into a nine-year-old bluestocking. I had thought more along the lines of teaching her to write a pretty letter and play a pleasant tune upon the pianoforte, or even arrange a proper supper menu. What could anatomy possibly have to do with preparing my daughter to someday manage her husband's household?"

Eleanor felt herself stiffen against the all-too familiar and insular concept that to be a wife, mother, and gracious hostess were the very heights of womanly ambition. It was that same belief, one that taught young girls that naïveté was "charming" and helplessness was a longed-for virtue, that she, herself, had swallowed all her life like a spot of afternoon tea with her fingers held just so, but that had, in the end, only left her feeling betrayed and utterly vulnerable.

It was a mistake she had no intention of perpetuating to another generation.

"As a matter of fact, my lord," Eleanor said then, pulling back her shoulders to sit up straighter in her chair, "I do think that a basic education in anatomy is most beneficial to a woman, even, it could be argued, more so than to a man. For who is it, sir, who is physically charged with the task of bringing forth new life? How much less terrifying that would be for a woman who has a basic education in the mechanics of the thing instead of blithely floating along on the belief that babies are delivered by fairies in the middle of the night, left upon the mother's pillow cooing and smiling to be discovered upon awakening the following morning?"

By the time she'd finished her point, Eleanor's voice had risen to the point that even Cudu had lifted his head to look at her in wonder. Her bout of indignation had brought a most appealing color to her face, the enthusiasm that she'd spoken with lighting her eyes a deeper green.

Gabriel wasn't accustomed to anyone, much less a woman, standing up to him so boldly. Most everyone he encountered feared the very sight of him, agreeing with anything he said even if it opposed their own views.

He was, after all, the Devil of Dunevin Castle.

But not so this woman...

He looked away from her, focusing on the letter he had been in the process of responding to at her arrival, a bland and wordy bit of account from his solicitor in London, anything to take his thoughts away from the direction they were headed.

"Actually, Miss Harte, here in Scotland the belief is that the fairies come to steal babies at night, not to deliver them."

The governess mistook his attempt at diverting his thoughts for ridicule at something she so obviously felt strongly about.

Her eyes flashed green fire. "Scoff at it all you like, sir, but I know of what I speak. Ignorance is never an asset. It is a weakness that victimizes women far more than it ever protects them."

As he looked on her bold eyes and flushed cheeks, Gabriel suddenly found himself wondering what had happened to her in her life to make her feel the burdens of her gender so keenly. There was no doubt she had been raised among elite society. Her manner and speech told adequately of that and she was educated far above even the most privileged members of her sex.

Just who was Miss Nell Harte? Where had she come from? Was she perhaps even married? He didn't know why, but for the fleeting moment that thought filled his head, his shirt collar grew uncomfortably tight.

What should it matter if she were wed with a flock of offspring waiting for her at home? She obviously didn't wish to be wherever it was she had been, and she was the best candidate to teach Juliana the ways of society.

Even more so, she was the *only* candidate.

If she wanted to instruct his daughter in the patterns of the stars or the Latin name of every weed on the isle, so be it. When she had completed Juliana's education, she would go back to whatever—or whomever—she had left behind, and he could return to the solitude of his life with Juliana's future welfare secure.

"Once again you have proven your point, Miss Harte. I am convinced that Juliana could only benefit from the subjects you have mentioned. You may have full use of my library here whenever you wish. You should find the materials more than adequate for your purposes, as over the past generations, my ancestors were great collectors of the written word in a variety of subjects. If there is anything else you find you need, we can see about acquiring it from the mainland."

The governess looked momentarily taken aback. After another moment, she simply nodded in response. That small movement of her head brought a single tendril of chestnut hair to slipping from the stricture of her coif, trailing softly along her cheek, a cheek that looked as if it would be smooth as silk to the touch.

"Is that all?" Gabriel asked, fast growing aware of the increasing intimacy of the two of them alone in that room with only the woolly bulk of his dog stretched between them.

"Yes, my lord. I thank you for your refreshing open-mindedness toward Juliana's education. It is a most admirable manner of thinking for a man of your rank."

Gabriel wasn't sure whether he should take that as a personal compliment or an affront to his gender. He wasn't given the time to decide, for she stood then and turned to leave the room.

As she passed by his desk, he caught a scent, a captivating mixture of flowers and spice. She may as well have struck him cold.

Watching her as she walked from the room, Gabriel found himself noting the gentle sway of her hips beneath the muslin of her skirts. The room seemed to grow suddenly warmer. He realized a wholly primitive tightening in his belly. It startled him and frightened the living hell out of him all at the same time.

What the devil was he doing? He wasn't some untested school lad dreaming of having a go between the luscious legs of the headmaster's daughter. He was a man, a man who knew better, a man who had learned all too well the perils of giving in to his emotions.

He was a man who hadn't lain with a woman in longer than he could remember.

And now this woman had been on the isle, in his home, all of one day and he was sitting there contemplating the softness of her skin, at losing himself in her fragrance. Had he learned nothing after Georgiana? How many more innocent people had to suffer because of him?

In that moment, Gabriel knew what he must do. He would strive to become the son of his father, the great Alexander, cold and aloof, utterly unaffected. He would maintain that same hard-edged armor that had served the lairds of Dunevin for generations.

And that meant one very clear thing, as well.

He must avoid being in the company of his mysterious governess at all costs.

6

*G*abriel stepped from the jetty onto the deck of the weather-worn skiff bobbing lazily at the shore.

It had dawned a clear morning, cool and crisp, the sort of day that brought everyone out after too many days of having been tucked away by the warmth of a peat fire.

It wasn't often the western seaboard was treated to such favorable weather so late in the season. The waning months of autumn were more often than not obscured by low-hanging clouds or battered by the constant howl of fierce seaward winds. Thus, when they were blessed by such unexpected fair weather, it almost seemed like an unplanned-for holiday.

Gabriel had planned to spend the day closeted in his study answering correspondence and reconciling the estate ledgers. But upon spotting the boat from his study window, and watching as it was readied for its voyage to the mainland, he had decided that the ledgers could wait for a more inclement day.

The waters of the firth tugged at the small craft as Gabriel shaded his eyes against the brightness of the day, filling his lungs with the salt and mist of the brisk air. A day like this, spent out on the open sea, was just what Gabriel needed to clear his head, banish the images that had plagued him in sleep, images of a particular governess with glinting green eyes and a mouth that begged to be tasted.

Là math dhut, Dòmhnall," Gabriel called in Gaelic greeting to Donald Duncan MacNeill, one of the island's tenants, who was preparing the boat for departure.

The few crew members were yet on the shore, stocking up on fresh water and bidding farewell to wives and mothers who were pressing them to take extra clothing should the weather take a sudden turn.

Gabriel took a moment to peer out over the easterly horizon, looking toward the distant mainland that rose through the dawn's drifting haze. There, hidden behind the scattering of isles that made up the Inner Hebrides, lay their destination, the quaint coastal town and hub port of all of Argyllshire called Oban.

"This morning's wind should afford us a swift crossing," Gabriel said.

"Aye, my lord," Donald answered, speaking in his native Gaelic, even though, like Gabriel, he had learned English at an early age. "We'll surely make good time this day."

Donald was only a couple years younger than Gabriel's three-and-thirty, and had been born on Trelay, as had his father and his father before him. He had only left the isle for any length of time once in his lifetime, when at seventeen, he had gone to serve in one of the Argyllshire Highland regiments against Napoleon on the Peninsula.

Donald had returned within a year of leaving, though, after he'd taken a stray shot through his calf, from which he'd eventually recovered, but which had left him with a pronounced limp that had since christened him with the nickname of "Lame Donald" to those on the isle. He captained his crude craft twice weekly to the Scottish mainland, taking passengers to Oban, picking up the post, and retrieving supplies for the other crofters that couldn't be grown or manufactured on the isle. In appreciation for his performing this charitable duty, the other folk of the island saw to his small stock of cattle and sheep, and the potato and barley crops that would feed Donald and his young family through the coming winter months.

As he stood on the deck of the small sailing skiff, Gabriel was anxious to be away, unwilling to waste another moment of the day's glory. The small crew of four had already boarded and were ready at their various stations. In minutes, the final details for their departure were completed.

"Shall I help you to shove off?" Gabriel asked even as he reached for the twisted root rope that tethered the skiff to the rocky pier.

"Aye, my lord, that would be—"

MacNeill hesitated, looking out past Gabriel toward the distant castle hill. "A moment, my lord."

Gabriel turned from the hawser to see two figures making their way quickly down the pathway toward the jetty. They were too far away to see clearly, but both were dressed in skirts and cloaks, with one quite a bit smaller than the other. The taller figure's arms were waving in an obvious effort to draw their attention.

This, Gabriel thought, was precisely *not* what he needed this day.

"Yoo hoo!" called out a reedy voice as the two figures approached. "Good morning, Lord Dunevin."

She was breathless from hurrying down the hillside and her hair had come loose from its pins. In the sunlight, it was burnished a rich auburn-brown and framed her cheeks and nose, and had pinked from the chill air most appealingly.

"I understand from Màiri that you are going to the mainland today," she said, stating the obvious, he gathered, in hopes for an invitation to join them.

Gabriel regarded her. "Yes, Miss Harte, we are."

If he at all thought his prosaic response would have deterred her, he was quickly proven wrong.

"Well then, I'm so glad we caught you before you departed."

Then, without waiting for an assisting hand, she stepped quickly onto the ship's deck, turning with a swish of her skirts to take Juliana's hand and help her on behind her. She then went for Donald, putting out her hand in greeting.

"How do you do? I am Miss Harte, Miss Juliana's new governess. I wonder if we might tag along to town with you today? It is such a lovely day for a sail."

MacNeill doffed his ragged fisherman's cap, revealing the crop of bright red hair that sprouted underneath. He grinned broadly. "Donald MacNeill at your service, Miss Harte."

The governess returned a bright smile, charming the Scottish sailor and his entire crew to their teeth. "Please, call me Nell. Everyone does."

Gabriel looked at her. "Pray, what are you doing, Miss Harte?"

Her easy smile didn't falter and she turned to regard him with eyes of curious unease.

"Why, I am taking your own advice, my lord."

"My advice?"

"Indeed. According to your cook, Màiri, I can purchase a pair of sturdy shoes in Oban quite cheaply."

"And I believe I told you that Fergus would see to it for you."

"Yes, you did, but I saw no reason to take him away from his other duties when I could see to the errand just as easily myself. I am also in need of some more suitable clothing and, well, Fergus couldn't very well have seen to the purchase of my underthings, now could he, my lord?"

An image of her clad in her chemise flashed suddenly to Gabriel's mind's eye. He scowled, although he certainly couldn't disagree that she needed clothing more befitting the isles. Even now, she was dressed in a high-waisted gown of checked light cloth and dainty heelless slippers, quite as if she were going off on a round of social calls instead of sailing up a windy sea lane. If she continued dressing like that through winter, she would catch pneumonia within a month's time.

"Besides," she went on, "this way I can be sure of the fit and with the weather so fine, I thought it a perfect first outing for Juliana and me."

Beside her, Juliana was looking at her father as if expecting him to refuse their passage.

Though his first sense told him he should, he also knew that Juliana had been shut away inside the castle for too many weeks without venturing out of doors. Even yesterday, the opportunity of a quiet moment by the sea had been spoiled by rain. Thus he couldn't argue against a healthy dose of sunshine and fresh sea air.

He also knew he couldn't very well just suddenly cry off from going himself without causing question, so instead he muttered, "Very well," and reached once again for the mooring ropes.

Once they were free, the sloop slid easily away from the pier, pulled by the swelling waves as her stout woolen sail filled with a bracing wind. The crew took their places at the thwarts, readying themselves at the narrow oars, and at Donald's command in Gaelic of *"Tiugainn!"* they pulled back in unison.

The boat heaved forward. They were headed out to sea.

As they sailed, the air was filled with the rhythmic sound of the oarsmen's chant, an ancient song that aided them in keeping their movements in sync. It was a practice long seated among the isles and various verses had been handed down through generations of seafaring men.

In between each stride, Gabriel was treated to an earful of Miss Harte's non-stop chatter as she told Juliana about things she knew, and alternately asked Donald about things she did not.

"You see this here, Juliana? This is the front of the boat, called the 'prow,' and the rear is called the 'stern,' is that not correct, Mr. MacNeill?"

Even before he could answer, she turned and asked further, "Oh, and what is that little island there called, Mr. MacNeill?"

"Oh, that be Eilean Olmsa, miss. There is a legend that says when the Bonnie Prince came to Scotland back in '45, 'twas there he first landed afore moving on northward to Barra."

"Indeed?" The governess's eyes lit with curious excitement as she scanned the rugged shoreline of the tiny islet as if searching for the lost Stuart among the rocks and overgrowth. "Do tell us the tale, Mr. MacNeill..."

While Donald began recounting the same stories of the Jacobites they'd been told since childhood, Gabriel busied himself with checking and rechecking the halyard on the opposite side of the craft, thankful for the brisk chill of the wind against his face and neck, anything to draw his attention away from those damnable green eyes.

This woman, this mysterious stranger, had a light about her, an indescribable radiance that shone in her tireless inquisitiveness and passionate nature. She had a face that displayed every emotion she felt like an open book. It was *intoxicating.*

The journey up the firth was not by any means a brief one; it would take them till late morning to reach Oban Bay. At no time during their journey did Miss Harte ever seem at a loss for words.

Juliana, in contrast, never uttered a sound. She sat as she always had every day for the past three years, staring at the far-off horizon, oblivious to all the activity going on around her.

Still, Gabriel couldn't help but be astounded by this new governess. She never gave up. Unlike any previous governess who had quickly detached herself from any social interaction with Juliana when she wouldn't respond, Miss Harte continued to talk to Juliana as if they were carrying on a nonstop conversation. She included her in everything that was going on around them, even asking her questions as if she had no notion that only one of them was conversing.

The next hours passed quickly. Just over halfway to the mainland, the skiff cut to where the firth began to narrow between the larger isles of Mull and Jura. The winds here began to pull the small craft more strongly along as they swirled and whistled through the moody sea corridor, sending a salt-sea spray shooting upward from the peaked prow with each wave they crested.

At the customary spot, the oarsmen suddenly stopped, stilling their movements and lifting their oars high in the air, allowing Donald to steer his way expertly over the choppy waves.

It grew quiet. Even Miss Harte seemed to sense the change, and they sculled further inward toward Oban. Soon, a distant and familiar roar began to rise from the east, growing louder, it seemed, with each swell they rode.

"*Och*," said Donald as he kept a firm hand on the ship's rudder, "sounds as if the *cailleach* is in a fine temper this morn, it does."

"*Cailleach?*" the governess repeated.

"Aye. Do you hear that, Miss Nell? That roar? 'Tis the Hag of the Isles, the roar of the Corryvrecken. 'Tis a most fearsome tidal whirlpool that lies off the northern coast of Jura there." He pointed toward the nearest coastline, where three distinct peaks rose through the hovering mist. "You and the little lassie there had best find a firm handhold. Sailing will likely get rough 'ere for a spell."

"Is it dangerous?" Miss Harte asked, eyeing the eastern horizon with some consternation. Her bubbling enthusiasm for their leisurely sail had suddenly waned.

"Aye, it can be, for those who dinna ken the ways of the waters of Lorne," Donald said. "'Tis called *Coire Bhreacain* by the Gaels, 'Prince Breacain's Cauldron,' and it comes from a legend almost as auld as these same isles. They say that hundreds of years ago, back when it were the Picts and the Gaels who dwelled on these ancient lands, there came a Prince named Breacain one day from far off Norway, seeking the hand in marriage of the beautiful daughter of the Lord of the Isles.

"But the Lord, he intended to truly test this young prince afore he'd give up the precious prize o' his beloved daughter. So he told the prince he must anchor his galley for the length of three days and three nights in the churning flood tide that roars a'tween Jura and Scarba. If he made it through the third night to morning, he would win the hand of the lord's young lassie.

"Many a sailing ship had gone to her grave in those treacherous waters, so to better prepare himself, the prince hied his way back to Norway to consult with the mystic sages. These wise men studied their ancient scrolls and prayed for direction to the Norse deities, then finally they returned to the prince with their advice."

Miss Harte's eyes were alight with wonder. "What did they tell him?"

"They bid him to take three ropes with him to the Kingdom of the Isles, one spun of wool, another of hemp, and the third made of the hair of pure and true maidens. Well, needless to say, many a Norse lassie gave over her silken tresses to the handsome prince for his rope, but what he dinna know was that one lass," Donald shook his head dolefully, "*och*, she wasna so pure. Unknowing of this, Prince Breacain sailed swiftly back for the isles, ready with his three ropes and confident to face the challenge that the Lord of the Isles had put to him."

Gabriel found himself staring in fascination at the expression of now breathless wonder on the face of Donald's one-woman audience. Forgotten was her unease at the roar that now surrounded them; she was utterly captivated by the old tale.

Gabriel, in turn, was utterly captivated by her.

"What happened when the prince went back?" she asked.

"On the first night," Donald explained, his voice growing hushed over the sound of the sea, "the rope made of wool broke, but the prince managed to weather the pull of the tide and see his way through to morn. On the second night, the hemp rope fared no better. Still Breacain prevailed. The third rope did hold fast through the third night just as the sages had promised, until a terrible storm arose from the west and the one strand that contained the hair of the impure maiden broke, weakening the rest of the rope. Just afore the dawn, the rope frayed and Breacain and his ship were carried away by the raging flood tide, doomed never to win the hand of his princess. But his faithful hound snatched the poor prince's lifeless body from the churning waters and dragged him to the shores of Jura, where he was then buried in the cave that bears his name to this day."

By now, the governess was staring at Donald with an expression of pure and utter veneration. Even Juliana had become entranced by the story, pulling her gaze away from the distance to give her attention to the lyric words of MacNeill.

Gabriel stood silently applauding the sailor's effort, for in the time it had taken Donald to relate that old and colorful tale, he had managed to sail them clear of any danger from the roaring flood tide. Even now, its howl was slowly fading into the mists behind them.

It seemed but a short time later that they were drifting to a halt at the busy pier in Oban.

Gabriel jumped off the skiff first to see to securing the mooring ropes, then immediately went back to assist the others onto the pier. The past hours had been a trial for him, being in such close company with Juliana after having spent the past months doing everything to avoid her. He had to continually remind himself of the dangers of so much as enjoying his daughter's company.

Thus when he felt the touch of Juliana's fingers in his as he helped her forward, he started. He stopped himself from a greeting smile, tempering it with a curt nod as she stepped onto the pier.

He reached lastly for Miss Harte, who stood waiting at the

skiff's prow. In the moment that she stretched her leg over the hull to the pier, the boat took a sudden lurch, pitching her forward and into his arms. She looked up at him in stark surprise, so near to him that he could feel the warmth of the sharp exhale of her breath against his chin, that same alluring scent of her immediately overrunning his senses.

She was staring at him, her eyes wide, dark hazel green, her mouth slightly parted. He could kiss her so easily, and somehow he knew she would let him, even as he knew he had to get away from her.

Immediately.

Gabriel set the governess to rights and stepped awkwardly away.

"We must leave no later than three of the clock if we're to make it back to the isle by nightfall," he said with more abruptness than he had intended. "Please mind the time."

Without waiting for her response, he turned away from her on the pretense of rechecking the tightness of the mooring hawsers, leaving her to stare in befuddlement at the unyielding wall of his back.

There was a steep flight of stone steps, slick from the sea mist, that led up from the busy pier to George Street, the main thoroughfare of the tiny hamlet of Oban.

The Highland fishing village had sprouted up within only the past thirty years or more, around the eastern curve of a picturesque sea-swept bay. It was scarcely more than a string of thatched cottages and lime-washed houses with high pitched roofs, and though there was no church, there were two small inns, a Customs' House, a distillery, and a scattering of other trades all centered largely on the fisheries that made up the bulk of the village's sparse economy.

Set at the foot of a towering, tree-lined mountain, Oban was sheltered from the keen Hebridean winds by the verdant isle of Kerrera across the bay, and dominated on its northern end by the fortress of Dunollie.

Donald told her that this ancient castle was the seat of the Clan MacDougall, now an abandoned ruin, although it had once been the stronghold of the kings of Dalraida. The present MacDougall chief still occupied the land, living in a house built of the castle's own stone right after the defeat of the '45. All that remained of the original stronghold was the ancient keep, standing like a sentinel above the sheltered cove at the precise spot where lofty mountaintop met endless sky.

Eleanor decided that it would be wiser to begin their outing with someplace familiar, and so she headed off first down George Street, walking the short distance to the inn where she had stayed earlier that week. She thought to ask the innkeeper's wife, Mrs. MacIver, where she might go to find her much-needed shoes.

They had to step quickly to skirt an oncoming pony cart and Eleanor took hold of one of Juliana's hands to direct her along safely. She did not, however, let go after the cart had gone, and was delighted to see that Juliana did not pull away.

When they entered the dimly-lit front parlor of the inn, there was no one immediately about, although Eleanor could hear muffled voices coming from the rear of the place. She looked down at Juliana and smiled, directing her to a small rustic-looking bench set beneath the front window while they waited.

Eleanor turned just as the innkeeper's wife came into the room, wiping her hands on her apron.

"*Och*, lass, but you gave me a fright just now. I dinna hear you come in, but I canna say I am surprised to see you either. I expected you'd be back. As I said to you afore, few have ever lasted more than a night's time on that accursed isle. But not to worry, we still have your room ready for you. Will you be wanting to stay for just the one night, then, or longer this time?"

Eleanor shook her head. "Oh, no, I'm sorry, Mrs. MacIver, but you are mistaken. I do not mean to take a room. I have decided to stay and serve as governess on the isle. I only just—"

Mrs. MacIver's eyes had gone wide as the harvest moon with disbelief. And then she spotted Juliana sitting behind Eleanor. Her mouth fell open in astonishment and it took her a full minute to find her tongue. "You mean to say you are going to stay there on that wicked isle and tend to that demon's child?"

Eleanor scowled unhappily at the woman. "I'll thank you not to speak in such an impolite manner in front of Miss MacFeagh."

"She *is* the demon's child, she is, sure as her da has stolen away her voice."

"That is enough, Mrs. MacIver."

"Then tell me, why doesna she speak like other bairns?"

"Perhaps because she has nothing to say. I would remind you that the fact that she doesn't speak does not prevent her from *hearing*, so I would ask you to hold your tongue against any further commentary, thank you. Now, if you would be so kind as to direct us to the village shoemaker, we will take ourselves off from your parlor and be on our way."

Mrs. MacIver shook her head dolefully. "*Och*, lass, but 'tis a grievous mistake you're makin'. A most grievous mistake."

Eleanor frowned. "The shoemaker, Mrs. MacIver, if you please."

The woman harrumphed, obviously displeased that she had failed to convince her to her nonsensical allegations. "He's down the road a bit on the bay side near to the end of town. Has a big black bear of a dog that lays by his door a'day, lazy as a lump in a pudding. Just look you for that beast and you canna miss findin' the place."

Eleanor thanked the woman and held out her hand to Juliana who took it quickly, no doubt as eager as she was to be out the door.

It was as she was reaching for the handle to leave that she first spotted the notice tacked next to the door in the precise place where she had days before discovered the advertisement that had taken her to Trelay.

This time, however, it wasn't any offer of employment.

NOTICE

A monetary reward of substantial sum is offered for
the safe return of one Lady Eleanor Wycliffe

of the esteemed Westover Dukedom.
The lady is of fair complexion with brown hair
and green eyes and was last known to be traveling
alone through the northern Highlands. Please contact
His Grace, the Duke of Westover, or his heir,
Marquess Knighton of Skynegal, with any information.
No expense will be spared in the search for her.

Eleanor felt a startling frisson run through her. Her family. They were hunting for her.

The notice had to have been posted within the past two days, since she had stayed at the inn so recently and had not noticed it before. She wanted to question Mrs. MacIver about it, to ask who had brought it and when, but worried any interest she showed might draw the woman's attention to the fact that the subject of the notice was quite obviously herself.

She was surprised, in fact, the woman hadn't realized it already, but perhaps somehow she hadn't been there when the notice had been posted.

Eleanor glanced over at Mrs. MacIver, who was busying herself with some flowers she was arranging in a small vase. Pretending to search through her reticule, Eleanor waited until the woman had turned her back for a moment, and then quickly snatched the notice from the wall, shoving it carelessly inside her bag.

Once outside, Eleanor paused a moment to calm herself. Her first thought was to return to MacNeill's skiff and simply wait there till it was time to leave, and she would have, except that she really needed to purchase her shoes. Perhaps it was the only notice posted, she thought hopefully. And if it wasn't, she would just have to make sure that she found and removed any others, starting, she decided, with the shoemaker's cottage.

As they started down the roadway in the direction Mrs.

MacIver had directed, Eleanor looked upward toward the mountains and noticed that the skies were beginning to cast over. She hoped that it wouldn't rain again.

They hadn't walked very far before they came upon a small, vine-clad cottage that had what looked like an open-ended barrel sticking out the top as a chimney. Lying in front was indeed a most prodigious black dog, sprawled before the door. His eyes were closed and his breathing was heavy, and he seemed to pay them no mind as they quietly approached. He didn't move, didn't so much as lift his head—

—until they were within a foot of him.

He jerked upright, placing himself between them and the door in one swift movement. In the next moment, he started barking like a hellhound.

Juliana froze at her side. Eleanor quickly put herself between the girl and the barking dog. Holding the child's hand tightly in hers, Eleanor took one cautious step closer toward the door. The dog bared his teeth and glared at her.

"Is anyone there?" she called feebly to the house, hoping to somehow alert the dog's owner inside, as if her quivering voice would do that more than this creature's unholy din.

There came no response, so she released Juliana's hand to step slightly to the side and closer to the single window. She tried to peek inside its filmy pane. "Excuse me, is anyone there?"

As she moved a bit to better see between the ragged curtains, Eleanor heard the dog give a low growl. She turned to look, drawing in a sharp breath.

"Juliana, no!"

Juliana had stepped forward and had extended her hand to within a few inches of the dog's grizzled snout. Eleanor's first instinct was to pull her from harm's way, but she feared that if she moved too quickly, the dog would become startled and lash out.

It was then she noticed that the dog was no longer growling. Instead, he had lifted his great snout upward, sniffing curiously at Juliana's outstretched fingers. Eleanor caught her breath, watching on. The dog gave a soft whine and then licked Juliana's hand, pushing his head under her fingers for a scratch.

Juliana smiled and stooped down before the beast, gently petting him.

"Aye, I thought I heard someone calling. Good day to you, miss."

A brawny man, perhaps in his later twenties, with muddy blond hair and amber-colored eyes, came around from the back of the ramshackle cottage. He wiped his fingers on a cloth before holding out his hand to her in greeting. "Seamus Maclean at your service."

Eleanor smiled and shook his hand. "Good day to you, Mr. Maclean. I am Miss Nell Harte, and this is Miss Juliana MacFeagh. We've come looking for some shoes."

"MacFeagh?" He eyed Juliana with much the same look as the annoying Mrs. MacIver. "Would that be the MacFeagh from Trelay?"

After the earlier conversation at the inn, Eleanor's defenses prickled immediately. "Yes, sir, that is right. We have come from Trelay. I am the governess on the isle now."

"Governess, aye?" His smile no longer gave the impression of friendliness. Instead, it seemed almost to mock her words.

Eleanor frowned at him.

"So this is her, the wee quiet one. Aye, though she carries the unfortunate mark of her da's coloring, she still has the light o' her mother's gentle beauty, she does."

Had this man known Juliana's mother? Perhaps the viscountess had come to town for shoes herself. His words, however, and the distinct emotion he spoke them with gave indication of a far more familiar relationship.

Maclean must have remembered then that they had come to give him business, for his tone changed almost in an instant. "You've come looking for shoes, you say?"

"Yes. A pair of half-boots, if you please, Mr. Maclean."

The shoemaker grinned broadly. "You're no' from the Highlands, are you, Miss Harte?"

She would have thought that her obvious lack of a Scottish accent would have given that bit of information away, but she simply shook her head and said, "I come from England, sir."

"A *Sass'nach*, you say? Well, I canna say I've ever seen or even heard of something called a ha'boot. Most Highland lassies dinna wear any shoes a'tall."

Eleanor drew a frustrated breath. "I see. Well, apparently I've come to the wrong establishment then. I'm sorry to have troubled you, Mr. Maclean." She turned to leave. "Come, Juliana."

"Aye, you must be from the Lowlands indeed, ready as you are to rush off e'en afore I've finished what I'm saying."

Eleanor stopped and looked at him, waiting.

"I cannot make you this ha'boot you speak of, but I can make you a bonny pair of Scottish brogues that'll serve you much better than those wee fancy slippers you're wearing now. I'll need to measure your feet first, though, to check the fit."

He walked over to the door of the cottage, opened it and stepped back, motioning for Eleanor to proceed ahead. Eleanor hesitated a moment, hoping she wouldn't regret having come, wondering if she dare trust him long enough to stay. She decided her need for the shoes outweighed her misgivings. She nodded for Juliana to come and started for the door.

Eleanor ducked inside the low doorway and found herself standing in a single cluttered room that took up the entirety of the cottage's interior. A crudely-built hearth was set against the far wall, looking more like a haphazard stack of flat stones, the smoke from which filled the room more than it escaped through what was indeed an open-ended barrel chimney. A blackened kettle simmered there and variously shaped tools and utensils hung in a scattered mixture from every spare bit of wall space. Piles of leather hide stood on one table. Forms, wooden and in the shape of a foot, were cluttered in one corner.

Thankfully, there was no sign of another notice like the one she had removed from the inn. She rather doubted he could find room for it on the wall anyway.

Maclean crossed the room to quickly dust off a small wooden bench by the hearth and then motioned for her to sit while he retreated to the far corner for some things.

Eleanor removed her slipper and made to hand it to him when he returned.

"Wha's that for?"

"For you to measure my foot with, sir."

Maclean grinned again, shaking his head as if she had just said something amusing. "I canna form a brogue from that bonny bit o' nonsense."

He sat down on a small stool before her and held out his hand, quite obviously expecting her to deliver her foot into it.

Maidenly modesty apparently had no place in the Highlands.

Eleanor lifted her foot to his waiting palm while making certain that the hem of her skirts went no higher than her ankle.

Maclean moved his hands deftly over her stockinged foot, testing several leathern shoe forms against the length of it. There was no attempt at delicacy in his touch. Rather the manner in which he worked was filled with a casual familiarity that made Eleanor increasingly uncomfortable.

When she felt his hands move upward under her skirts past her ankle to her calf, Eleanor stiffened. "I beg your pardon, sir, but..."

"That's enough, Maclean."

Eleanor drew a startled breath at the sudden and unexpected

voice coming from behind them. She turned to see Lord Dunevin standing just inside the cottage doorway, filling it with his imposing stature, his face crossed by a stern frown.

The dog, she realized, had never made a sound to forewarn of his arrival.

"I believe you have sufficient measurement to make the lady a competent pair of brogues. Now get on with it."

Maclean scoffed, his eyes fixed coldly on the viscount. "Ah, well, when I awoke this fine morn I'd never have believed I'd find the Devil of Dunevin Castle standing in my parlor door. How does the mighty Lord 'Done-Her-In' fare these days?"

Dunevin's eyes narrowed perilously as he advanced into the room. His dark head nearly glanced the smoke-blackened rafters above them. "We've a boat to catch in order to return to the isle by nightfall, Maclean. Just get the lady her brogues and be quick about it."

The men faced each other through a tense moment. Still grinning that cold smirk, Maclean then turned to Eleanor. "I've a pair a'ready made that'll suit you in the back. I'll take but a moment, lass."

He stood and departed through a door at the rear of the cottage.

Alone now with only the heavy silence between them, the viscount looked at Eleanor, his expression grim.

"You would be wise, Miss Harte, not to allow a Scotsman such liberties, and especially in front of my daughter."

Eleanor stared at him, dumbfounded. "Liberties? I beg your pardon, my lord, but Mr. Maclean was fitting me for a pair of shoes. Yes, he did become a bit too familiar and at the moment you interrupted, I was on the very verge of rebuking him."

"A man like Maclean would care very little about your polite rebuke." He glanced quickly at Juliana before saying, "I will await you outside."

Eleanor didn't know who she wanted to cosh on the head more, Maclean for his crudeness, or Lord Dunevin for his unfounded accusation. He made it sound almost as if she had been flirting with the Scots' cobbler. Even worse, he had inferred that she could not handle herself, that all would have been lost had he not happened upon the scene when he had to save her.

She fought against the urge to inform him in no uncertain terms that she was quite capable of taking care of herself, that she had had the situation well in hand. Instead, she could but set her feelings aside and smile when she noticed that Juliana was watching her. She waited silently for Maclean to return.

He did, after a handful of minutes, carrying with him a pair of the leather-laced shoes the Highlanders called brogues.

Eleanor slipped one of the thin-soled coverings easily over her foot and then pulled tightly on the leather thongs that criss-crossed the top of her foot to tie it. The shoe fit with the snug-ness of a glove, the softly treated leather molding itself delicately to the contours of her foot. Despite his impolite behavior, Maclean certainly knew his trade.

As she took a few steps to test the fit, Eleanor noticed that the sides of the shoes had been left unstitched in places. Maclean must have noticed her uncertainty in looking at them and explained.

"The sides are left open like that to allow water to escape, else you'd be sloshing about like an otter whenever it rains."

They were certainly like no other shoes she had ever worn before, but as she became accustomed to the flexible fit of them, Eleanor found she quite liked them.

"Thank you, Mr. Maclean. They are very nice. I especially thank you for making them so quickly. What do I owe you, sir?"

He was putting away his tools, his back to her. "Three shillings. They wear out quite easily, so for that price I'll make you up another pair and send it over the next time MacNeill makes the crossing."

As Eleanor reached to place her coins on his work table, Maclean turned to look at her. Gone was the smirking grin and mocking amber eyes. Instead his expression had turned unexpectedly grave.

"Be careful on that isle, lass. 'Tis a mournful, forsaken place. If you should ever find yourself in danger, always remember *Uamh nan Fhalachasan,* 'the Cave of the Hidden.' Ask Màiri where it is. There is a secret chamber at the back of it that even he"— the cobbler glanced at the door where the viscount had just departed—"dinna know of. Keep it to yourself, lass, and tell no one of it. Dinna make the same mistake that Lady Georgiana did."

His stare was so intense that Eleanor could only manage a short nod, averting her eyes nervously as she turned and called for Juliana to follow her.

As she made for the door, Eleanor wondered that the confrontation earlier between Maclean and Lord Dunevin had had less to do with her than it had to do with whatever history there was between the two men, a history that she suspected had something to do with the former viscountess.

As they emerged from inside the cottage, Eleanor was more than a little surprised to see that Lord Dunevin was still waiting for them outside.

"The brogues fit well?"

He seemed to have forgotten the unpleasantness from inside the cottage.

"Yes, indeed, my lord. They are most snug and comfortable."

"Good. I'll escort you to the pier then," and he started down the dirt path leading away from the cottage.

"Oh, thank you, my lord, but Juliana and I are not yet finished with our sightseeing. We've yet nearly another two hours and I thought to explore the ruins of Dunollie before finishing my shopping in town. I do appreciate your kind offer, but I believe I can take it from here."

He mumbled something she didn't quite hear. "I beg your pardon, my lord?"

"I said I will accompany you to wherever else you need to go."

Eleanor thought for a moment, then nodded, thinking this a good opportunity for him to spend some time in Juliana's company. Perhaps if he saw the progress she was already making with his daughter, he wouldn't be so reluctant to spend time with her himself. In fact, Eleanor thought further, she would do whatever she could to prolong the outing for just that purpose.

"Shall we go, then?"

They spent the next quarter hour climbing the steep path that led up the thickly-treed hillside to the castle ruins. The view over the secluded bay and distant isles there was truly breathtaking, a rich palette of colors—greens, purples and reds—that stretched for as far as the eye could see. The viscount pointed out the isles of Mull and Lismore and the Morvern Peninsula, clearly seen from this lofty vantage, making it easy to see why this particular site had been chosen for the fortress. Built at a time when most all travel was done on water, anyone approaching within the distance of ten miles would be easily spotted.

While they were there, climbing about what had once been the seat of ancient kings, they encountered the present MacDougall chief, Patrick "Peter" MacDougall, who had watched their approach from the house he occupied a short distance away. Despite his advanced age of nearly eighty years, he had made the walk up the hill to greet them and had spent nearly an hour telling them wondrous tales of the MacDougalls throughout history. Eleanor thought him a warm and genial host.

Leaving Dunollie, they made their way back down the hillside path to town. As they strolled quietly along George Street, each lost to their own thoughts, Eleanor couldn't set aside the nagging sensation that they were being watched.

And they were.

One place in particular drew the curtains closed when they

passed and children who were playing at Tom Tiddles scattered as their mothers called them in. Every quaint cottage and house they passed along the way was like so many of the lines of decorated ladies at a London ball, whispering to each other from behind their lace-edged fans.

It was utterly ridiculous, Eleanor thought, this unfounded fear an entire town had of the viscount. He was a man, not a monster, out merely taking a pleasant stroll in fine weather with his daughter. For his part, Lord Dunevin pretended not to notice the villager's actions, still the frown he wore deepened the further along they walked.

Eleanor stopped at a couple of the waterfront shops to purchase lengths of sturdy woolen for skirts, a few pair of thickly knit stockings, and chemises made of the white twilled cloth called *cuirtan* that Màiri had advised her to get. She ordered several and tried to ignore the shopkeeper's dismayed expression when she learned they were for delivery to Trelay. She was relieved, however, to note that no other place in the village had another notice posted about her missing.

By the time she finished, Eleanor had spent nearly all of the coin Lord Dunevin had given her as an advance on her salary, but there was still enough left for one more item, one she had purposely saved enough to buy.

They came to a small shop nestled near the pier, a haberdashery of sorts whose front window was filled with everything from wooden spindles to timepieces. Eleanor had remembered the place from her previous visit to the village, had remembered something in particular she'd seen.

"Excuse me, my lord, but there is one last place I wish to stop."

Lord Dunevin glanced quickly at his timepiece. "The hour grows late, Miss Harte."

"I'll only be just a moment, my lord. I promise."

He nodded curtly and Eleanor turned for the shop, which by now Juliana automatically followed her into. While Juliana was gazing at some small painted pictures of sailing ships set up near the back counter, Eleanor quickly made her purchase, thanking the shopkeeper with a smile as she turned to leave.

With this last purchase tucked under one arm, Eleanor returned with Juliana to where Lord Dunevin awaited and they walked in relative silence to the pier.

Donald MacNeill was standing ready at the skiff, chatting amiably with a fellow boatman, when they approached. MacNeill smiled at Juliana in greeting and spoke quietly to her as he helped her on board, in sharp contrast to the many villagers they had encountered that day who had looked on the child quite as if she carried the plague.

Once Juliana was settled safely upon one of the thwarts, Donald then reached to assist Eleanor aboard. "Tha's a fine pair o' brogues you've gotten there, Miss Harte."

"Thank you, Mr. MacNeill. Mr. Maclean tells me he will have a second pair ready by the time you come to the mainland again."

"Then I'll be certain to fetch them for you."

Eleanor nodded her thanks and joined Juliana.

It had been a pleasant day despite the boorishness of Maclean, Mrs. MacIver, and the villagers. There had been several occasions during the course of the day when Eleanor had noticed Juliana actually listening to her and not lost to her own silent world. Eleanor had delighted in her progress to reach the child, a sign, she believed, of even better things to come.

"Juliana," she said as she sat beside her on the skiff's small bench seat, "I have something to show you."

Eleanor removed the cloth covering from the small extending spyglass she had just purchased at the haberdashery. "Do you know what this is?"

Juliana took up the brass piece in her hand and studied it closely, turning it over several times in her hand. She looked at Eleanor.

"It is called a spyglass." Eleanor took it and extended it to its full size, about the length of a foot of interconnecting pieces. The light of responding curiosity that sparked in Juliana's eyes was her reward.

"You look through it on the small end here and it makes things that are faraway look closer." She pointed it out toward the isle of Kerrera as they sailed down the sound for the firth beyond. "Here, why don't you try it."

Eleanor sat back and watched on as Juliana placed the glass near her eye and looked out at the horizon. Brow knit in concentration, the child looked, drew back and looked again, taking the glass away time and again to compare the true distance with the one she saw through the glass.

"Amazing isn't it? Do you like it?"

Juliana simply stared at her, but her eyes spoke her agreement clearly.

"Then it is yours."

Juliana remained still through a quiet moment. Then she did the most extraordinary thing.

She smiled.

It wasn't a wide, ear-reaching grin, but instead the shy tentative smile of one who had gone too long without doing so. Eleanor thought to herself that she would have paid the cost of one hundred spyglasses if it would have taken that to see this one moment of Juliana's happiness.

"Look there!" She pointed outward, watching as Juliana went back to peering through the glass. She sat back on the seat, relishing the sea air against her face, the freedom of gliding over the waves. It was then Eleanor noticed Lord Dunevin sitting across from them.

He was watching Juliana and her smile, unaware of Eleanor's silent scrutiny. His gaze as he stared at his daughter was filled with such softness, such unconscious longing, that Eleanor could feel his emotion almost as clearly as if it were a tangible thing.

This was not the face of a man who didn't care for his child.

Lord Dunevin loved Juliana with the tender adoration of a true father, but for some imperceptible reason, he just didn't want anyone else to know it.

And that left Eleanor with one lingering thought.

Why? What was it that made him hide his affection, as if he was somehow afraid to let anyone else know how he truly felt?

---

8

*T*he journey back from Oban was uneventful, quiet and touched by a vibrant sunset, mixed pinks, purples and oranges shimmering over sleepy gray waters that glistened like glass in its ebbing light.

The image of Trelay, limned by mists and colorful light, was one of the most beautiful Eleanor could ever imagine having seen. She stood on the ship's deck, relishing the wind on her face, awed by it all as they sailed their way to dock at the jetty.

The coming back seemed to take twice as long as the getting there, and they arrived at Dunevin shortly after dark. But Màiri had been ready for them.

A simple supper of barley bannocks, cheese, and sliced roast pullet was waiting when they returned. As they ate, Màiri asked about their outing, thrilling over Juliana's new spyglass, making plans with Eleanor for the woolens she'd purchased, and then she filled Gabriel in on the doings at the castle in his absence.

Soon after their meal, the day's activities began to make their effects known, bringing on quiet thought, wide yawns, and fast-drooping eyes.

They retired early, and once again, Eleanor had gone down to the kitchen after seeing Juliana to bed for a cup of tea with Màiri. Once again she returned abovestairs to find Juliana missing from her bed, curled asleep in her mother's bed, and joined her there.

Early the following morning, they shared a simple breakfast of oatcakes and tea, sitting at the small table by the warmth of the kitchen hearth while Màiri flitted about the place in preparation for the baking she would do for the upcoming Michaelmas holiday.

The festival of St. Michael, patron saint of the sea, would bring the month of September to a close, the traditional end of the harvest, when rents were paid and thanks were given for a bountiful crop.

Màiri's two married daughters, Alys and Sorcha, had come that morning from the mainland to help their mother to prepare. While they checked that there would be enough meal and other food stuffs for the traditional Struan Micheil cake that would be the highlight of the celebration, Màiri sat with Eleanor and Juliana, telling them of the sacred holiday.

"Ev'ryone on the isle takes part in the celebration," she explained, "beginning on the Sunday afore St. Michael's Day, a day we call *Dòmhnach Curran,* when all the women and young lasses of the isle of every age gather the wild carrots from the fields. 'Tis a tradition that is long seated in the isles. You and the wee one must take part with us, too."

Eleanor was delighted to accept.

The weather had continued fair so after finishing their breakfast, Eleanor saw that Juliana was dressed warmly enough, then tied the thonged laces of her new brogues snugly, and the two of them set off for the craggy hills beyond the castle. They would pass the day exploring through Juliana's new spyglass.

As they crested the first hilltop, Eleanor turned back once and thought she spied a figure standing at one of the castle windows. At their distance apart, she could not see that the figure was the Lord Dunevin, nor could she see his troubled frown as he watched their departure, his thoughts haunted by another such outing three years before, one from which only one had come back.

The sun seemed content to hide its morning warmth behind a mottled covering of autumn clouds, the wind blowing in off the firth briskly, tugging at the ends of their overcoats as they walked. Eleanor wore the warmest gown she had, an ashen gray with heavier skirts and sleeves. Her new woolen stockings provided ample warmth against the cold, but she had brought along a spare pair for them each just in case they might need them.

Within a half an hour, the carefully wound chignon into which Eleanor had fashioned her hair that morning had grown slack, drooping further and further down the nape of her neck. A quarter hour more and Eleanor gave up the effort of keeping it confined altogether, pulling the pins that secured it from her hair and letting it fall in a loose tangle about her shoulders.

As they walked along, they stopped now and again to investigate some curious speck on the far horizon with the spyglass, only to find numerous herring boats, an occasional shearwater soaring close to the water's surface in search for a fishy snack, and the bobbing rounded head of a gray seal who curiously seemed to be following them.

Juliana constantly stopped to peer at the creature while Eleanor chatted pleasantly to her about the island landscape, remarking on the abundance of wildflowers they encountered this late in the season. As they went, they gathered woodruff and other herbs for Màiri to freshen the linen presses, tucking them in a small willow basket she had given them before they'd left.

It was a most pleasant day.

As they made their way over brae and glen, they met with several of the tenants of Trelay. The whole of the island was governed by Lord Dunevin, and those who lived outside the castle proper occupied land that was divided into separate crofts, or small holdings, which they farmed both to feed their families and to earn their living.

Most often, the crofters would not earn enough from the land to sustain themselves, so they would supplement their incomes with secondary trades such as fishing, kelping, weaving, or in providing other services, as Donald MacNeill did in delivering the island post and ferrying goods and people between Trelay and the mainland.

The crofts they passed stood mostly on their own, not in clusters as was common in the villages of England, and they usually consisted of a thatched-roof cottage built alongside a "drystane" enclosure used for keeping sheep and goats. The materials used for constructing the cottages came from the land itself, stones of every size and shape heaped one upon another to form patchwork walls around an earthen floor and beneath a heavy roof. Some had a crude chimney, or *lum*, through which the smoke from the perpetually-burning peat fire escaped. Others simply allowed the smoke to hover above their heads, making its way out slowly through the small crevices and openings in the thatch while turning the rafters inside a glistening black.

While some might look on such seemingly impoverished conditions of living as miserable, the crofters, Eleanor found, were a happy, congenial folk. All greeted them with friendly smiles and welcoming warmth, stopping in their work in the fields to wave and call out in Gaelic greeting.

Whenever they happened close upon a cottage, they were immediately invited inside to partake of whatever refreshment was at hand, freshly drawn milk, tea, whisky even, despite the fact that for some, it was all they had. Everyone treated Juliana with the respect due the daughter of their laird, calling her the "Wee MacFeagh," and if they felt any awkwardness about the fact that she didn't speak, they certainly did not show it. Lord Dunevin was only spoken of as a good laird, a chief who saw after the well-being of his people, a reaction so very different from the mainlanders they had encountered the day before.

It was while they were visiting with the family of Donald MacNeill, the boatman who had taken them across to Oban, that Eleanor began to hear more of the history of the island and its reclusive, mysterious laird.

Eleanor was sitting at a sturdy oaken table, enjoying the warmth of a fresh cup of tea in her hands while Donald's eldest son, introduced to them as "Donald the Younger," took Juliana out with him to watch as he brought in the sheep from where they grazed.

Donald's wife, Seòna, was stirring a savory-smelling stew that simmered in an iron kettle over the hearth fire. Their toddler son, whom they called "Wee Donald," played happily with a ball of yarn at his father's feet. It was tradition in the isles, they had explained, to name sons for father and grandfather to ensure that an honored name carried on.

Seòna was a young woman with soft brown hair that she wore pulled back from her cheerful face beneath the netting of a snood. Her feet were bare beneath the colorful plaid of her skirts and she wore a saffron-colored chemise beneath a dark-colored bodice that laced loosely at the waist, for she was with child, one which she hoped would be born a lass, she said, for she could come up with no other fitting nicknames for another Donald.

"'Tis a good thing, your coming to the island to look after the wee MacFeagh," said Donald then, nodding over his cup of tea, and echoing the words of Màiri that first night Eleanor had been on the isle.

"Aye, a verra good thing," Seòna added as she tossed bits of the potato she'd been chopping into the stew. "'Tis been too long since we've seen a new face on the isle, it has."

"Were there many governesses at Dunevin before me?" Eleanor asked. She noticed that Donald cast a momentary glance at his wife before responding.

"Not many, one or two"—he paused—"three or more, but then Lady Dunevin has been gone to us these three years past. Afore she died, she cared for the wee one herself with the help of a maid."

"Who has cared for Juliana since then, when she hasn't had a governess?"

"Màiri mostly. Sometimes his lairdship's ghillie, Fergus. He's a man who has served the lairds of Dunevin for generations. 'Twas an honor for him to see to the wee one, it was."

Eleanor nodded, watching Juliana outside the small window as she knelt to pet the sniffing nose of one of the fleecy lambs who had just come in. She wondered that perhaps Fergus's outwardly gruff manner toward her was due more to having her, a stranger, suddenly assuming responsibilities he'd formerly held.

"Has Lord Dunevin been laird of the isle for very long?"

"Only the past ten years or more," Donald answered on a nod. He offered her an oatcake fresh and hot from the fire. "He was on the Peninsula and at university afore that."

"Lord Dunevin fought against Napoleon?"

Eleanor knew a number of her family's acquaintances who had gone abroad to serve, Robert Edenhall, now Duke of Devonbrook, Bartholomew Tolley, all friends of her brother, Christian, whom she had known since childhood. She wondered whether any of them might be acquainted with Lord Dunevin.

"Aye, the laird was the fiercest soldier I've ever seen," Donald continued. "We were together at Corunna. The man lost three horses beneath him but he ne'er faltered. 'Twas as if the enemy shot somehow couldna touch him. A loss to the regiment, it was, when he left us."

"He was injured?"

"*Och*, no, lass. He was called back to Trelay when his brother Malcolm died suddenly and left him as the new laird. The MacFeagh are one of the oldest of all the clans in the isles. The last living direct descendent of the MacFeagh couldna risk his life 'gainst the French. Lord Dunevin had his duty to the clan and the people of this isle and so came home to wed Lady Dunevin and settle in. Then the wee one came and all was well, until..."

Just then, Donald the Younger and Juliana came into the cottage from outside. Eleanor wondered what Donald had been about to say, but decided it was a conversation that would be better kept for another time.

She turned a warm smile on Juliana whose face had touches of color at her cheeks from the brisk wind. Her eyes, framed by the wisps of her dark hair that had blown loose from its ribbon, were vibrant and animated.

She didn't need to say a thing for Eleanor to know she had enjoyed her outing with the young Donald; it showed clearly in her expression.

"Well, we have taken up enough of your time," Eleanor said, rising from her chair. "It is past time we were heading back to Dunevin now. Thank you so much for your hospitality."

"Would you be needin' Young Donald to walk you the way back?" MacNeill asked. "It grows late."

Eleanor shook her head, pulling on her overcoat. "I believe we can find our way, but thank you for the kind offer."

Linked arm in arm, Donald and Seòna bid them farewell, inviting them back for another visit whenever they wished, which Eleanor could already guess would be often. She had enjoyed herself at the simple croft very much. They were warm and friendly people, and one of the few families on the isle who spoke English as well as the native Gaelic.

Outside, the sky had already begun to darken with the twilight, even though the hour was just late afternoon. Eleanor and Juliana had not made it any further than the crest of the first hilltop before Donald the Younger came following from behind with a wooden pail swinging in his hand.

"Ma sent me to fetch some milk for our supper. If you dinna

mind it, I thought I'd walk with you since we seem to be headin' the same way."

Eleanor smiled and nodded, turning to wave her thanks to Donald who stood watching from the cottage doorway behind them.

Donald the Younger was twelve and already stood taller than his da, whose red hair had been passed on to his son. His lanky arms were muscled beneath the linen of his sark from his constant work on the croft. A bright lad, he knew every landmark they passed and pointed out a good many of them, recounting the legendary tales surrounding each seemingly insignificant rock or tree that dotted the endless landscape.

"That there," he said, pointing out a large rounded stone that rested alone, looking quite out of place, on the machair. "That is 'The Lifting Stone.' 'Tis said that the stone was thrown 'ere all the way from Eire by the great Fingal himself. It was used as a test of a man's strength though only few could move it and none certainly in this lifetime. And that," he said pointing outward toward what appeared to be a small recess on the side of a far hill, "that is one o' the MacFeagh's Hiding Places."

"One of them?" Eleanor asked.

"Aye. Legend has it that the last great MacFeagh, Malcolm MacFeagh—not the laird's brother, but another Malcolm—was hunted down by enemy Macleans there. They chased him from spot to spot and finally caught him hiding in a cave with his great black hound. There were two entrances to the cave, as there are even to this day, and he stood guard at one entrance with his mighty claymore while the hound kept watch at the other, but they shot him through with an arrow by way of an opening in the cave roof. It's been since then that the MacFeaghs lost their ruling place over the three isles and were exiled here to Trelay."

"But why did the Macleans wish the MacFeagh harm?"

Young Donald simply shrugged. "*Och*, 'twas a long standing feud, as most feuds are, the reasons for it lost over time."

Eleanor was suddenly reminded of the shoemaker in Oban, Seamus Maclean, and the obvious hostility between him and Lord Dunevin the day before. She wondered if their enmity was a last, enduring remnant of this same, age-long feud.

While Donald had been telling his tales to Eleanor and Juliana, he had nearly filled his wooden pail from the black cow who stood sedately grazing. He had clearly inherited his father's gift for storytelling. His chore completed, they started for the shore, chatting as they went about ancient clans and bitter feuds and the like. The sun was nearly gone over the western hills, and the mist that seemed ever to cling to the isle had begun to drift in slowly off the sea, dappling the landscape around them.

As they approached the shore, right at the point where the grassland gave over to sandy dune, there stood a curious, conical-shaped hillock, nearly as tall as Eleanor, surely man-made for as perfectly shaped as it was.

"What is that?" Eleanor asked, standing by as Donald proceeded closer toward it.

"Oh, that? 'Tis just a *sithan*," he answered as if it were as common as an English hedgerow.

Eleanor waited quietly for the explanation she knew had to be coming, her mouth falling open when, as without so much as a "Watch me now," Young Donald proceeded to pour a goodly portion of the milk from his bucket into the top of the hillock where a small opening had been formed.

He poured until the milk nearly overflowed it, then stood and waited several moments while it slowly receded into the ground. He then turned to Eleanor and as matter-of-factly as one could possibly speak, said, "'Tis for the *sith*."

She looked at him, incredulous. "*Sith?*" was all she could manage in response.

"Aye, 'the Still Folk.' They live in those small hills. We of the isle call them 'Fairy Knowes.' 'Tis a long known fact that if you offer the wee folk some o' your own milk, they will ne'er bring their mischief to your house. 'Tis they who make the green fields grow so rich for the cows to live on so that we will have their milk to sustain us. 'Tis only fittin' then that we should give some of our bounty back from whence it came."

Had she been talking to him thus in one of the numerous London ballrooms that had been the setting for her life before coming to Trelay, Eleanor would have believed the boy a likely candidate for Bedlam. Still Folk? Fairy Knowes? But somehow, standing on the shore of this rocky, mist-swept isle, where the unknown was as much a part of life as the known, she couldn't entirely dismiss his superstitious logic.

Even as they turned to walk away, bidding Young Donald and his half-filled milk bucket farewell, Eleanor found herself looking back to the peculiar grassy mound just once, to see if maybe something strange and unexpected had suddenly appeared.

Like a wee person.

As they continued on their way back to the castle, the skies seemed to be growing darker by the minute, the mist settling in thickly, making it difficult to tell if they were still heading in the right direction. Juliana began to walk closely by Eleanor's side, her small hand soon finding its way into hers as they picked their way over a rocky, desolate mull that was slick from the incoming tide.

Eleanor tried to ease Juliana's growing apprehension by chatting to her about Young Donald's unusual stories, all while secretly hoping that the next hill they climbed would be the one she had turned back from hours earlier to look at the castle.

She wasn't too terribly worried, though, for she knew that eventually, even if they were walking in the wrong direction, they would arrive at one of the crofter's cottages who would be more than happy, she knew, to offer them shelter until the morn.

They had to climb a cragged outcropping in order to continue on their course and Eleanor stopped to help Juliana up before her. Then, grabbing a handhold on the rough granite while tucking her toe onto a footstep, she pulled herself up behind.

Through the swirling mist, she could see Juliana standing several feet in front of her, looking out toward the distant sea that crashed on the rocks below them. As Eleanor came up beside her, she could see that the child's eyes were fixed widely, her face suddenly an ashen white.

"Juliana, what is it?"

Juliana did not move, not even to look at her, in response.

Eleanor looked out across the water to see if she could find what had so caught the little girl's attention, but saw nothing through the dense swirling mist. She reached for Juliana's hand and tried to lead her away, frightened by the strange look in her eyes.

"Come, Juliana. Let us get back before it grows much darker..."

It was almost as if the child's feet had taken root to the ground, so fixed was she on that distant shore. She wouldn't budge.

Eleanor murmured to her, soothing her, trying everything she could think of to draw her away, but to no avail.

In the very next moment, Juliana began to tremble.

Eleanor knelt down beside her, patting her hand. "What is it, Juliana? Are you cold? What is wrong? Please, tell me..."

Juliana wouldn't respond. Eleanor was quickly growing panicked now, too panicked to realize the uselessness of her words. Her heart began beating anxiously as she looked all around, trying to find something, anything, to pull Juliana's attention back to the present. It was as if she were fixed in some terrible trance, unreachable even though she stood right beside her. Eleanor stood, helpless, desperate, as she searched the thickening darkness around them.

Blessedly, after several moments, she spied a flickering lamplight glowing off in the distance, but she couldn't leave Juliana standing there alone, trembling so fiercely. She cried out for help, praying that whoever it was would understand her enough to come to their aid.

Seconds later, the lamplight began to move in their direction. Eleanor blinked back her growing alarm as a figure of a man of middling age who she immediately recognized as one of the crofters they had seen earlier that day, emerged from the darkness and mist.

He spoke to her in Gaelic, but she had no way of responding. All she could manage was to wave her hands about.

"Please, go find Lord Dunevin...the laird...MacFeagh..."

Finally, the man nodded to her. He pressed his flickering *cruisie* lamp into her hands and turned, jogging off into the thickening darkness. Eleanor simply stayed at Juliana's side, trying once again to calm her, talking softly to her, begging her to come away and return home to the warmth of the kitchen fire, where she promised Màiri would be waiting.

She had no notion of how much time had passed. It could have been moments. It could have been an hour. The next thing she realized was the thundering sound of approaching hoofbeats and Cudu's bellowing howl.

"It is all right now, Juliana. Do you hear that? Your father is coming."

Eleanor turned just as Lord Dunevin crested the hilltop, pulling his mount to a halt close by. Cudu trotted forward from the mists, going at once to sniff at Juliana's hand.

Still she did not move.

"What are you doing here?" Dunevin barked at Eleanor as he leapt down from the saddle. "You should have been back to the castle hours ago."

The emotions that Eleanor had managed to keep at bay all that time suddenly gave way as she sobbed out her response. "We were walking back—and we had to climb up from the shore, here —but Juliana, she just stopped and wouldn't move—and then she began shaking like that. I couldn't quiet her no matter what I tried to do..."

"Just get her out of here!"

Lord Dunevin's face was darker than the skies around them, and she suddenly was reminded of the name she'd heard him called. The Devil of Dunevin Castle. Eleanor was frozen by the change in him. When she didn't immediately move, without a word of warning, he stalked forward and seized her roughly about the waist, lifting her heedlessly onto the back of his horse. He then took up Juliana who still stared frozen and trembling out to sea, and lifted her to sit before Eleanor.

"Take her back to the castle."

"But I don't know the way—"

"Now!"

The viscount clapped his horse on the flank and the beast sprung forward, nearly dragging Eleanor and Juliana both to the ground. Eleanor grabbed for the reins and a handful of the horse's mane while clutching Juliana tightly against her, praying that the horse knew its own way back to the castle in this darkness.

Tears stung at her eyes as its hooves ate up the distance. The wind was biting against her face but she barely noticed. She was fast growing senseless.

It seemed as if in moments, they had arrived at the castle courtyard.

As the horse slowed to a walk, Eleanor called out for help. She slid from the saddle, gently guiding Juliana down before her. Màiri came running from inside, pulling off her tartan wrap to place it gently around Juliana's still shivering shoulders.

Without a word, Màiri led Juliana inside. Eleanor followed behind to the nursery where the two women quickly removed Juliana's shoes and coat and eased her back onto the pillows on her bed.

They tucked a woolen blanket up around her but she was still trembling, though not as violently as before. Her eyes, however, were yet fixed in that same frightening, frozen stare.

"What in heaven's name happened to the lass?" Màiri asked on a whisper.

Eleanor shook her head, utterly at sea. "I truly do not know. We had gone to visit the MacNeills and were just walking back to the castle. All was well. I was chatting to her about something, I don't even remember what, and we had to climb some rocks. I helped her up first and when I came up behind her, she was just standing there as if she had turned to stone. She wouldn't move no matter what I tried to do. She just kept staring off like that. When she began to shake I grew so frightened. Has she ever done anything like this before?"

Màiri's eyes were suddenly grave with a most haunted darkness. She nodded. "She has. Only once. 'Twas the day her mother disappeared."

Eleanor felt as if all sense of strength suddenly left her body. She had to grab onto the bedpost just so that she wouldn't crumple to the floor.

The housekeeper shook her head. "I'll fetch some tea with a bit of the valerian in it. 'Twill help to calm her and I've a notion it would do you some good, too."

Eleanor could barely manage a nod as Màiri turned to leave the room.

Alone with Juliana again, she'd never felt more helpless. She wanted to know what had brought on this sudden change in the child's behavior. Had she said something, done something, wrong? Even more, she wanted to know what she could do to bring Juliana out of it. She felt so helpless, so alone, so *lost*. She would do anything to take that hopeless look of shock from that child's sweet face. Anything...

On instinct, Eleanor sat on the bed beside Juliana and drew her up gently into her arms, rocking her as her own mother had her as a child when she'd awoken in the night from a terrible nightmare. Softly, she hummed to her while smoothing a hand over her hair, closing her eyes and silently wishing that Juliana would come around.

After a few minutes, the trembling quieted, but Eleanor stayed as she was, rocking and humming, quietly soothing this child who had so easily and so quickly stolen her way into her heart.

Gabriel took the steps to the nursery two at a time, his jaw set, his hands clenched in anger. He had spent all day standing at his study window, watching the hills and waiting for them to return. The longer they had remained gone, the darker his mood had become until, when night had begun to fall and the mists had drifted in off the sea, he'd convinced himself that history had once again visited its damnable curse upon him.

He'd already had his horse saddled and was readying to go out in search of them when Angus MacNeill, a crofter on the isle and cousin to Donald, had come running breathless into the court-yard, telling him in Gaelic where they were.

As he spurred his horse around, racing off in the direction Angus indicated, Gabriel couldn't help but blame himself. It was he who had brought this on, he'd told himself. If he hadn't begun the day before to loosen his reserve, allowing himself to enjoy the sight of Juliana's delight in the spyglass Miss Harte had given her, none of this would have happened.

The progress the governess had made with Juliana so quickly after her arrival had truly astounded him, certainly, for none other had been able to breech the protective wall that Juliana had surrounded herself with after Georgiana's death. Even worse, though, Juliana's progress had begun to give him hope, hope that their lives might be better, no longer cast in the shadow of fear.

Why could he never learn?

Now, less than a couple of days after hiring her, he was on his way to dismiss the very person who had finally managed to reach his daughter. He had been so angry at himself for relaxing his guard the day before. Coming back to the castle, he had turned that anger on the governess, thinking to dismiss her for his own failing.

But as he stepped into the nursery doorway and opened his mouth to speak the words that would send that remarkable woman out of their lives, his voice died in his throat. The helpless fury that had built with every step back to Dunevin instantly vanished.

Standing there, watching her as she held his daughter, giving Juliana all the love and compassion she had been denied after the loss of her mother, he knew he could no more dismiss her than he could keep himself from loving his own child.

For the smallest of moments, he would have sworn that he was watching Georgiana again sitting on that bed, rocking their daughter to sleep as she had so many times. A tenseness overtook Gabriel inside as he fought to control his conflicting emotions. He had thought that by keeping himself away from Juliana all those many months since Georgiana's death, he had been protecting her from being touched by the curse that seemed ever to plague his family. But trying not to love someone, a child of one's own flesh, was like a living hell!

Standing in the doorway, Gabriel looked on the two of them for one moment more. Then, without a word, without a sound, he turned and walked away, his angry words forgotten. Followed by the soft tune she'd been humming, touched by the way she had gently stroked Juliana's forehead as she drifted off to sleep, Gabriel knew that he'd only been fooling himself.

9

*E*leanor stood framed in the doorway of Lord Dunevin's study, watching him quietly from across the room. He hadn't noticed her arrival. His head was bent over the parchment on which he was writing—scribbling—and she couldn't help but wonder if he might be composing her dismissal from her post.

He had sent word through Fergus early that morning, requesting her attendance *as soon as was convenient.* That had been two hours ago. She had delayed purposely in coming, taking time at their breakfast and then afterward sitting with Juliana in the schoolroom for a time, reading a bit of poetry aloud. After the events of the previous day, there could be no favorable reason for his wanting to see her. Dunevin would dismiss her, Eleanor was convinced, because of what had happened with Juliana the day before. She could not, however, put it off indefinitely.

A single streak of sunlight reached in through the mullioned window beside him, precisely lighting the desktop where he wrote. She wondered fleetingly if he had chosen that particular placement for the desk because of it. As Eleanor watched him, he swept a hand carelessly through his dark hair, pushing it back as he rubbed his eyes. He was a man so very different from any other she had known. All her life, she had been surrounded by men of polished gentility, a good many of them fops who pinched snuff till they sneezed, wore high starched collars that made them look like ostriches, and who fretted for days over which leg they should put forth in a bow to make themselves look most fashionable.

But this man, this dauntless and inscrutable Scot, he was as far from that image as was possible.

No mincing buck he, Lord Dunevin was a mixture of the unconventional and the noble with an infinite strength of mind as well as of body, primitive in a way that only added to his mystery. He was rugged, yes, even imposing, but that was countered by a quiet strength that need never be demonstrated, who didn't need to bluster and pose in order to go noticed in a crowd. His commanding height and presence alone did that.

But it was his eyes, she decided then, that were most compelling. Dark, intelligent, they had the striking ability of being able to convey with but a simple glance exactly what he was thinking without his needing to utter a word. Those same eyes could, however, in the very next moment, become as unreadable, as vague as a moonless night. Lightness somehow seemed to elude him. She wondered what caused him to guard his heart so closely. She wondered what the touch of his hands would be like.

Where in heaven had that thought come from...?

Eleanor shook her head, returning her attention to the situation at hand, that of his summons for her there that morning.

She knocked softly on the door jamb. "You wished to see me, my lord?"

The viscount looked up from his paper, his stare immediately catching her. He removed his spectacles, set down his pen. "Miss Harte, please come in."

His voice was stiff, matter-of-fact, unemotional. She walked into the room slowly, trying to ignore the lurking sense of dread that weighted her footsteps as she crossed to sit in the chair before him.

Smoothing her skirts over her knees, Eleanor lifted her eyes to look at him. He regarded her for several moments, silent, his hands clasped before him on the desk, his mouth set in a stark line.

Oh, most certainly he was going to dismiss her.

"Miss Harte, as you might have already guessed, I have called you here to discuss yesterday's incident with Juliana."

"My lord, I—"

He held up a hand. "Miss Harte, please, allow me to finish."

She pressed, "*No, my lord. I have something to say first.*"

Eleanor sat forward in her seat, looking away from his startled expression. She focused instead on a small porcelain curio of a dolphin that stood at the corner of his desk. If this was to be it, she had every intention of speaking her piece before he sent her packing.

"There is no need for you to finish, sir. Indeed, I already know what you are going to say."

The viscount sat back in his chair, folding his arms before him, one brow raised in question. "Do you now?"

"Yes. You think to dismiss me from service as Juliana's governess because of what happened yesterday, but I'll have you know I have no intention of abandoning that child."

She was letting her emotions get the better of her, she knew. She had to temper them. Eleanor looked at him directly, softening her next words.

"I know you believe you made an error of judgement in hiring me, but you are wrong. I can help Juliana. You saw her when she was looking through that spyglass, how she had begun to respond. I don't know what happened yesterday, what I did to cause Juliana to react the way she did, but please do not allow my carelessness to put an end to her progress. You need not pay me, my lord. I will stay on without wages and continue to work with Juliana regardless."

The viscount sat quietly considering her words as the clock behind him ticked off several long moments. His face gave no hint of his thoughts, no indication of whether she had succeeded in persuading him. Finally, he answered her.

"Very well, Miss Harte. You have convinced me to your opinion. You will stay on. With wages."

"Oh."

Gabriel watched as an uncertain moment of confusion played across the window of her face. She was like an open book, her thoughts so easily readable. She had expected more of a debate from him, obviously. No doubt she had spent the morning preparing, mentally rehearsing all sorts of arguments to combat his reasons for dismissing her. She was puzzled at his ready agreement, perhaps even wondering if she had heard him right. And then she looked at him.

It hadn't taken her long at all.

"You weren't planning to dismiss me, were you?"

He shook his head, hiding his mirth behind a disguise of nonchalance.

"But why did you let me go on like that, saying all those things to you, knowing in the end it wouldn't matter...?"

Because I wanted to watch the fire light up your green eyes...

Gabriel hastily cleared his throat against that sudden vagrant thought. "If you will recall, Miss Harte, I attempted to explain, but you would hear none of it."

That drew her more upright in her chair, her head cocking slightly to the side. Gabriel tried to ignore the single twisting curl of sable brown that fell against her shoulder.

"Oh. You are right. I apologize, my lord."

"No apology is necessary. However, I do need to give explanation for Juliana's behavior yesterday. In truth, it was through no fault of yours, Miss Harte. Has anyone yet told you of Lady Dunevin's death?"

She looked at him. "Only that she was out walking with Juliana one day and vanished without any apparent explanation."

Gabriel nodded solemnly. "They had gone out, much like you had yesterday, for a walk. I had gone out to find them when they hadn't returned and it was on that particular precipice you had climbed yesterday where I found Juliana without her mother, standing trembling in much the same manner. I can only presume that Lady Dunevin slipped from there and Juliana could do nothing to help her. It was a terrible, unavoidable accident. Juliana had never gone back to that place since."

"Until yesterday."

The governess's voice was filled with remorse. The light in her eyes grew dim and she shook her head regretfully. "I am so very sorry."

"Please do not blame yourself, Miss Harte. You couldn't have known. I hold myself wholly responsible. I should have told you of it before you went out."

She sat for several moments, her brow slightly furrowed as she reflected on all he had just told her. Gabriel allowed himself the silent pleasure of her presence.

Somehow, if it were possible, she looked more lovely this morning than ever. She had pulled her hair back and pinned it high upon her head in a topknot of curls that framed her face. It was a style that revealed the slender grace of her neck, the arch of her brow, the soft curve of her cheek.

Gabriel wondered what she was thinking. Did she doubt his explanation of Georgiana's death? Did she, like so many others, believe he had somehow done away with his own wife?

But when she looked at him again, he did not find any hint of suspicion, nor the condemnation he had seen so often in the eyes of others. What he saw behind those green depths was profound compassion and something else, something tender and honest and impossible to describe.

The impact of just that look startled him, and his reaction must have shown on his face, for she suddenly stood from her chair.

"Well, you no doubt have much to do," she said. "I won't keep you any longer."

Thinking it was probably better that she go, he agreed. "Yes, thank you, Miss Harte."

She nodded and turned and Gabriel resumed his letter writing, continuing his scribbling thought in response to his steward in London.

And in regard to...

"My lord, if I may trouble you just another moment."

Gabriel lowered his pen, glancing back at the door, where she was standing with her back to him now as she faced his bookshelves on the other side of the room.

"Yes, Miss Harte?"

She said to the shelves, "I wonder, does your library contain any Gaelic literature?"

It was not a question he would have expected. "Yes, of course. Poetry mostly, though." He was intrigued. "Do you read Gaelic, Miss Harte?" He didn't recall her having mentioned it during their interview.

She shook her head, letting go a resigned breath. "No, I'm afraid I do not."

She did not move to leave. Gabriel continued watching her as she surveyed the many titles in the tall bookcases.

"Is there a particular shelf on which I might find them?" she then asked. "The Gaelic books, I mean."

Gabriel stood from the desk and crossed the room to join her. "Something in particular you are looking for?"

"A grammar would be ideal, but I'd probably be expecting too much..."

Curious now, Gabriel surveyed the shelves for her. "There, on the topmost shelf."

She smiled at him. "Oh, yes, thank you, my lord. Please do not allow me to keep you from your business. I can reach them with the steps."

Gabriel pulled the rolling library steps from the corner, setting them beneath the shelf she sought, then returned to his desk and his letter while she picked through the books on the shelf. He had only written a sentence or two more before he found himself glancing back to where she was sitting now on the topmost step. Her feet were tucked neatly beneath her, and she was skimming one of the books she had lying open across the tops of her knees. That bit of her hair had fallen into her eyes and her mouth was moving in silent recitation of what was written there, her brow knit in intent study.

"Miss Harte?"

She lifted her head, looking at him from behind the stair railing. "Yes, my lord?"

"May I ask what you are doing?"

"Certainly. I realized yesterday when Juliana and I were walking about the isle that very few of the people here are familiar with the English language. It was most distressing when I attempted to communicate with Mr. MacNeill that I needed help with Juliana. Since I am in essence the stranger here, I thought perhaps in my spare time, I might endeavor to learn more of the native tongue."

Gabriel found himself intrigued. "And you mean to do this simply through reading?"

"Indeed. It worked quite well with Latin."

"Do you mean to say you taught yourself the Latin language?"

"Well, mostly, although I did have the benefit of my—" She stopped herself. "Few ladies are permitted instruction in such a masculine tongue, my lord. English and French have for some reason been deemed the only languages fit for the female mouth.

But I love to study history and so much of it is recorded in Latin, I determined that I would learn it."

Gabriel found her logic refreshing. "But I'm afraid you won't find the Gaelic as amenable to your efforts. It is an auditory language; it must be learned with the ear, not solely with the eyes."

"Oh, I see." She thought for a moment. "Perhaps...?" She shook her head against her thought. "No, that wouldn't likely be appropriate."

"What were you going to say, Miss Harte?"

She hesitated, reluctant. Finally, she answered, "I was going to ask if perhaps you would be willing to introduce me to the language, at least some of its pronunciations and conjugations, then perhaps I would be able to continue from there on my own. At least to get a rudimentary understanding of the language. But you are a very busy man with many more significant obligations than to remedy my ignorance."

Her suggestion actually intrigued him, partly because of her lively enthusiasm for learning, a thing most ladies did not have, but mostly because of his own love for the natural language of his heritage—and a bitter regret that since the failed Jacobite rebellion and the proscription that had followed in the century before, the Gaelic language was slowly fading into obscurity all across his homeland.

Gabriel left his desk, crossing the room as he motioned for her to come down from the library steps. He took the book she had been reading, a collection of ancient and modern Gaelic poems and songs, and glanced quickly through the pages.

"Come, Miss Harte, sit for a moment. I'm not that busy that I can't stop for a moment to enjoy a bit of poetry."

Her face brightened as he motioned for her to take one of the two chairs set nearest the window.

"The primary difference between English and Gaelic," he explained, "is that some of the consonants do not always carry the same sound, depending on where they are in a word. So, in order to learn Gaelic, you must forget a great deal of everything you were ever taught about English."

He glanced at her. Her eyes were absolutely alight with enthusiasm. He found himself struck by it.

"For example," he continued, "let us first discuss the letter *B*. When it is found at the beginning of a word, it carries the much same sound as the English *B*." He glanced at her again, "As in the word 'beautiful.'"

Their eyes locked for a single brief moment. The room grew suddenly warmer and it had nothing to do with the fire in the hearth. Gabriel reluctantly pulled his attention away from the emerald sea of her eyes.

"However, when the letter *B* is found elsewhere in a word, it carries the sound more of an English *P*. To make matters even more confusing, often you will see the letters *BH* together in Gaelic. They can make the sound of an English *V* or *W* as in this word here: *leabhar*."

"Le-orr," she repeated easily. "'Tis almost like the word 'lower' in English, but prettier. What does it mean?"

Gabriel held out his hand to her, handing her the—

"Book."

She nodded, smiling. "Cudu," she said, glancing at the carpet where the hound napped. "Is that Gaelic, as well?"

Gabriel nodded. "It is from the Gaelic *Cù-dubh*."

"What does it mean, my lord? Surely it must be the name of some great ancient hero like Fingal or cuChulainn?"

"I'm afraid it isn't anything quite as romantic as that," he replied. "Quite simply, it means 'black dog.'"

She laughed at that, a rich, delightful sound that hadn't echoed past these walls in a long time. The music of it was more seductive than anything he could remember.

"You are jesting, my lord. Teasing me, surely."

He looked at her.

"Oh, goodness, you are *not* jesting, are you?"

Gabriel shook his head, looking down at the hound who, as if listening to their conversation, rolled onto his back with all fours in the air. He couldn't resist a small scratch to the beast's belly, smiling as one leg twitched reflexively against the movement of his fingers. "It was the only name he would ever come to, after trying a score of others that were much more illustrious."

Gabriel glanced up at her. Her eyes were sparked in the sunlight. His pulse leapt.

"Would you perhaps read a page to me, and then translate it to English so that I might get a sense for the flow and intonation of the words?"

Gabriel swallowed, nodded. "Very well. Choose one."

She flipped through several pages in the book, browsing them before settling on one. She laid the book upon the table between them so that they could both read together, he aloud, and she following along on the page.

Their heads were bent closely as Gabriel began to recite the poem she'd chosen, an ancient Erse verse titled *Aisling air Dhreach Mna*—'Vision of a Fair Woman.'

As he spoke the words in his native, lyrical tongue, she bent her head closer to the page as if to somehow absorb the words written there. As she did, he was caught by the scent of her, that exotic perfume that had struck him before. Gabriel soon found himself reciting the poem from memory instead of reading off the page as he studied her face, her inquisitive eyes, her mouth, the gentle curl of her hair. When he finished, he repeated the verse for her in English:

> *Tell us some of the charms of the stars...*
> *Soft and fair as the mountain-snow;*
> *Her two breasts were heaving full;*
> *To them did the hearts of heroes flow.*
> *Her lips were ruddier than the rose;*

Tender and tunefully sweet her tongue;
White as the foam adown her side
Her delicate fingers extended hung...
Unfolding their beauty in early spring...
And her eyes like the radiance the sunbeams bring.

Every attribute could have been describing her. When he finished, he watched in expectant silence as she lifted her eyes slowly to meet his.

The very air around them had become charged. They were so near to one another, eye to eye, face to face, their breaths mingling between them. In that moment, he knew what she would do. And he knew that he would let her.

Gabriel sat perfectly still as Eleanor leaned toward him, closing the space between them to touch her lips softly to his.

He closed his eyes. Her mouth was still beneath his, the stillness of a maid who had never before kissed, or been kissed. Gabriel tipped her chin softly upward with his fingertip and deepened the kiss, drinking her in.

She responded, instinctively opening to him.

Too many years of living in emotional exile, of being feared and reviled and haunted by the very world around him, came together in a single moment of freedom. This woman, this one incredible creature, did not, had never seen him as the monster everyone else did. With her, for the first time in his life, Gabriel could truly forget the darkness of the past, the legacy of his family history, and simply live.

But the forgetting could only last as long as their kiss went on. It was knowing this and hating it both at the same time that brought Gabriel to reluctantly pulling away from her.

He felt the warmth that had wound between them vanish almost immediately. He watched her face as she hovered between dream and reality. Slowly her eyes drifted open and she stared at him, wordlessly, unwilling to shatter the moment they had shared together.

Without thinking, he spoke softly, saying her name. "Eleanor..."

It struck her like the shock of a chill wind, drawing her up and away from him as she blinked. She was so stunned, she never realized he had not called her "Nell," but had used her true Christian name.

"My lord, I am so sorry." She put a hand against her mouth. "I — I don't know what caused me to do that." She pushed abruptly away from the table, nearly tipping her chair back in her haste to be away. "Please forgive me."

Gabriel shook his head, to tell her she had nothing to apologize for, that she had done nothing wrong but something so right, but she had already turned and was rushing from the room.

He wanted to call her back, even as he realized he could not.

They'd stolen a moment, a brief breath-stealing instant in time where the darkness that followed him had ceased to exist behind the warmth of this woman's kiss. It had been joy and light and freedom all at once. Yet, as always, the clouds of reality had returned.

No matter how much he wanted, he could not outrun it.

He was the Devil of Dunevin Castle, the Dark Lord of Trelay.

She was a creature of gentleness and light.

What had he to offer her other than the darkness, the anguish and misery that were his inherited cross to bear?

10

*N*early every spare moment over the following fortnight was taken up with the preparations for the St. Michael's Day, or Michaelmas, celebrations. The castle kitchens were hectic with activity from early morning till late into the night, and Eleanor and Juliana took part as often as they could when they weren't involved with their lessons or other activities.

As governess, Eleanor wouldn't as a rule have been involved in the work of preparing, but she defied convention, throwing herself into whatever task was at hand to occupy herself, making certain she always had *something* to do, if only to keep her from remembering what a fool she'd made of herself with Lord Dunevin.

Even now, she couldn't quite understand what had happened that ineffable morning, what had caused her to do something so bold, so *brazen*, as to kiss Lord Dunevin outright like she had.

At first, she had told herself that she'd simply, inexplicably gotten caught up in the rich lyricism of his voice, the beautiful cadence of the poem he'd read to her that day. Even now she could see it so vividly, the way he'd been looking at her so intently, his eyes captivating and dark, his voice warm and beautiful, she'd all but forgotten that he'd been reading from a book and not speaking those fluid words to her directly.

It was only later, as she lain awake in the middle of the night reliving those few magical moments, that she realized she had wanted him to speak those words to her, wanted it so badly, she'd somehow convinced herself he truly had.

As if a man like him, handsome, noble, incredibly mysterious, would ever recite those words to someone like her. To the viscount, she was little more than a member of staff—an utterly foolish member of staff, at that—even though, in truth, she was more.

However had she gotten herself into such a complicated situation? To the rest of the world outside this far-off isle, she was Lady Eleanor Wycliffe, the missing heiress to the Westover fortune. Had they met one another in a London ballroom instead of on this distant isle, would things have been any different? She wondered what he'd think, what he'd say, if he knew the truth.

Shaking away that most troublesome thought, Eleanor turned her attention to where it was needed more, to Juliana, who sat on a high stool at the central kitchen table, helping Màiri to roll out a fresh batch of bannocks for supper.

Blessedly, Juliana seemed to have overcome the frightening episode on that dreadful precipice, and within days had begun taking part in the Michaelmas activities. To avoid any further upset, Eleanor had made certain they did not return to that part of the isle on any of their excursions. Instead, they kept close to the castle proper and immersed themselves in reading, music, sewing and various other exercises, many of which Eleanor employed to show Juliana how she might express herself differently than through speech.

With the help of Màiri and Donald MacNeill, Eleanor's first venture was to undertake the re-painting of the schoolroom walls, forever banishing the drab beige-green behind a fresh pristine coat of fresh whitewash.

The difference of doing just that had been astounding, but Eleanor had had another thought, as well. Using some of the natural dyes for coloring the local wool, they created other paints with which to further adorn the walls. By mixing and trying different colors, a diverse palette of hues was created and once ready, Eleanor then set the task to Juliana of what should decorate her walls.

"This schoolroom is *your* place," Eleanor had told her, handing Juliana several small brushes made from birch branches and bent grass, as well as a collection of different pointed leaves and feathered quills to paint with. "Cover it with whatever you feel inside."

After a few tentative efforts depicting a flying gull and a shy flower, Juliana finally set to the project, deepening her focus to create a scene Eleanor soon recognized as Trelay, the heathery hills, the rugged sea, and atop it all, the tower of Dunevin looking out like a faithful sentinel. She spent hours at it, showing true interest for the first time in something other than that window. While she painted and colored, Eleanor would read to her aloud from Shakespeare or Virgil, or spend some time herself practicing the Gaelic pronunciations Màiri had been teaching her.

Since that day in the viscount's study, Eleanor had only seen Lord Dunevin a handful of times. She and Juliana no longer took their meals in the dining parlor with him, but instead spent more and more time with Màiri in the kitchen. If it seemed odd to Màiri, their sudden company there, she said nothing. She accepted Eleanor's explanation that she simply sought to balance Juliana's education of the running of a household by showing her firsthand the inner workings of the kitchen, the true heart of any house,.

If Eleanor did see the viscount, it was only in passing, with a pleasant "Good day to you, my lord," as she and Juliana went about their daily routine. He, too, seemed content to avoid their company. If she needed something from his library, Eleanor waited until she was certain he was away from the castle before going to his study. It wasn't a difficult thing to do, for the estate was involved in the business of the harvest and preparing for the coming winter, so he was rarely there during the day.

Time passed quickly. While occupied with her activities, Eleanor could successfully hold her thoughts about that day and their kiss at bay—at night, however, when she would lie in the darkness with a sleeping Juliana beside her, she would find herself thinking back on that morning, the curious siren's song of his voice as he had read her those words written centuries before, the glory of that fleeting kiss.

She knew now that her mother had been right. That kiss had been every bit as wonder-working, as mystifying and enchanting as Lady Frances had promised it would be. She truly had forgotten for that moment how to draw a breath. It had been nothing at all like Lord Monning's son, James Crockett, whose sloppy fumblings the night of her first London ball had only brought her to giggling when he'd struck his forehead on a low-hanging tree branch after he'd backed her against the outside balcony banister. Nor was it anything like the polite parting peck on the back of her gloved hand that had been the all of what Richard Hartley had ever attempted with her.

Whatever it was that had possessed her to kiss Lord Dunevin as she had, it had been more magical, more incredible than she could have ever possibly imagined. It defied definition, filling her with warmth and softness and hope all at once. Everything about that day, the two of them, had felt so right, so real, so...as it should be.

But then, all at once, their kiss had ended, pushing the world back into place with a jarring nudge, and leaving her awash with horror at what she'd done, the humiliation, and haunted each night by the memory of it.

Eleanor wondered if the emptiness of it would ever go away,

the feeling of having lost something that in truth she'd never possessed, but had for one moment stolen. Would the memory of the touch of him, the warmth of his breath, ever go away?

She resolved that she would simply have to keep herself constantly occupied until it did. And thankfully, there was much to do for the approaching holiday.

That Sunday before St. Michael's day, Eleanor and Juliana had joined a gathering of the other women and girls from the island who had assembled on the castle courtyard. Armed each with a special three-pronged *mattock*, the entire assembly of them, dressed in colorful skirts and bodices, their hair bound beneath bright kerchiefs, made their way to the thriving fields outside the castle proper.

There, Màiri and Seòna MacNeill instructed Eleanor and Juliana in the ancient method of cutting the special *torcan*, an equally-sided triangle around each wild carrot, before pulling it from the earth and dropping it into the bag that hung from their waists. Lilting songs were sung in Gaelic as they worked, with Eleanor understanding more than a few of the words, and there was much gaiety, and a touch of rivalry as to who would get the most and finest of the carrots.

Once, Eleanor pulled out a forked carrot and within seconds she was surrounded by the others, all smiling and congratulating her in bubbly Gaelic for such a find was a sign of great luck, she was assured.

Afterward, when they had returned to the castle, the carrots were washed and tied in bunches with a scarlet-colored thread, most of them then stored away until the feast day later that week. But at Dunevin, Màiri explained, it was a tradition for one carrot to be chosen from each bundle and included with that evening's meal.

Eleanor and Juliana helped Màiri in the kitchen all through that late afternoon, preparing a special supper that would be attended by all the people of the castle, the viscount, Màiri,

Fergus, Eleanor and Juliana, the groomsman, Angus, from the stables, as well as Donald MacNeill and his family. It was a private custom for the laird's family, repeated through each generation. The more formal celebration on St. Michael's Day would come later that week on Friday when all of the island families would take part.

As a young girl growing up in the sterile and socially proper Wycliffe home, Eleanor had never felt a true part of the inner workings of the household. The separation between servant and lord there had always been a most definitive thing, and she had rarely seen what went on beyond the green baize door.

Here, on Trelay, that division was less distinct, and because of it, there was more a feeling of all hands doing their part.

For Eleanor, the notion of something as simple as baking before coming to Trelay had meant nothing more than simply writing out the instructions for the cook on what to prepare for that evening's meal. But here at Dunevin, baking meant putting her own hands into a soft oatcake dough, kneading it, rolling it out for cutting. She even baked it herself, turning it—only once— on the iron *greideal*, savoring its pleasing scent as it mixed with the smoky heat of the peat fire crackling beneath it.

This community, this belonging, was a feeling that affected not only Eleanor, but Juliana as well. Even now, as they stood together in the kitchen, Màiri's aprons doubled about their waists, their faces dusted with oat flour, a light of elfin delight shone in Juliana's dark eyes that was extraordinary.

Looking on her as she carefully cut out the rounded cakes, Eleanor came to realize that in the short time she'd been there, this enchanted place and its wistful native daughter had stolen completely into her heart. It was as if her life before had been merely a stopping-off point, a brief respite on a journey to a place where she would find... she would find...

"Well, it looks as if we're about ready t' serve," Màiri said, interrupting Eleanor's thoughts before she'd had the chance to decide the answer.

Eleanor and Juliana quickly removed their aprons, splashing away the flour dust from their faces at the small wash basin in the corner. Màiri handed Juliana a willow basket that had a fresh batch of warm bannocks tucked beneath a linen inside.

"You can carry this, lassie. Miss Harte, Mrs. MacNeill, and I will see to the rest."

Together, the four of them made their way from the kitchen across the vine-draped arcade to the castle's donjon.

In the dining room, Lord Dunevin and the others had already gathered around the crimson light of the fire that blazed in the stone hearth. The table had been freshly polished and set with plateware of delicate china, glimmering silver candleholders, the likes of which a number of the guests had never seen.

Night had already come and the moon hung high and bright in an uncommonly cloudless sky. The wind blew in softly off the firth. It was a fine ending to a most pleasant day.

"'Tis time to sup," Màiri said cheerfully to the others as she and Seòna began to set out the fare, each dish a singular representation of food grown on the isle. There was kail brose, a sort of thin porridge, with tatties and herring, roast grouse, stewed turnips, and the traditional haggis, which Màiri had promised Eleanor tasted much better than it looked. An assortment of warm bannocks and scones, a fresh cranberry tart, and a flummery had been prepared for dessert.

The meal, however, would start with that day's harvest of the carrots picked that morning and stewed in a tasty broth. It was the tradition.

Fergus served while Màiri and Seòna finished arranging the various dishes about the dinner table. Donald MacNeill the Younger took the seat beside Juliana while Eleanor took the chair across, nearest the head of the table where the viscount sat. Eleanor smiled when she noticed Young Donald's eyes nearly as wide as the dish before him as he looked on uncertainly at the assortment of flatware before him. Eleanor took up her napkin, unfolding it in her lap before subtly pointing out the proper utensil to him.

He grinned his thanks, his face coloring nearly as red as his hair. The viscount took his seat beside her. Eleanor glanced at him briefly.

He was dressed more formally than was his custom, wearing a rich coat of dark green over a white linen shirt with knotted cravat and the kilt. As he lowered himself into his chair, their eyes caught. Her heartbeat immediately thudded, and she smiled nervously.

Was he, like she, remembering the kiss they'd shared?

"Miss Harte, good evening," he said, nodding to her.

"Good evening to you, my lord."

When everyone was finally seated, Lord Dunevin stood, and raised his glass of claret in a toast.

"Today we celebrate another successful harvest at Dunevin. We thank the Lord for keeping us safe and in good health and for feeding our families well with this good food."

The others around the table all raised their glasses, saying "Aye," before they drank in unison.

Eleanor chatted amiably with Seòna. Talk was of the coming festivities for St. Michael's Day, at which, Seòna told her, there would be horseracing, much dancing and music.

As she was speaking, Eleanor took up her fork; since she had found the lone forked carrot that morning, she was given the honor of leading the meal. She tried not to notice the eyes of everyone looking on around her as she went to take the first bite. Until a voice sounded out, halting her.

"Stop!"

Eleanor froze, the fork poised just outside her mouth. She turned in surprise to regard Lord Dunevin, who had just spoken so sharply.

"Is something wrong, my lord?"

Without a word, he plucked the fork from her hand. "Do not eat it."

He stood, crossed the room, and tossed the carrot into the fire. "None of you eat any of it."

Màiri looked at him in alarm. "My lord, what is the matter?"

Gabriel had gone from his seat and was circling the table, taking each person's plate. "The bite that Miss Harte was about to take was not a carrot. It was *iteotha*."

A gasp rose from around the table.

Iteotha. Eleanor repeated the word he'd said to herself. It wasn't one she was yet familiar with.

"I do not understand," she said. "What is it?"

But no one would answer her. Instead, they all looked around the table at each other.

When all the plates had been cleared away, Lord Dunevin returned to his place at the head of the table. He clasped his hands before him and looked at her gravely. "It was hemlock, Miss Harte."

Eleanor's mouth dropped. "Hemlock?"

He nodded. "It is very similar to the wild carrot of the isle in appearance and only someone familiar with both can tell the difference between them. Had you or anyone else here eaten it, the results could have certainly been fatal."

Eleanor was taken by a sudden chill and instinctively wrapped her arms around herself. A moment later that she realized Lord Dunevin had just saved her life.

"But, my lord," Màiri explained, her voice trembling with upset, "I checked them, each and every one. I always do."

"Màiri, I'm sure it was only an accident," Eleanor said in effort to calm her. "I probably picked it myself. I wouldn't have known the difference whereas you and the others would have recognized the plant in the field."

Màiri shook her head. "But we havna seen any of the *iteotha* here on the isle in years." She began to lose the battle to her tears. "Sweet Mary in heaven, 'tis just like when we lost the laird's own brother, Malcolm..."

The viscount looked at Donald MacNeill. "Is he on the isle?"

MacNeill hesitated before he slowly nodded. "Aye, my lord. I brought him over just this morning."

"Who, my lord?" Eleanor asked.

Dunevin's fingers were gripping the stem of his glass so tightly, Eleanor thought sure it would snap.

"Seamus Maclean," he said as if the very words brought a bitterness to his mouth. "His family lives here on the isle and he comes each year to spend Michaelmas with them."

"But we did not see him at all today."

His dark eyes shifted suddenly to her. "I would not be so eager, Miss Harte, to jump to the man's defense."

"I am not, sir," she said. "I just cannot think of a reason why Mr. Maclean would wish to poison me."

"You cannot know if it was you he'd intended the hemlock for. Any one of us could have taken that first bite. You, me, Màiri, even Juliana..." His voice dropped off suddenly.

Eleanor knew exactly what he was feeling, how the mere suggestion of such a terrible harm coming to his daughter filled him with a sense of fear. She felt it, too.

"But why would Mr. Maclean want to poison anyone at this table?"

Eleanor looked at the myriad of faces around her. Oddly, none of them seemed to be as confused as she was. They all looked as if they weren't too terribly shocked even and she realized that she was still the outsider here. She also realized that there was something more to this that no one else was saying.

And then she remembered the story Young Donald had told her that night when they'd been walking back to the castle.

"You cannot truly believe that he would do something like this because of that senseless feud?"

Lord Dunevin's eyes narrowed. "Who told you about...?"

Eleanor noticed that Donald MacNeill shot his son, Young Donald, a stern look, easily figuring out where she had heard the tale.

She quickly sought to divert the man's attention.

"But you can't very well accuse the man without some sort of proof."

"I've proof," Fergus suddenly said from his place at the other end of the table. The grizzled man stood from his chair. "I saw that Seamus Maclean flirting with young Catriona after the carrots were gathered this morn."

"My sister's Catriona?" Màiri asked, obviously horrified.

"Aye."

This all simply made no sense to Eleanor. It had to have been a ghastly mistake, nothing more. A stray root of the hemlock must have somehow gotten tossed in with the other carrots without anybody noticing. There had been so much singing and merriment that morning in the fields, so many hands picking through, surely that had to be it.

Wasn't it?

The others sitting around the table were now eyeing the other dishes, wondering, no doubt, if anything else had been tampered with.

Finally, the viscount spoke.

"Màiri, I know you worked very hard on this fine meal for us all, but I'm afraid I cannot risk anyone's well-being on the chance that something else might have been tainted. We'll have to dispose of it all. I am truly sorry."

Màiri's eyes were filled with tears as she nodded quietly in agreement. "I've some cheese and a mutton ham in the larder we can partake of instead, my lord. I know it hasna been touched by anyone but me."

The viscount nodded, and Màiri, Seòna, and Fergus began the task of clearing away the waste of their unfortunate feast. The mood in the room had turned most grim.

Eleanor looked to where Lord Dunevin yet sat at his place heading the table. His eyes were focused blankly on the glass of claret before him, his expression troubled.

"What will you do?" she asked, trying to push aside a vagrant image of warring clansmen heaving mighty claymores in bloody battle to exact revenge.

"What choice have I?" he answered in quiet torment. "I can simply watch and wait to see if he will try again now that this effort has failed."

11

*I*n the days before Michaelmas, Juliana became more fully engrossed in her wall painting, until it seemed she wanted to do nothing else. Even the promise of Màiri's sweet treacle bread and a cup of warm milk early that chilly morning wouldn't entice her away.

She would spend hours at it at a time, silently drawing, never tiring, adding freely to the mural as she enhanced the image first with tangled, wind-swept trees and distant shadows of the various standing stones that peppered the island landscape. Later, figures of some of the more familiar inhabitants of the isle began to take shape, scattered here and there about the idyllic setting.

The painting itself was really quite good. Even at her young age, Juliana showed the keen eye for detail that was the mark of many a talented artist. It was uncanny, really. Even more remarkable was that somehow, without any instruction, she seemed able to capture the very personality of each figure she drew simply by the manner in which she illustrated them.

There was the family of MacNeill, all standing outside their small thatched croft, fleecy sheep teeming around them like land-locked clouds while Donald sailed by on the murky waters of the firth in his small skiff.

At the opposite corner, Juliana had brushed in the imposing structure of Dunevin, the figure of the viscount standing high in the castle tower with Cudu flanking his side, a pair of silhouettes against the sullen clouds that stretched across the sky overhead.

Below them, the tender figure of Màiri stood on the castle yard, her trademark apron tied around her waist as she tossed bits of crumbs to the scattered chickens while Angus, the groomsman, watched on from the open stable door.

Each day, some new image would appear on the mural. Just when Eleanor had thought she'd finished, Juliana would add in something more to it.

The day before, she had spent a great deal of time drawing the small, round-headed figure of the seal who often followed them when they walked, peeking out from behind the water's surface. And that morning, she had begun sketching in yet another set of figures, this time a pair of them standing closely together at the edge of the shore while a third waved to them from a rocky mull overhead.

At first, Eleanor had thought the two figures nearest the water were meant to depict her and Juliana, with their skirts hitched up to their knees as they had waded out to gather periwinkles for Màiri's stew several mornings ago. The water had been so cold their toes had tingled for some time afterward.

But when Juliana had enhanced the figure that was waving to the two from afar with dark hair and eyes, dressing it in a pale green frock very similar to one of her own, Eleanor realized that the one waving was meant to be herself. The other two, she surmised, were likely meant to be Juliana herself and Young Donald, who had joined them in the winkle pool that day.

It was that part of the painting Juliana was now perfecting, her head bent closely to the wall as she traced in some careful detail with the tip of a feather dipped in black. Guessing that she would be involved in the project for some time, Eleanor had just decided to spend some private time on her Gaelic studies when Fergus suddenly appeared at the schoolroom door, his weather-worn face nearly eclipsed by the tilt of his ragged blue bonnet.

"Màiri says 'tis time to come down to bake the *strùan* cake now."

The man always spoke so matter-of-factly, never stating anything beyond what was necessary to get his message across. At first, Eleanor had thought the man hadn't liked her, his manner was so brusque and at times even callous. She had since decided that he simply spoke with everyone that way.

Eleanor nodded to him. She had forgotten that she had asked Màiri if she and Juliana could help with the baking for the St. Michael's Day feast the following day.

"Thank you, Fergus. We shall be right down."

As she set aside her book, Eleanor noticed the Scotsman staring with keen interest at Juliana's mural.

"It is very good, isn't it?" she said.

"Aye," he answered, looking intently at Juliana, who had turned to face him. "A good likeness, indeed."

Juliana turned away then, stowing away her paints and brushes.

"Has the laird seen this?" Fergus asked.

"No, not yet. I thought to wait until Juliana was finished before showing it to him."

The quizzical look in his eye brought her to wondering. "Do you think Lord Dunevin might be angry that we painted over the walls without asking him first?"

Fergus shrugged. "I canna say what the laird would or wouldna like. The laird is the only one t' tell you that."

And with that, the man turned and shuffled out of the room.

Eleanor looked over to where Juliana stood by the window. The expression on her face looked somehow bothered. "Oh, do not worry, Juliana. I'm sure your father won't mind that we painted over the walls. In fact, once he sees the wonderful work you've done, he'll congratulate us on what an improvement we've made."

She seemed to ease at that, and Eleanor smiled. Together, the two of them made off for the stairs.

The kitchen below was ablaze with light from a scattering of candles, *cruisie* lamps, and tin lanterns, and the glowing hearth whose welcoming warmth could be felt all the way to the outer corridor. The pleasing smells of baking and fresh herbs filled the air, mingling with the earthy wooded scent of the fire. Màiri's two daughters, Alys and Sorcha, both robust and ever cheerful like their mother, were already there, helping to get things prepared.

Though they each had taken husbands from the mainland, the two young women visited their mother on Trelay often, coming over on Donald MacNeill's skiff since the death of their father five years before, when Màiri had given up the family croft for a pair of rooms off the kitchen at Dunevin.

Sorcha, with what must have been her father's dark hair and high forehead, was the elder of the two and currently in the later stages of pregnancy, Màiri's first grandchild. She looked the picture of maternal contentment, with soft eyes, rose-tinged cheeks, her hand frequently at rest on her swollen belly. The family had been doubly blessed for Alys, who more resembled their mother and was perhaps a few years younger than her sister, had brought the news just that week that she, too, was expecting to deliver her first child late the following spring.

Eleanor found herself looking on the two, Alys even younger than she was herself, both married and now establishing their own families. She wondered wistfully if the time would ever come when she would know what it was to be a wife, a mother...

"I think we're a'ready now," Màiri said, handing Eleanor and Juliana each one of her voluminous aprons.

The process of baking the traditional Michaelmas *struan* was as celebrated as the time-honored cake itself, created through a series of steps and ingredients that was followed stringently each year.

First, oats, barley and rye were ground together into meal in equal parts in the circular stone quern that stood in the kitchen corner. It was the custom for the eldest daughter to bake the cake; this year, Màiri passed that honor on to Juliana, teaching her the proper way to moisten the meal with some milk, tossing in a handful of bogberry and caraway, adding a dollop of honey as they shaped it into its traditional three corners onto the heated flagstone where it would bake.

The fire itself was fueled not by the usual peat, but by symbolic branches that had been gathered earlier that day, oak, rowan, and bramble, woods that were considered sacred among the isles. While the cake gained in consistency, Màiri and Juliana took the three basting feathers they'd plucked from one of the Dunevin cockerels, and applied a smooth batter of eggs, cream and butter to form a custard-like covering that glistened in the firelight.

After being blessed, this sizeable *struan* would be shared by everyone at the feast the following day. Any leftover meal was made into smaller individual cakes for those family members who were absent or had died.

While Màiri set out each tiny cake, quietly mentioning the name of each departed member of their families, Eleanor couldn't deny feeling a touch of sadness. It reminded her of the bitter separation from her own family so far away.

So many times over the past weeks, Eleanor had wanted to write to her mother. She'd begun countless letters, thinking to assure Lady Frances not to worry, that all was well, but just couldn't seem to find the words any further than the salutation.

What could she say? If she revealed to her where she was, Eleanor knew Lady Frances and Christian would both come immediately to Trelay to fetch her back, back to a life that no longer felt anything but false. The truth was Eleanor wasn't ready to go back, not now, not yet. Juliana had made such progress, especially recently. She needed Eleanor, but even more than that, Eleanor needed her.

In Juliana, Eleanor saw so much of herself. Though she hadn't lost the will to speak, from the time she'd been a girl, Eleanor had somehow stopped being heard. She had seen only what others had wanted her to see, had done what had been expected of her without really wondering, without questioning. Only now did she understand why they had never visited the old duke, her grandfather, even though he'd lived less than a mile from their London house. Only now did she recognize the tense hostility, the bitter resentment that had always simmered below the surface.

It was this realization that had helped Eleanor to come to terms with the truth of her birth, that had allowed her to forgive her mother and Christian for the decisions they had made in keeping it from her. Had it been Christian who had been born in her place, Eleanor couldn't honestly say that she wouldn't have made the same sacrifices he had to protect her. Society was cruel to anything less than ideal; in the same way that Juliana was shunned for her silence, Eleanor would have been shunned for her bastardy. And how easily she herself could have faced the same circumstances as her mother, wed to a man she obviously had not loved, living day in and day out with unhappiness, and the resentment it would breed. How many of her acquaintances from Miss Effington's school had done just that? Countless many—even Amelia B. hadn't been able to avoid it.

After Michaelmas, Eleanor promised herself. After Michaelmas when the harvest was complete and life on the isle settled in for the winter, she would write to her mother and assure her all was well. She would not tell her where she was, but would promise to explain when the time was right. Lady Frances would understand, for she of all people realized that there were times when things were better left unsaid.

It was with that thought that Eleanor shaped her own batch of the tiny cakes, silently designating a name for each: *Mother... Christian... Grace...*

By the time they had finished with the baking that night, the moon was high in the star-dusted sky and several dozen little cakes were set out in neat rows to cool on the trestle table. Before leaving the kitchen that night, Màiri broke off a tiny bit of the Michaelmas cake from the bottom edge, tossing it to the fire, 'as an offering' she said, 'to safeguard the house against the evil deeds of the underworld for the coming year.'

The festivities were to begin early the following morning with the circuiting of the isle's ancestral graveyard in a gesture meant to honor those who'd departed.

Shortly after dawn, Eleanor and Juliana came quickly down the tower stairs, munching their morning bannocks as they tied on their bonnets and headed off to join the others already gathering on the green outside. Màiri and her daughters were awaiting when they came into the great hall below.

"Have they already begun?" Eleanor asked, hoping they hadn't slept too late.

"Nae, not as of yet, lass. But we'd best hurry else we'll miss the morning blessing."

They headed off across the hall to leave, but Eleanor hesitated when she happened to spy Lord Dunevin through the open door of his study, standing at the window.

"What is it, lass?" Màiri asked when she noticed Eleanor had not joined them at the door.

Eleanor walked Juliana over to her. "Is Lord Dunevin not planning to join in the festivities?"

"*Och,* no. The laird doesna ever come down for the revels."

"Whyever not?"

Màiri's expression grew clouded, her voice dropping to a

quiet murmur. "Come, lass, you remember the terrible things Seamus Maclean said to you? About the laird? The mainlanders talk to the island folk, too, stories get passed around, and well, the laird just believes 'tis better for everyone if he stays 'ere at the castle."

"Oh."

But Eleanor was still staring at the study door, mulling Màiri's words over in her thoughts. Gossip or no, it wasn't right that he should stay locked away from one of the most important events taking place on his own isle, with his own people.

He was the laird—*their* laird. For too long, they had been listening to the false words of others, superstitious nonsense that had been added to and embellished for so long now, there was no longer any fragment of truth to the stories.

The viscount was not some black magic wizard who had cast a terrible spell on his own daughter to steal her voice. He had never been responsible for crop failures, foul weather, or the fact that one of the mainlander's cows had a white marking shaped like a lightning bolt on its neck. The people of the isle had spent too much time now believing Lord Dunevin to be something he'd never been. It was past time they were acquainted with their true laird.

Màiri bent down to help Juliana tie her bonnet in place. "Shall we go, then?"

But Eleanor didn't move. "Màiri, why don't you take Juliana and go on ahead. I'll catch up with you shortly."

Màiri looked at her, knowing immediately what she planned to do. "Very well, lass. We'll see you on the hill. But dinna be disappointed if you fail to sway him. We've tried in years past to no success."

Eleanor nodded to them, watching as they all departed, baskets in hand. Only when they had gone, closing the door behind them, did Eleanor turn for the viscount's study.

Lord Dunevin was still standing at the window when she

walked quietly into the room. Even at a distance from him, she could see his stance was tense, like a collie watching over his flock, sensing a predator but unable to see it. His arms were folded before him, and he looked as if his thoughts were troubled. He had said nothing more about the near-accident with the carrots at dinner earlier that week, but Eleanor knew the incident preyed heavily on his mind. It had preyed heavily on the minds of them all.

As Eleanor came fully into the room, Cudu lifted his head from where he lay on the carpet, rising up on all fours to walk over to greet her. Lord Dunevin noticed the dog's movement and turned. He glanced at her only briefly, and said nothing before returning his attention to the scene outside the window.

She said to his back, "I thought certain you'd be outside on the green, my lord, readying to ride that great beast of a horse of yours to victory in the race this morning."

The viscount shook his head. "No, my place is here where I can watch over it all. Didn't you know? That is what laird's do."

His tone tried at levity, but he wasn't fooling anyone. Most especially not her.

"Keeping yourself away only gives them that much more to talk about, you know."

"I beg your pardon?" He turned to her as if trying to feign that he didn't know what she was talking about when, in truth, he knew very well.

Eleanor moved to join him at the window. "I was just thinking that if you took part in the festivities of the day, assumed your true and rightful place as laird of these people, they would all see that there is nothing to those ridiculous stories the mainlanders keep bandying about. But keeping yourself a silhouette in a tower window only implies that you have something to hide." She stared directly at him. "Which you surely do not."

Gabriel turned then to fully face her. Vibrant green eyes that somehow saw straight to his soul blinked back at him. His insides tensed just to look at her. He thought again of how closely she had come to eating that hemlock, how the curse that plagued his family had nearly worked its wrath on another, this time an innocent bystander. He knew she believed it was merely a terrible accident. Did she yet realize that her life was at risk solely because of him?

Or was that her purpose in coming there? Why had she come there this morning, suggesting he do something he had longed to for years but had never dared even consider? To test him some-how? Did she think to see if he would admit that there was indeed something for him to hide?

But as he looked into those eyes, losing himself in them, Gabriel knew that her intentions were only true. Reflected he saw something he had never seen in the eyes of any other.

This woman believed in him.

He told himself she was too naïve, too unaware of the danger she was in. It was that same naïvete that had allowed her to kiss him that day, in this very room, having no earthly idea that as she had been falling dreamily under the spell of that sentimental old poem, she had at the same time been kissing a demon.

"Tell me, my lord," she said then, breaking him from his thoughts, "what would it take to get you to leave that window and walk with me to the hill to stand with the others?"

A bloody miracle, he thought to himself.

"A round of piquet, perhaps?" she asked then.

Eleanor crossed the room to the gaming table without even waiting for him to respond and opened the drawer, removing a deck of cards from inside. She arched a brow above a most cunning smile.

"I propose these stakes," she said. "If you should best me, you can stay there at that window all day and watch the day pass from afar. You can allow the people of your isle to continue to believe false tales and implausible conjecture about you. But, if I win, then you must accompany me to the hill and take part in the festivities today. Including," she concluded, "racing your horse on the course later today."

At first, Gabriel thought she was jesting, until she cut the deck and began to shuffle the cards. She had no idea of what exactly she was proposing. He, the Dark Lord of Dunevin, take part in the Michaelmas celebrations? It was impossible.

His next thought was to decline her proposition, tell her to leave him to watch as he always had before, alone and haunted by memories, even as he turned from the window and headed for the gaming table.

Perhaps, he would just accept her wager and best her at the hand. It would serve her right. He was, after all, an excellent piquet player.

But so, apparently, was she.

Six deals later, she had thoroughly trounced him.

Gabriel sat back in his chair and stared at her in stunned disbelief. "Wherever did you learn to play like that? You play with a ruthlessness worthy of White's!"

Eleanor took up the cards proudly, shuffling them with the ease of a practiced gamester. "I learned from the aunt of a very close family friend. Instead of spending our afternoon visits pouring tea, she and I played at cards. She is quite a sharp." She stood then, setting aside the deck and pulling on her gloves in an obvious prelude to leaving. "Are we ready then, my lord?"

"Ready?"

"Yes. To leave. We wouldn't want to be late."

She didn't even address the possibility of his refusing. Gabriel looked at her, contemplating his decision. He had never been one to walk away from a debt. She had beaten him fairly. And, he reasoned further, that if he was down in the thick of things, he could keep closer watch on Seamus Maclean.

So he would go.

"On one condition," he added.

She turned to him, her eyes alight beneath the brim of her bonnet. "Yes, my lord?"

"That you cease with the 'my lord's' and 'sirs.' Anyone who was able to best me so ruthlessly at cards should certainly be given the freedom to call me by my given name."

"But, my lord, is that at all a proper manner of conversing for someone in your employ?"

"It is proper if I say it is."

"Oh."

When next she spoke, her voice was noticeably softer. "But I'm embarrassed to say I don't even know what your name is."

His eyes held hers. "It is Gabriel."

She smiled softly as if the name pleased her. "Very well, *Gabriel.*"

It was the first time in his life that the sound of his own name brought his pulse to skipping.

"Well, then, shall we go?"

He turned from her then, and took up his coat.

As he pulled it on, she said from behind him, "But I must insist that you must do the same. It is only fair."

He turned to face her. "Very well, Eleanor."

Eleanor.

For the briefest of moments, she feared the end of her charade as Miss Nell Harte. She searched his eyes. Had he somehow learned the truth of her identity? Had he seen a notice like the one she'd taken from the inn wall, one she'd somehow missed?

But she saw nothing in his eyes to indicate that he'd chosen that name for any reason other than it was the more formal version of 'Nell.' If he had known the truth, if he had seen a notice and somehow figured out it was her described there, he surely would have revealed it to her long before now.

They left the study then and walked quietly together down the graveled pathway leading to the hill where the others had already gathered for the blessing of the *struan* cake. As they took their place among the small congregation of others, Eleanor noticed the looks of surprise and wonder at Gabriel's unexpected attendance. She could feel the stiffness of his reaction even as he stood beside her among these people whom he governed, but who he had avoided for so long. After a few minutes, when he saw that there were no protests, no bitter remarks whispered amongst the gathering, he began to ease.

Those that knew him, like Donald MacNeill or Màiri, simply looked astonished, pleasantly so, that he had decided to join in. Others, those who had rarely if ever seen him in person, looked on him as if they weren't quite sure how they should feel. It had to be difficult, she assumed, to think on the man suddenly standing amidst you as the devil incarnate.

Only one person, Seamus Maclean, showed any hint of contempt as he glared at Gabriel from where he stood beside what appeared to be the members of his family.

Gabriel and Eleanor stood quietly with Màiri and Juliana as the cleric began to speak in Gaelic, blessing the day and the fruits of the harvest, the prosperity of the isle, the health of the people and their laird. As if the very heavens realized the specialness of the day, a salt-scented gust of sea wind blew suddenly over the hilltop, dispersing the mist that hovered around them to reveal the rugged beauty of the ancient landscape while the cleric's lyric voice carried like a mystic song on the lifting breeze.

When the service was finished, not a single person moved from where they stood. Everyone turned as if waiting, and Eleanor realized that it was Gabriel's place as laird to lead the circuit around the final resting places of those no longer a part of the isle. It was a tradition he had avoided for too long.

He looked at Eleanor, sensing the same, but reluctant to take such a forefront so soon after emerging from the shadows of his long-held obscurity.

She smiled at him and watched as he took a deep breath and walked slowly to where the cleric stood waiting.

But even after he had gone forward, the others waited, watching her now.

"You must go with Miss Juliana and follow the laird," Màiri whispered quietly to her. "The laird and his family all walk together. 'Tis tradition."

She nodded and took Juliana's hand, walking slowly after him. The others fell into place behind her.

They walked in a quiet procession once around the grave-yard filled with ancient carved crosses and stones from centuries past before they dispersed to allow each family to make their own private offering to their departed loved ones. St. Michael's morn was a time for remembering, for reaffirming one's roots, for knowing from where one had come. It was a security, a pride, Eleanor thought, that she would never truly know.

Some offered prayers, others bits of cake and bread. Eleanor found herself kneeling beside the stones of those graves whose families were no longer a part of the isle, pulling stray weeds and smoothing away scattered bits of leaves and twigs.

It was just as she was readying to make her way back down the hill when she felt Juliana loosen her hand from hers and begin to walk away on her own.

"Juliana?"

But the little girl just kept walking, crossing the green to where the laird's ancestors were interred at a separate parcel of the cemetery, higher up on the hill.

Eleanor didn't try to stop her, but followed quietly after her, watching as Juliana paused before the beautifully carved stone cross that symbolically marked the final resting place of her mother. With all the innocence and tenderness of the child she was, Juliana reached down and placed a single daisy flower she'd picked, laying it gently at the base of the cross. Eleanor was so moved by the gesture, her eyes clouded with tears, that she never heard him approaching.

"'Tis a man with little conscience who can stand before the graves of those he put there."

It was Seamus Maclean's bitter voice that hissed closely to Eleanor's ear, like a menacing cloud had just come to cover the sun's light. Angrily, Eleanor wiped a gloved hand across her eyes and turned to face him.

"Even less of a conscience is shown by the man who would disrespect the significance of such a day in order to satisfy his own resentment."

The two stared at one another through a tense moment before Seamus' father came up alongside, taking his son by the arm and urging him along. "Away, lad. 'Tis no good will come of this."

Seamus yanked away from him. "No, Da, she needs to know." He turned to Eleanor, his eyes flashing. "He's the devil tha' one. I tried to save the other lady, but I was too late. He will lure you into his trap sure as he did her. It's in his eyes, lass. Dark as the depths of hell they are. No life behind them. Get you away now, afore it is too late."

Eleanor simply stared at the man in stony silence.

Maclean gave a bitter smile, shaking his head at her lack of reaction. "Look you up there at all the crosses and headstones of those who have perished at the hands of the MacFeaghs. The evidence speaks for itself, lass. See how many have gone to their graves because of that godforsaken clan. Dinna be another to join them, lass. Hie yerself away afore it is too late for ye."

Loath to listen to his spiteful insinuations any longer, Eleanor turned away from him and headed off up the hill to join Juliana. But as she wove her way slowly through the carved stone crosses and wind-battered headstones that peppered the hillside, she found herself glancing unwittingly at the names and the dates that had been inscribed upon them.

There was *Liùsaidh MacFie, died aged seven and ten,* in the sixteenth century, *Iseabail, infant daughter of Alexander MacFeagh,*

Murchadh Macfie, born 1710, died without issue 1733, and the least weathered of the stones which read *Georgiana MacFeagh, Lady Dunevin, taken from this lonely isle in 1817.*

There were so many, one could see why it would be difficult to put it off to unfortunate coincidence. Still, as she gazed across the hillside to where Gabriel stood conversing with the cleric, she could not bring herself to give credence to Seamus Maclean's terrible accusations.

There had to be some other explanation for the incidents that had darkened this place and these people. But what was it?

Eleanor felt a tugging on her arm and turned to see Juliana's sweet dark eyes looking up at her. And then she knew.

The answer to it all lay with this one child, hidden behind a wall of frightened silence. Only Juliana knew the truth of what had happened to her mother. Only she had been with her last before she'd disappeared. Somehow, some way there had to be a key to unlocking it.

And Eleanor determined that she would find it.

12

*A*fter the morning's more spiritual observances, the mood of the day shifted, like the pale light of dawn giving way to the sun, from a feeling of thoughtful remembrance to another soon filled with lively merriment and high celebratory spirit.

Winter was coming to the islands, and Trelay had been blessed by a bounteous harvest that would see them all through the meager months ahead. Thus, St. Michael's Day was a day of rich reward after months of toilsome work. This was a day of giving thanks for a season of abundance and prosperity at a time when other districts of the Highlands and western seaboard were struggling against land clearances, steadily increasing rents, and economic failure.

Out on the green that stretched in a lush fusion of soft meadow grass, white clover, and dandelion like a carpet from the castle proper to the lower shoreline, games and amusements had been set out for the children to play with while the adults took part in the *odaidh,* the St. Michael's Day traditional horse race.

Gabriel had taken himself off shortly after the ceremony that morning and hadn't returned since. Eleanor hoped that he hadn't changed his mind about taking part in the rest of the day's activities, retreating back to his study window to watch from afar. She couldn't, she knew, press him to stay, but inwardly she hoped that he had been encouraged by the reactions of the islanders, many of whom had even approached him that morning on the hillside to wish him well.

For the *odaidh*, the horses would run on a sandy stretch of rugged shoreline that extended from below the castle's walls to the stone jetty that served as the island's pier. It was a length of about a quarter mile, uneven terrain that was peppered with an assortment of natural obstacles, everything from timeworn standing stones to dense clumps of sea moss and scattered pieces of driftwood that had washed up with the tide.

As the others made their way down the hillside to where the racers were at that moment assembling on the strand, Eleanor looked, shading her eyes as she studied the faces of the others. Màiri noticed her searching and came up beside her, tucking her arm loosely around her waist.

"If you ask me," she said with her usual infinite wisdom, "'twas a miracle you convinced the laird to come out e'en this morn, lass. Be happy you managed to accomplish that. He's been apart from this all so long, it may take him some time to feel comfortable 'ere."

Eleanor simply nodded, trying to stave off her disappointment, and turned to help with the other activities.

For the children, Màiri and Seòna had furnished tubs filled with a sudsy mixture made from crushed soapwort stems and various other herbs that they could pour into little carved wooden 'pipes' to blow clumps of bubbles all about the place. Later that evening, there would be games of "Hoodman Blind" and "Tigh," while the adults danced at the *cuideachd*.

While the older children pranced around, trying to see who could blow the biggest bubble, Wee Donald and some of the younger ones sucked on spoonfuls of sugar that had been twisted into bits of paper for a special treat. Eleanor was heartened to see that the other children took Juliana into their collective fold, accepting her muteness without any outspoken remarks and with only a little curiosity.

When a boy of about six asked Juliana her name, she responded with a silent stare. A moment later, another little girl named Brìdghe, very near Juliana's age with curly blonde hair and bare feet beneath the ragged hem of her woolen skirts, took it upon herself to act as Juliana's attendant, introducing her to the others as 'My friend, *Jwee-lhanna*.' Even now, they lay on their bellies, ankles crossed behind them and noses nearly to the ground, one dark head bent closely to one light, searching through a thick patch of clover for the one bearing the charmed four leaves.

Would that the mainlanders they had encountered that day in Oban could take a lesson from the perspective of a child, Eleanor thought, watching them with a soft smile.

When it came time for the race to begin, Eleanor walked with Màiri and Seòna to the edge of the course to stand with the others already assembled. It looked as if most every family on the isle had come out for the festivities that day, for easily two hundred or more spectators of all ages stood along the periphery of the race's course.

A line of nearly a dozen riders had congregated at the starting point, a motley assortment that included most every sort of beast from riding horse to pony, plow horse to nag. There was even a mule that looked quite as if it might doze off at any moment, its head hanging low to the ground, its eyes blinking to a snooze. They were all without both saddle and bridle, the riders by tradition made to direct their mounts by means of their seat and skill, and a simple leading rope.

"I wagered old Angus MacNeill a batch of blaeberry scones

that your Donald would win this year, Seòna," Màiri said as they waited for the race to begin. "I even gave Donald a special bit of sugar with mint for his mare with the promise of another if she can beat that Seamus Maclean's nasty old hack to the finish line."

"And what is your prize from Angus if Donald should win?" Seòna asked with a tilt of her brow and a mischievous grin.

It was a subject of frequent mirth among the women that Màiri's interest in the widowed crofter was a little more than friendly acquaintanceship. She often asked after him to Seòna and Donald, and Old Angus could often be found sitting in the Dunevin kitchen, sharing a wee cuppa with Màiri while she worked.

"If I win, Angus has to turn a reel wit' me at the *cuideachd* later tonight."

At Seòna's sidelong glance, she added, "I ken what ye're thinkin' by the look on your face, Seòna MacNeill. Dinna be getting' any matchmakin' thoughts into that pretty head o' yours. 'Tis simply because I miss the dancin' so much without my Torquil 'ere these past five years."

Seòna glanced knowingly at Eleanor. "And I suppose all those cakes and fresh bannocks you keep takin' over to Angus' croft are because you worry the man canna feed himself?"

Màiri lifted her chin stubbornly, but her plump cheeks pinked modestly, and she gave a slight smile while Seòna and Eleanor chuckled behind her.

"*Wheesht*, you brazen lassies, the race is nearly ready to start."

The riders were poised to set off when Young Donald, who was readying to strike the signal to start using a tin pan and a stick, suddenly lowered his arms, looking up toward the castle heights. Everyone turned at once to look at what had caught his attention, just as a lone rider, silhouetted by the sun, started coming down the hill toward them.

A murmur of excitement immediately bubbled through the crowd.

"Well, you'd better get to baking those scones, Màiri Macaphee," Seòna said. "I think your chances for winning that wager just went astray."

Eleanor's heart drummed at the sight of Gabriel making his way down the hillside toward them. With the wind tugging at his hair and the late morning mist curling around the legs of his dark, prancing horse, he looked quite like an ancient Highland warrior readying to do battle. She felt the urge to rush over to meet him, but held it in check as he quickly closed the distance to the shore.

"Sweet heaven," Màiri said, shading her eyes along with all the others against the light of the sun. "'Tis the laird. He's goin' to race this year."

Word spread quickly throughout the assembly, sending a headlong rush of excitement rolling across the brae like the swift autumn wind. Even the children stopped in their play to watch as Gabriel directed his great hunter past the astonished faces of islanders to the starting point.

The stallion was a magnificent animal, well over seventeen hands and a sleek black, with but one white sock on his right hind. Young Donald was staring with his mouth agape as Gabriel took his place in line.

"I hope you don't mind an additional rider," Gabriel said, urging his horse forward alongside Donald MacNeill's mare, who looked rather like a pony beside the viscount's taller hunter.

Like the other riders, Gabriel had changed from his fine coat and dress kilt into a pair of the traditional riding trews that hugged his legs almost like a second skin beneath his linen sark. Gone was the austere lord to be revered and watched from afar. In his place was a man who fit in easily with the others, every bit the Scot. Eleanor could but stare.

She smiled, appalled to feel herself blushing like a giddy schoolgirl when he glanced over to her, and shyly looked away. That smile faded when she happened to notice the fierce look that had crossed Seamus Maclean's features as he glared at Gabriel from the other side of the line of riders.

Noticing her watching him, Seamus suddenly backed his horse from the ranks.

"Maclean," Donald MacNeill called to him, "what're you about? Are you for quittin' the race even afore it's begun, mon?"

A chorus of Gaelic whispers soughed through the gathering.

Seamus spat into the ground at his horse's feet before responding. "Nae, Donald MacNeill. I just see nae good reason to waste my time t'day. 'Tis obvious to all 'ere who'll win the race now. 'Tis the mon with all the money who can afford to buy himsel' the best piece of horseflesh."

An astonished silence followed. People shook their heads in disbelief that Seamus would dare direct such open hostility toward the laird. Others simply stared.

A threatening wind blew in off the shore, whistling through the stark coastal trees. No one moved and made a sound. Quickly did the festive mood of the gathering change.

Though Seamus Maclean didn't himself live on the isle, his elder parents did, leasing land directly from Lord Dunevin. As such they were at his mercy. Few lairds if any would be tolerant of such an open show of disrespect. In fact, any number would make an example of this blatant insolence to serve as a reminder to the others of the true order of things.

Eleanor stole a quick glance at Seamus's father and mother who stood across from her. They were of an advanced age and the looks on their faces were stricken with their fear at their son's actions, telling of the gravity of the situation.

It was only through Gabriel's grace that they had a home to rent and land to sow; it could just as easily be taken away without cause, without warning, without recourse. At a time when Highland lairds were swiftly clearing their lands of their tenants for the more profitable venture of sheep farming, words like those of Seamus were both imprudent and perilous.

Everyone watched Gabriel for his response, waiting in tense silence. When it came, even the gulls flying overhead fell silent.

"If it was my horse you coveted, Maclean, you should have taken advantage of the opportunity to steal him last night for today's race."

He looked at Eleanor then, explaining. "Miss Harte, there is an ancient custom that on the eve of St. Michaelmas, any horse may be appropriated for the race the following day without fear of punishment, provided the horse is returned afterward unharmed. Most of the men here spent the night watching over their own horses and ponies in the fields."

He glanced a moment at the mule beast, who had, in fact, by now dozed off. "Well, except perhaps for Olghar there. No doubt he left the byre unattended all night in hopes some unlikely fool would take that lazy beast off his hands."

Several of the islanders laughed at that, while the mule's owner, Olghar Macphee, grinned at Gabriel's jest. "Och, but he's a fine beast, m'lord. Dinna be fooled. We're certain to take the prize of last of the pack today."

The crowd began to ease, sensing their laird's leniency.

"I posted no guard on my hunter," Gabriel went on. "I even left the stable unlocked because I hadn't planned to race today and thought perhaps someone else might like to borrow him, but no one bothered to take him. It doesn't seem fair now not to let him stretch his legs today with all the other horses. I had no choice but to come and ride him myself in the race."

Murmurs of agreement arose from the assembly gathered. Others turned angry glances and muttered curses at Seamus Maclean for his failed attempt at ruining the happy gathering.

"But," Gabriel went on, "I will make this concession to you, Seamus Maclean, so that it cannot be said that the race was run unfairly in my favor. My horse will bear the weight of two riders through the course while everyone else rides alone. That should sufficiently even the stakes."

Those islanders who understood English seemed to agree, translating Gabriel's offer to Gaelic for the others. All around the crowd, people began to nod and comment on their laird's integrity and sportsmanship. One man even suggested that Olghar's mule beast, as dispirited as it looked, race riderless to even the odds the other way, eliciting a chorus of good-natured laughter.

Eleanor was so busy looking around at all the others, reading their reactions, that she never noticed Gabriel had directed his horse over to where she and Juliana stood with Màiri and Seòna. Only when he was standing right beside her and she felt the nudge of his horse's muzzle against her arm did she turn about.

"Well?" he said, looking down at her from the back of his great beast.

It wasn't until she noticed that the eyes of everyone around her were focused solely on the two of them that she realized what it was he was proposing.

"You wish me? To ride with you?"

Gabriel never had the chance to answer her for cheers of encouragement immediately erupted from all sides, urging her on.

Before she even comprehended what was happening, Eleanor felt herself being hoisted somehow up and onto the horse's back, turning to sit before Gabriel with her legs dangling over one side. She stared at him in astonishment.

The stallion jigged at the arrival of its new rider, getting accustomed to the added rider.

"Hold tight, lass," Gabriel whispered to her on a half-grin. "This will likely prove a bumpy ride."

He turned his horse without using his hands, guiding it solely with pressure from his legs back into its place in the line of other racers. Eleanor threaded her fingers into the wiry hair of the horse's mane, her heart already racing, hoping that she wasn't unseated the moment they started off.

"Riders at ready!" Young Donald called out then, raising his tin pan gong once again as he readied to strike the starting signal.

Eleanor felt Gabriel tighten his arms around her, took a deep breath of the mingling scents of formidable horse and even more formidable man that surrounded her, and held it. She closed her eyes just as Donald lowered his hand to strike the gong.

She felt the horse's muscles bunch in expectation beneath her.

The signal resounded.

They leapt suddenly forward in response.

That same breath she'd been holding left in a gasp of pure exhilaration as she was thrown back to meet the solid wall of Gabriel's chest. She fought to remain seated, her hands soon letting go of the horse's mane and working their way around Gabriel's arms as he urged them on even faster.

The wind bit at her cheeks and nose, stinging her eyes as her hair tumbled helplessly from its pins, but she barely noticed. All she could see, all she could think about, all she could feel was the man whose arms were around her, holding her securely.

They were racing at pace across the rough terrain, but Eleanor had never felt safer in her life. She could let go, she knew, and still he wouldn't let her fall. He would never let her fall. But none of that mattered. She didn't want to let go of him. She wanted to feel the strength of his arms beneath her hands, the warmth of his body, the salt spiced scent of his neck as she allowed the motion of the horse beneath them to push her further and further back until she was leaning fully against him.

With the spray of the tide dampening their faces, they bounded over a fallen stone, thundering over brush and marram as they began to close in on the jetty that stretched its way outward from the shore in front of them. At the jetty, they would have to make a sharp rollback, retracing the course to where they'd begun and where the burgeoning crowd of islanders awaited, cheering on the racers even now behind them.

As they came to the jetty, there were three of them running

closely together, Donald MacNeill, Seamus Maclean, and Gabriel's hunter carrying them both. It would make the sharp turn on this narrow strip of shoreline even more difficult to accomplish, but Gabriel showed no signs of slowing.

Neither did Seamus or Donald.

If anything, they all urged their horses on faster, hooves cutting deeply into the wet sand and graveled shell beneath them as they raced closer and closer to the rock pier.

Once at the point where they had to make the turn, Seamus cut left inland toward the green of the machair, while Donald cut right, galloping out in a wide arc to where the waves lapped hungrily at the shore. Gabriel would have to make an even tighter turnabout, a difficult maneuver without the use of a bit to direct his horse. As he went into it, leaning and tightening his legs around the stallion's girth, Seamus cut him off suddenly from the side, making it that much more difficult to pivot.

The hunter faltered, uncertain, throwing his head and nearly unseating them both. Gabriel had to pull on the leading rope to bring them to a sudden stop or else risk sending one or both of them plummeting to the tumbled rocks of the jetty. As he managed to set them each to rights and turn the horse back in the other direction, Seamus set his whip hand to slapping against his own steed's flank, shouting out an curse in Gaelic that frightened the poor beast into a panicked gallop as he headed for the finish line.

Gabriel snaked an arm around Eleanor's waist, pulling her even more closely against him so that she was sitting atop his thigh and quite nearly across his lap. His chin brushed her temple, the roughness of it rasping against her forehead as he looked down at her.

"Hold tight to me, lass, for we're about to sprout wings."

Eleanor barely managed to get one hand around his arm before he set his heels to the hunter's sides and they were off again, hooves flying, wind screaming in her ears as they rode through the foam and raced down the pebbled shoreline in relentless pursuit of the other two riders.

They overtook Donald MacNeill first whose mare was visibly tiring, her shorter legs no match for those of the other two larger horses. Gabriel's hunter ate up the distance between them easily, galloping past in a flurry of sand and sea spray to the encouraging shouts of Donald himself as he cheered them on.

They pounded over the shoreline, drawing slowly closer to Seamus and his steed a distance ahead. A screen of pebbles and sand from the horse's flying hooves in front of them began to pepper them. Eleanor turned her face into Gabriel's neck to avoid the debris, the scent and the heat of him going straight to her head.

She never even noticed when they hurtled past Seamus's horse in a quicksilver flash as they closed in on the finish line. Not until she heard the uproar of cheers from the crowd around them did she realize they had just won the race.

Gabriel slowed his horse, first to a trot and then to a walk, taking them along the brae of the heathery hillside beneath the castle. Even after they had stopped, Eleanor hadn't let loose of him, not until they were surrounded by a crowd of the islanders all cheering and congratulating them on the exciting victory.

Gabriel let go of the leading rope, loosening his embrace, and swung his leg around, dropping to the ground. As the others crowded thickly around him, he took Eleanor by the waist and eased her gently to the ground before him, tightening his hold around her again when her legs threatened to buckle suddenly beneath her.

"Steady now, lass," he said softly to her. "You seem to have lost your land legs. I thought that sort of thing only happened at sea."

At sea...

They were the perfect words to describe the unusual way she

felt at that very moment. Her senses were giddy, her thoughts so much in chaos she could only manage a weakened smile.

"A kiss from the lady for the winner," called out a sudden voice that sounded curiously similar to Màiri's.

As if in a dream, Eleanor could but watch, wide-eyed and bewildered, as Gabriel lowered his head to hers and kissed her there before all.

A chorus of cheers resounded around them, but Eleanor barely heard them. Somehow, in the space of those few moments, they had gone from governess and lord now simply to woman and man, all propriety, all stricture between them departed in the very blink of an eye.

The sounds of the rest of the world around them, the crowd, the wind, the crash of the surf on the shore, all of it faded into a haze. The only sound she could hear was the rapid drum of her own heart, beating a rhythm all its own as she gave herself over completely to the kiss and the man whose mouth touched hers.

It was over far, far too soon.

As Gabriel pulled away, his dark eyes captured hers and held her suspended. Eleanor knew in the very next moment what it was that had caused this to happen.

She had fallen in love with Gabriel.

It was nothing like the cordial affection that she had once felt for Richard Hartley, what she had thought in all her maidenly ignorance had been the beginnings of love.

What she felt for Gabriel was something else, something infinitely more. It was fire, it was gale, it was bottomless sea all at once. Even now, she wanted him to kiss her again no matter who stood around them, and never stop, not even when the moon had risen high in the sky and the magic of the night surrounded them. She wanted to feel his hands against her, the heat of him touching her in places she had never been touched. She wanted to lose herself in the dark endless depths of his eyes every day for the rest of her life.

It was utterly consuming, this sudden realization she faced about herself. She wanted to love this man who the world had forsaken and heal his tortured heart. She wanted to spend her days living on this island, watching Juliana grow and helping her to find her way in the world. She wanted to breech the distance between father and daughter and show them the way back to each other again.

She wanted all this and more, so much more, but first Gabriel would have to know the truth of her, of her ancestry, of her reasons for running away from the life she'd lived before. She would have to tell him she was not really Miss Nell Harte, but that she was Lady Eleanor Wycliffe, the illegitimate Westover heiress—even if doing so might very well destroy whatever future they might have had.

Her troubled thoughts must have shown clearly on her face for Gabriel stood before her then, looking down at her with eyes filled with concern.

"Is something wrong, lass? You look as if you're not pleased we won the race."

She looked up at him, uncertain at what she knew she must do. What would he do if she were to tell him right there, that moment, that she loved him? Would he think her fanciful? Would he think her a fool? Even worse, would he turn away?

Would he be angry she had lied to him, leading him to believe she was someone she was not?

It was the risk she had no choice but to face. What she felt for Gabriel was too real to surround with a lie. She would have to lay her heart, her life, her future on the line to him, but not here, and not now.

This wasn't the time or the place to tell him. This was a day of celebration for so many reasons, not the least of which was his own "coming out," his re-emergence into his rightful place in the world.

So, instead, Eleanor simply smiled, looking into the eyes of the man she loved, and shook her head, saying quietly, "I always knew you would win."

For he had won more than just the race that day.

He had won her heart as well.

13

*M*any agreed there hadn't been such a fine Michaelmas on the isle in more years than most could remember. Others attributed the unusually clement skies to the unexpected, but wholly celebrated, appearance this year of the isle's reclusive laird.

After the excitement of the race that morning, the islanders had retreated inland from the shore to the verdant machair beneath the castle heights where the men and boys of the isle then squared off into teams for the traditional game of "shinty."

It was a competition steeped in tradition. The men were armed with the slender curved *caman* stick with a small wooden ball made from an elder gnarl the size of an apple. The play of the game was both hard and fierce as each team labored to drive the ball successfully into the opposing team's hail, marked clearly by two makeshift stacks of stones on either end of the sporting field. There were scraped knees, bruised heads, and for one, a broken front tooth. Rules were unwritten, although ancient custom prevailed. Tempers would flare, disagreements often erupted, sometimes coming to blows, but always it was the play of the game that decided the true victor.

When the sun had descended and the skies had darkened too much for further play, the assembly retired back to the Dunevin courtyard for the feast, the Michaelmas lamb and the *struan* cakes that had been baked by the women the night before.

Each of the island families brought food from their own crofts to contribute, and tables were filled to bursting— numerous cheeses, partan pies, cakes and scones, howtowdie, puddings, and biscuit-like treats called whim-whams. Heather ale and birk wine flowed freely, loosening tongues and freeing gay spirits. All around there was a feeling of good cheer. By the time night had fallen on St. Michael's day, the dancing was well under way.

On the moon-kissed courtyard outside the castle donjon, burnished in muted torchlight and whispering shadows, circles of dancers moved in whirlwind harmony, hands clasped, arms linked, weaving in and out of one another in time to the lively tune of the piper, drum, and fiddle. Brightly colored skirts swished and swayed around bare feet and slender legs. Hands clapped. Feet stomped. Laughter and gaiety filled the air, while in the far-off corner, sitting alone at the end of one of the many trestle tables that had been brought out from the great hall for the feast, the laird of Dunevin watched over it all with thoughtful eyes.

It had been a day of celebration for many reasons. As laird, Gabriel was protector and ultimate caretaker for every person— from eldest graybeard to newborn nursling—on the isle. He was lord, master, benefactor, their trials were his trials, their safe-keeping his bounden duty. Being an island community only made them that much more vulnerable. Today, however, was a day when he could find peace in knowing that the people of his island, the island that his ancestors had safeguarded for centuries, would have sufficient food and shelter to last them through the harsh months ahead.

It wasn't always so across the Highlands. Throughout the

western seaboard and further out even to the more remote isles of Lewis and Harris, places once inhabited by great Gaelic kings, were being wholly abandoned out of necessity, the land no longer affording the barest sustenance for the people who had lived there through generations. The industry of kelping, which so many had grown to depend upon to make their living, was steadily declining since the defeat of Napoleon, leaving them with only the unpredictability of farming or herring fishing on which to survive.

Even worse, the people on some of the other nearby isles were at the very mercy of a system that offered them little in the way of protection against greedy tacksmen and absentee landlords who valued pounds far above the livelihoods of their minions. Gabriel refused to adhere to this new system of estate management. Despite the darkness of their past, the MacFeaghs, lairds of Dunevin since time immemorial, had always been as one with the needs of their people—patriarchs of clan and kin—and he meant to see that tradition preserved.

All through the day and evening, Gabriel had been approached by the people of his isle, people who had avoided him just as much as he had them for the past three years since Georgiana's unexplained death. It was almost as if he had been away on a journey to far-off lands, returning just now to their welcome.

Across the courtyard, Gabriel watched his daughter, Juliana, who would one day take his place as benefactor on this lonely isle. The change she had undergone in the past weeks was beyond astounding. Not a month before, he had thought her lost forever, an empty shell of a child who shunned human contact. To look at her now as she sat playing with another little girl, Brìghde Macphee, whose parents had changed the spelling of their own last name years earlier in order to differentiate their family from his, could only be called a miracle.

The two of them together were the picture of innocence,

skipping together in a circle beneath the flickering light of the rush torch beside them. Their faces were kissed with smiles, their eyes alight with excitement. It was just one of so many revelations that had touched this special Michaelmas celebration.

What was it, he wondered, that was so very different? Was it simply the festive mood of the day? The thankfulness for an abundant harvest? But even as he wondered this, Gabriel knew the reason for this sudden rebirth stood now among the line of dancers, clapping her hands in time to the music, the torchlight reflected in those green eyes.

She called herself Miss Nell Harte. He had hired her in hopes that she would prove a suitable governess for Juliana, someone who would teach her the social accomplishments she would need to one day be wife and mother.

Instead, the woman had proven herself an angel in disguise.

Gabriel watched Eleanor quietly now as she linked hands with Young Donald MacNeill amid a burgeoning circle of other dancers, trying to mimic the steps of a lively reel she had only just learned, laughing at herself when she misstepped and trod upon his toes. Her thistle-down laughter was like music to his ears, madrigal that had been unspoken at this castle too long. Her smile shone brighter than the harvest moon overhead...

"I ken what ye're thinkin', laird."

Gabriel broke from his romantic musings, looking beside himself to where Donald MacNeill had suddenly appeared. He arched a bland brow. "You can read thoughts now, can you, MacNeill?"

The man simply stared at him, seeing right through his attempt at feigned detachment. "Have I no' known ye since we were lads, laird?"

"Aye, you have."

"Did I no' fight with ye at Corunna 'gainst Napoleon?"

"Aye, you did."

"Then I think I can say that I ken what ye're thinkin'"

There were few on the island who would speak so openly to Gabriel, just as there were few who knew Gabriel, really knew the true MacFeagh, and not the legendary Dark Lord of Dunevin that people on the mainland filled their children's nightmares with. It could be said that Donald MacNeill was the closest person Gabriel had to a true friend on the isle.

MacNeill fell quiet for a moment, then added, "If my young Donald was ten years older, you'd have you a sure fight on yer hands. I think the lad's smitten wit' her."

Gabriel turned to look at MacNeill, his expression suddenly grave. "And a better man for her he'd be."

Donald shook his head, scratching his rusty hair beneath his natty bonnet. "How is it a mon as rich as you can be so bloody stupid?"

"I ask myself that same question all the time. You would think I'd have learned well enough. I thought I had learned, after Georgiana. I let her get too close and just as all the times before, she suffered because of it. I cannot allow myself to repeat that mistake again with this lass."

No matter how deeply she might speak to my soul...

"That's not what I mean and you know it." MacNeill's words were sparked with feeling. "That old witch's curse only has its power because you give it that power." He tapped a finger to his forehead. "You give it the power to rule you in 'ere. You fight it every day in yer mind. Ye're consumed with it." Then he flattened his hand against the front of his woolen shirt. "But it's here, in yer heart that you must finally put that curse to its rightful rest, laird. Banish it and be on with yer life afore you end up old and bitter, dying alone just like..."

"Just like my father," Gabriel finished for him.

MacNeill stared at him, fearing he'd gone too far, touching on a subject of great anguish for Gabriel.

The great Alexander MacFeagh had been what some would call a medical miracle—walking, talking, breathing, while devoid of any hint of a heart. He had lived to the ripe old age of seventy-nine that way.

Gabriel had been four the first time he remembered seeing the man, his dark hair and fierce stolid eyes sending the lad backing away to the safer haven of his mother's skirts.

"Ye've coddled the lad, woman. Look at him! I ne'er should have given over his care to you like I did. Should have raised him like I did young Malcolm here, to be a mon worthy of the name MacFeagh. Ye might as well start dressing him in skirts and tying ribbons in his hair!"

With twin looks of disgust, his father and his brother had turned away from Gabriel that day, their laughter echoing across the courtyard as they went. But Gabriel would never forget that day.

It was another three years before he saw his father again. Never again did he back away from him, but Malcolm had grown into manhood, as fierce and heartless a man as their father, and so Alexander had had no need for another son.

Gabriel looked out at the swirling sea of dancers on the courtyard while silently considering Donald's words. Most of his life, he had been surrounded by people who had either feared, ridiculed, or reviled him. His mother had died shortly after he'd turned seven and from then, he was sent away to a series of boarding schools. To be forgotten. No one had ever dared believe in him.

But since this mysterious governess had come into their lives, he found he now began to wonder what it would be like to have someone to share this island with, someone who held his same affinity for its people and their ways, someone who wouldn't flinch when he touched her, someone who set his pulse to racing just with a simple look from her eyes. How easy it could be, he thought, watching as Eleanor linked arms now with old Angus, taking a twirl with the ruddy-cheeked Scotsman while Màiri and the others around her cheered. How easy it would be for him to fall in love with her...

But he could not erase history no matter how much he wished it, the dark history that plagued him still. It was a history that put her at such great risk.

Gabriel noticed that the dancing had stopped and everyone was moving off from the center of the courtyard to sit at the tables or stand off in the evening shadows. He saw Eleanor making her way to the small dais where the piper and the fiddlers had assembled, carrying something tucked under her arm.

Màiri came forward from the gathering then to stand and face the others.

"Aye, but ye're all in fer a treat now, you are. It took some doing—" she glanced at Eleanor beside her, smiling, "—but I've managed to convince this sweet lass to share the talent she has that she's been hiding from us all."

Gabriel found himself sitting more forward on his seat. He watched as Eleanor stepped forward to stand at the front of the musician's platform. In her hands she held something, slender and dark. When she lifted it up, he realized it was a flute she meant to play. The entire courtyard hushed as she took her first soft note.

The dulcet tones of an old Scottish air familiar to everyone seated there drifted sweetly from her fingertips, whispering across the courtyard, filling the air with ancient magic, and entrancing everyone seated before her. Like the famed piper of Hamlin, her sweet music drew each listener in, each note of her plaintive tune swirling across the assembly like a siren's song.

Gabriel stood, completely forgetting Donald MacNeill beside him as he walked slowly from the shadows, spellbound as she played on, her eyes closed, lashes resting lightly on her cheeks. Not typically a ladies' instrument, Eleanor played the flute like she'd been born to it, her fingers moving easily through the notes. Many around the courtyard had closed their eyes, swaying softly to the rhythm of the breathy melody. Others simply stared as if afraid to so much as blink lest the vision before them suddenly vanish.

When she finished, ending the lilting tune on one gentle, sweet note, there was silence for a moment afterward. Nobody moved or uttered a sound. It was as if she had lulled them into a dream. Then, as if suddenly awakened, they applauded, cheering out, standing and surrounding her with their praise.

Eleanor smiled shyly, bowing her head before she turned to back off the dais.

"Nae, dinna go just yet," called the piper, who struck up a lively tune, accompanied by the fiddler. "Play wit' us, lassie!"

Eleanor stood as they began to play and listened for a few moments, following the tune, memorizing its notes. After the first chorus, she joined in and everyone got up at once to dance. Just as quickly as the mood had shifted to one of softness and whispers, it had turned back to the liveliness and vigor of before.

Gabriel saw Màiri standing off to the side of the dancing with Seòna MacNeill beside her, watching the dancers as they whirled and skipped. Quietly, he walked over to them.

"Good e'ening, laird," Màiri said warmly. "'Tis a fine *cuideachd* we're havin'. Is no' Miss Harte a bonny fine musician?"

Gabriel couldn't take his eyes from Eleanor. She had somehow come more alive while playing, her expression alight as she tossed her head with the trill of her tune. "Indeed, she is quite an accomplished flutist. I had no idea."

Màiri grinned. "Nae a'one of us did. I only happened to be walkin' out one night late and heard the loveliest of strains coming from out on the hillside. I thought to me'self that it must be the faeries, for who else could there be making such magical music on a moonlit night? I stole closer to catch a wee look at them and was astounded when I found not any o' the wee folk, but our own young miss sitting atop a stone, playing a lovely song all alone. She said she'd played her fife since she were a wee lassie, that it often gave her ease, but that she mostly played for herself. It took a lot o' convincing to get her to play for us all t'night."

"Well, I'm pleased you did."

Gabriel watched then as Eleanor, who had finished playing with the others, crossed the courtyard, heading for the door that led inside the castle. He waited through the next dance, and when she didn't immediately return, he decided to follow after her.

Excusing himself from Màiri and Seòna, he headed for the castle door.

Màiri glanced sidelong at Seòna, her mouth touched with a small cunning grin. "Keep the ghillie occupied for a while, won't you, Seòna dear? His master will no' be needin' him tagging along behind him this night."

Seòna nodded knowingly, and headed across the yard to where Fergus was sitting with some of the other islanders, chatting over a mug of ale. Always a most resourceful lass, she soon had the man engaged in a conversation that he had no hope of extricating himself from.

Her work done, Màiri glanced up at the top window in the castle tower, whispering to herself, "St. Michael, if ye're a'listenin', 'tis time for you to work your magic."

ELEANOR SET THE SEPARATE PIECES OF HER FLUTE INSIDE ITS velvet-lined wooden case, smoothing a fond hand against the polished rosewood and the silver keys that still shined as if new, before tucking it back inside the chest of drawers in her small chamber. It had felt good to play, to lose herself in the music, to be a part of the celebration of this very special day.

She stopped for a moment, smiling as she thought back on the happy scene yet engaged outside, the ending of a time of coming together for all, and the hope for a new beginning, too.

She turned for the door and started down the hall to leave, but hesitated outside the open door of the schoolroom. Across the room at the window, she could see the glow from the torchlight in the courtyard, could hear the laughter of the revelers and the plucky tune of the fiddle, echoing into the night.

She crossed the room to the window seat Juliana was so fond of and looked out onto the scene below. She spotted Juliana sitting with Màiri and Brìghde, and smiled to herself. Of all the wonderful things of that day, theirs had to be the most special. For that day, Juliana had found a friend.

It was inexplicable. All day, the two girls had interacted with one another as easily as if they were carrying on in conversation, but Juliana never had to speak a word or even make a gesture. Brìghde, a most precocious child, spoke to her, answered her, questioned her, and somehow knew exactly what Juliana would have said had she said it herself. It was as if Juliana had spent all those years of silent anguish in the loneliness of isolation waiting for this one girl, and from the moment they'd met, it had all magically melted away as the two of them played and danced the night away together.

It was just one of so many mysterious things that happened on this ancient island, for which there was no reason, no logical explanation. Wee folk, faeries, kelpies, even ghosts that wandered aimlessly in the mists at night, there was something about this place that seemed somehow supernatural, an enchantment that made one believe in things they'd never believed before.

And it was that same Gaelic mysticism that had delivered her heart to Gabriel.

All through the day, her thoughts had been filled with him, wondering what he would do, what he would say if he knew her feelings. She wished she could look in a pool of water, or a cup of tea like one of those fortune tellers who set up tents at the country fairs, and see what the future held for her, for them.

As she sat looking out on the castle courtyard, she remembered something Màiri had told her earlier that day, that if a maid said the name of the man she loved to the St. Michael's moon, he would come to her in a dream.

Silently, Eleanor stood before the window, staring up at the moon and the stars and the endless sky stretching out over the turbulent sea. She whispered softly to herself.

"...Gabriel."

Almost in the same moment, she heard a soft sound behind her. She turned and her breath left her in a rush when she saw that he was suddenly standing there, before her.

Had she conjured him up?

She didn't speak. Nor did he. Cloaked in the near darkness, they simply stared at one another in silence.

Was he real? Or was he some flight of her imagination? At that very moment, Eleanor didn't even care. Just looking at him, having him there, made her feel alive.

Gabriel crossed the room slowly then, coming to stand before her at the window. His eyes watched her closely, his features etched in the muted moonlight. He looked as if he wanted to say something, but knew not what.

It was precisely the way she felt, too.

To convince herself he wasn't a wildering dream, Eleanor reached up, touched him softly on the side of his face, tracing her fingertips along the scuff of his jaw, delighting in the texture of him. His eyes held hers captive, his skin warm to her fingertips, and she could see his pulse beat against his neck in the moonlight shadow.

She wondered what it would be like to touch her mouth to him there. She wondered if it were possible for her to take flame just standing before him. Until he stepped even closer, to where his legs brushed her skirts. He took her face on either side with his hands and tipped her mouth upward for his kiss.

And then she wondered no more.

Eleanor closed her eyes and melted to him, flattening her hands against the cambric that covered his chest as he kissed her more deeply than she could have possibly imagined.

He smelled of the open air, salty and fresh, and of the smoke from the rush fires that burned even now on the courtyard beneath them. She felt his hands curve around the back of her neck, upward through her hair to dislodge its pins, caressing her until his fingers were overflowing with a riot of loosened curls.

Eleanor dropped her head back into the cradle of his hands, drawing in a breath deeply as he moved his mouth downward, over the line of her chin, down the column of her neck, to bury his face in the curve of her shoulder. Her limbs had turned to limpid honey and she felt herself falling with him as he lowered them both onto the scattered cushions of the window seat behind him.

"Oh, lass, we shouldn't be doing this."

His burr was more pronounced now, mesmerizing her as it rolled so easily off his tongue.

Eleanor rose up before him, sitting on her knees, and reached for him, sliding her hands around his waist. She rested the side of her face against the solid warmth of his chest and whispered to the night.

"I wished for you to come to me in a dream, and now you are here. Do not wake us from it so soon, Gabriel. Forget about the rest of the world outside this room. Forget who I might be, who you are. Let us just have this one night to keep us for the rest of our lives."

They were all the words he needed to hear.

Gabriel took Eleanor up against him and dragged his mouth across her shoulder, tasting her as his hands trailed downward to work the small buttons that lined the back of her gown. She felt the bodice loosen around her, felt it fall, and suddenly wanted it gone, wanting nothing between them.

The moment he touched her, closing his hand over her, she was seized by a riot of sensation. It whirled throughout her as she wanted to draw him to her as closely as possible, to touch him, to know his body like her own. She wanted him to touch her.

Eleanor threaded her fingers through his hair and pressed her hips against him, desperate for him as he shifted them on the window bench. He eased her back onto the cushioned seat and then he came to stand before her, cast in muted moonlit shadow.

He looked anxious. He looked uncertain. He looked as disconcerted by the fire between them as she was.

"I love you, Gabriel."

She said the words even before she realized she had. Her heart stilled for the briefest of moments as she watched his eyes expectantly for his response.

Perhaps it was the darkness, the shadows, the play of the light, but it looked as if his expression shifted from one of desire to stunned denial. A chill came over the room in an instant, dousing the flame between them with one, swift gust.

"Gabriel...?"

He shook his head. "You don't know what it is you're saying."

"But I do know. I've never known anything more."

He moved away, closing his eyes. Eleanor felt the pall of his rejection all the way to her soul.

She wrapped her arms around herself, covering her nakedness, suddenly ashamed in the face of his unyielding response.

Gabriel looked at her once more before he cursed out loud in Gaelic at the darkness. He struck his hand against the surface of the wall where Juliana had painted her mural. "It cannot be. It can never be. Don't you see? I cannot forget who we are, no matter how much I might want to."

Because she was the governess, a member of staff...

Tears began to well in Eleanor's eyes, burning, and inside,

deep inside her, something twisted. She just stared at him, silent, awash with humiliation and heartbreak, her throat so tight she couldn't utter a word as he turned, vanishing from the room just as quickly as he had come.

And then, as if waking from a dream, she was left sitting alone and forsaken at the window.

14

Gabriel looked with bleary eyes onto the despairing darkness of his study. He blinked to clear his fatigue, and glanced at the small clock on the table beside him. Its face indicated an hour far too early, nearly dawn, in the muted moonlight.

The hearth at his feet no longer flickered, unattended the past hours that he'd spent slumped in his chair, locked behind the isolation of his study door, trying to banish the image of Eleanor's stricken eyes from his memory.

The brandy he'd drunk earlier had not numbed his senses as he had hoped it would. Instead it had only given him a dull headache behind thoughts that remained far too damnably clear for his liking. He'd wanted to lose himself, his thoughts and regrets, behind a dim drunken haze. He'd wanted to surround himself with obscurity, anything to put what had happened, what he'd done—what he'd *not* done—forever out of his mind.

Nothing he'd tried, not the brandy nor the darkness nor the sullen isolation, had succeeded, and he knew no amount of denial would ever take away that last moment between them, the hopeful sound of her voice when she'd spoken those three telling words.

I love you...

And his rejection of them.

No one in his life, not Georgiana, not even his mother that he could remember, had ever spoken those words to him before. They were words that offered everything of another person, their heart, their body, even their soul, words that made up poetry, filled pages in books, became plays acted upon the world's stage.

They were words that asked and hoped, begged and waited— waited for an expression of the same feeling in return, words that were a most precious gift, that made a person the most vulnerable, but that, because of the past, he could never allow himself to accept.

As he sat in that chair, glaring at the carpet beneath his feet, Gabriel cursed the bloody ancestor who had first brought down this darkness upon all of them centuries before. It was fortunate the man was already dead, for at that moment, Gabriel felt certain he would kill him.

But he couldn't, he knew, do anything more about it, except...

Gabriel got up from his chair, crossed the room to the corner trunk, suddenly intent on taking that damnable scroll of parchment, the one that had haunted him and his ancestors for so unbearably long and consign it to the place it truly belonged. He yanked at the key, pulling the silver chain from around his neck, and unlocked the trunk to open it. Taking up the scroll from inside, he read the ancient witch's words one final, woeful time.

For nine hundred years, and then one hundred more,
any creature or beast you allow past your heart's door,
will soon slip away and suffer death's most telling stone,
while helpless you watch on, forsaken and alone.
Only here on this misty isle might the truth be found,
St. Colomb's staff will loose the curse by which you are bound.

One of pure heart and eye will right the wrongs of the past,
to bring about an end to the suffering at last!

Nine hundred years be damned, witch!

With a sour frown, Gabriel dropped the lid on the trunk, making a hollow thud, and turned for the hearth behind him. But he stopped mid-stride when he noticed Cudu getting suddenly to his feet and trotting over to the door. He sniffed at the space underneath, whining softly, and turning to look at Gabriel in the pale light. He pressed his nose to the door again and sniffed some more. After several more whimpers, an insistent scratch, the dog gave out a mournful, unearthly howl.

"Dè tha ceárr, Cudu?"

Gabriel walked over to him to see what could be bothering him.

The dog scratched at the door again, groaning at Gabriel to open it. As soon as he turned the handle, Cudu darted through, moving swifter than Gabriel had ever seen him go, heading at once to the tower stairs across the hall.

As a rule, the dog was historically indifferent—very little if anything ever disturbed him—thus Gabriel decided he would follow to see what had caused the beast to become so agitated.

He never even realized when he dropped the tattered scroll heedlessly to the floor.

They clambered up the first flight of tower stairs and the moment Gabriel opened the door at the top, Cudu sprinted off down the hall, heading in a straight line for the next set of stairs as if he were somehow mysteriously being pulled there by an invisible source.

He did the same when they reached the third level, and it was as they were coming to the door at the top of the stairs that opened onto the fourth level that Gabriel first noticed the acrid smell of smoke.

He pulled the door open and Cudu scrambled through,

rushing on to the last set of stairs—the stairs that led up to the nursery level of the castle.

And Gabriel then knew a moment of true panic.

The circular stairwell that led to the nursery was filled with grey smoke that grew thicker the nearer he came to the top of the stairs. Cudu was panting more from upset than exhaustion, scratching at the threshold beneath the door as if to dig his way through.

"*Gabh nam*," Gabriel said, shooing the dog away.

He reached for the door handle, noticing it was warm to the touch. But when he tried to turn it, he found the door staunchly locked.

Gabriel stared at it, baffled. Something wasn't right. How had the door gotten locked? He hadn't even known there was a key.

He jiggled the handle again, pummeling the door in a moment of frustration when it refused to yield. Perhaps Eleanor had found a key somewhere, he told himself, in her chamber or in the schoolroom, and had locked the door as a measure of safety.

Safety from what?

Gabriel pounded on the door.

"Eleanor...Juliana...wake up! Can you hear me?"

There came no response, but he could hear a faint crackling sound coming from the other side of the door—like fire feeding on wood.

Bracing himself against the solid wall of the tower behind him, Gabriel lifted his foot and kicked at the door hard—once, then again—before it finally gave, bursting open. He was met by a wave of raw heat from the other side, his panic building when he saw the flames licking at the walls of the schoolroom, reaching out into the hallway in front of him.

Gabriel shouted out again, calling for Eleanor and Juliana both, but still there came no reply. He ran for the first door, Eleanor's chamber, and slammed himself against it, shouting out her name again.

The room was dark inside, no window to light it, and filled with so much smoke, he could barely see.

"Eleanor!"

There came no reply. He crossed the room, kicking at the furnishings, tossing anything he encountered out of his way, only to find an empty bed.

"Damnation!"

Gabriel turned and rushed for Juliana's door further down the hall. Again he found the bed empty. Where in perdition were they? He looked down the hall to where the flames were burned steadily from the schoolroom.

No...

He tried to go in, shouting out to them again, but the fire was too great, the smoke too thick, the heat from it all too intense. What if they were inside, trapped, somehow unable to answer him? With the door to the stairs locked as it was, their only other way out would have been the window. But it was barred. They wouldn't have been able to escape. Could they be lying there among those flames overcome by the smoke? Where else could they have gone?

Gabriel snatched the coverlet from Eleanor's bed and began to beat at the flames, trying futilely to fight his way further inside the schoolroom. He needed someone to help but daren't leave. As he attacked the flames again, he heard a voice coming suddenly distant to him.

"Gabriel?"

He stilled, listening in the darkness. "Eleanor? Where are you?"

"I am at the stairs."

The stairs? His query was immediately superseded by his profound relief that she was safe. "Juliana? Where is she?"

"She is with me. What is happening?"

"Run down to the courtyard. Find Fergus and anyone else who is there. Tell them there is a fire in the schoolroom."

Blessedly, a good many of the islanders had decided to pass the night in the great hall or in the stables rather than make what was for some a long trek home in the darkness to the opposite side of the isle. Within minutes, a succession of them began arriving above stairs and soon, they had a team running buckets of water up each flight of stairs while still others dropped ropes from the windows on the middle castle floors to take up more.

Fergus soon joined Gabriel and together they alternated running buckets up to the nursery floor to try to douse the flames. When he managed to advance far enough into the room to see, Gabriel threw a chair across the room, breaking out the lone window to allow the smoke to escape.

Outside on the courtyard, Eleanor gasped, watching the smoke billow out from the castle tower overhead. The orange light from the fire glowed against the muted morning sky. She tried to think of what could have possibly caused the fire to start, especially at that hour, as the celebration had gone on well into the early hours of morning. She and Juliana had been out of the nursery all day, involved with the Michaelmas festivities, so the hearth had never been lit. When they had left the nursery that night, she had taken the candle with them to light their way down the stairs to the viscountess's bedchamber where they slept.

It was some time later when the smoke coming from behind the bars of the window had finally slowed to a scudding drift. Inside, the flames had mercifully been extinguished.

It had taken hours to put out the fire; the morning had now broken on the eastern horizon, shining its colorful mixture of morning light through the drifting haze of dull smoke. Out on the courtyard, Màiri flitted about like a nervous mother hen, bringing damp cloths from the kitchen to wipe soot from faces and fresh water to ease the smoke-stung throats of those who were seated about. If not for the help of the other islanders, the fire would surely yet burn, and the ancient stronghold might have been destroyed.

Eleanor didn't see Gabriel when he first came out onto the courtyard, but when she noticed him talking with Fergus by the stables, she had to stifle a gasp. His clothing was scorched, his face blackened from the fire and smoke he had fought. He was coughing and looked ready to drop from exhaustion, yet he stayed out on the courtyard for some time, thanking each one of the islanders who had helped, informing them all that because of their efforts, the fire had been successfully confined to the uppermost tower floor.

They were fortunate. With the exception of a few minor burns, raw throats, and stinging eyes, there had been no injuries. Though the damage in the schoolroom was extensive, the rest of the castle remained intact; it would take quite a bit of effort, but the upper floor could be rebuilt.

Later that day, Eleanor sat quietly in Gabriel's study, looking through the books in the library while Juliana napped in one of the armchairs, when Gabriel finally approached her.

"I had hoped to find you here," he said, coming into the room behind her.

Nearly all evidence of the event that morning was gone. He'd bathed, changed his clothing, although his face still bore a certain redness from the intense heat of the fire. His expression, however, looked as if he carried the very weight of the world upon his shoulders.

Eleanor set aside the book she'd been reading, and came down the library steps. "I had come to do some reading while Juliana rested. But I had also hoped to talk to you."

"And I you." He looked at her. "But, please, you first."

Eleanor took a seat before his desk, folding her hands gently into her lap. The gesture suddenly reminded her of that first day when she had come to the isle, of the apprehension she had felt at meeting him. How long ago that somehow seemed. How different things were now.

She looked across at him and was seized by the memory of the night before, his arms around her, the passion of his kiss, not a handful of hours earlier. She tried to forget the humiliation of having blurted out her inmost emotions so stupidly, tried to forget the sorrow of watching him turn away from her. How utterly ridiculous she must have seemed to him, professing her love when what had happened between them was likely no more to him than a dalliance between master and servant.

She drew herself up, keeping her voice matter of fact. "I wanted to talk to you because I'm sure you are wondering why Juliana and I were sleeping in the viscountess's chamber last night and not in the nursery."

"The reasons why matter very little now against my utter relief that you were."

"Still, I think you need to hear my explanation, if only for Juliana's sake."

Eleanor paused, searching for the words. "The first night I came to Dunevin, I discovered Juliana missing from her bed. I eventually found her, in her mother's chamber, and instead of forcing her to return upstairs to the nursery, I decided it would be better to allow her to remain. It was obvious she had been going there for some time. I gathered that sleeping in her mother's bed offered her some sort of comfort. So, instead, I stayed with her."

"Right down the hall from me every night." Gabriel shook his head. "I had no idea she was going there."

"I don't think anybody did. But how fortunate it is that she had after the accident of the fire last night."

"Yes. The fire." Gabriel sat behind his desk. "That is what I wanted to talk to you about. That fire was no accident, Eleanor. It was set—deliberately."

Eleanor took a moment to grasp what he was implying. "But how can you be so certain?"

"Because the door leading to the nursery off the stairs was locked—from the outside. I'm assuming you didn't lock it when you came down to Georgiana's chamber."

Eleanor shook her head. "I didn't even know there was a key."

"Nor did I. So that would indicate that someone else had locked it—with the intent of keeping you and Juliana inside. They could have no notion you weren't asleep in your rooms. Had you both been there, with the window barred as it was, you would have been unable to escape."

He paused a moment before going on. "There is more, too. I also found a cruisie lamp turned onto its side on the floor in the nursery room where the fire first started. The oil would have quickly ignited the carpet to allow the flames to spread."

"A lamp? But who—?" Eleanor looked at him then, knowing his thoughts even before he replied. "You suspect Seamus Maclean?"

"He was very cross after losing the race yesterday morning. In fact, he left the festivities without returning. He did not participate in the games all day, nor did he come later for the feast and the dancing. No one has seen him since he rode in the race yesterday morning. And lost."

"Perhaps he returned to the mainland."

Gabriel shook his head. "Unless he swam there, someone would have seen him sailing out of the bay. Because of the range of the currents off the channel, the jetty is the only safe place to disembark from the whole of the isle."

"But his parents. Surely they can tell you if he was with them last night at their croft after the *cuideachd*."

"I have already sent Fergus off to bring them here to Dunevin so I can question them, with Seamus—if he is there. We should know very soon just where Maclean was when the fire broke out."

Gabriel stood from his desk then. "In the meantime, however, I have come to a decision." He looked at her. "A decision that effects both you and Juliana. I have decided to send you to London to stay until the repairs on the castle can be made, and I have determined who it was who set the fire and can deal with the matter accordingly."

"*London?*" Eleanor didn't bother to hide her dismay at this most unexpected announcement. "But why so far away?"

"Because it is far enough that Seamus Maclean cannot harm you or Juliana there. It isn't just the fire, Eleanor, but the incident with the hemlock, too. I cannot take a chance a third time. It is better this way. There will be no possibility of him reaching you there."

"So you believe it is me he seeks to harm?"

"I cannot pretend to deny it is a possibility." Gabriel looked at her. "Both incidents have directly involved you. Nor can I fail to do whatever I can to protect Juliana. So to London you will go. With the ready resources in the city, you can continue Juliana's education there more adequately than you can here. I own a townhouse there, part of the Dunevin viscountcy. It is usually let to others for the season, but at this time of year, it is always vacant. I will draft a letter for you to take to my solicitor, Mr. George Pratt on Buckingham Street. He will assist you with hiring the necessary staff and will secure you whatever funds you might need."

"It sounds as if you mean us to stay there for some time."

"It could take some time to repair the damage from the fire. Winter is coming. It may have to wait until the spring."

Eleanor frowned. "Somehow I believe that is a convenient excuse. Juliana and I could easily move to the lower floors."

Gabriel shook his head. "Call it whatever you prefer, but I've made my decision."

Eleanor's emotions started to get the better of her, her eyes stinging with the threat of tears. She blinked them back. Annoyed at herself for giving in to such an utterly female response, she got up from her chair and crossed the room to stand at the window.

She stood there for several minutes, arms crossed before her, watching as Angus, the groomsman, took the ponies out from the stables to graze on the machair while he mucked out their stalls. She thought to herself how she had planned to teach Juliana to ride on the little gray one, a sweet pony mare Angus called "Marigold" for the calendula flowers she was so fond of eating.

There were so many things she had planned for them to do together. She had hoped to pass the coming winter months teaching Juliana how to stitch her first sampler. They had even promised Màiri to help make conserves from the cloudberry and bramble they had gathered.

Now they would be a world away from this place.

Eleanor spotted Màiri below her then, hanging out laundry to dry on the branches of the elder trees that grew around her herb garden. Even though the fire had been contained to the schoolroom, all of Eleanor and Juliana's things had smelled so strongly of smoke that Màiri had had to use poppy root and bracken ash to wash away its pithy trace. Eleanor mused bitterly that she had promised Màiri she would help with the chore of it. Instead, now, it seemed, she was going to be packing it all away to go to London—the very place, the very life she had run away from.

Eleanor turned from the window, suddenly angry at the way things were turning out, angry at Gabriel, too. "You are doing this because of me. Because of what I said to you last night." She started back for her chair, lowering into it. She tempered her cross tone. "I should never have said that to you."

"That has nothing to do with it, Eleanor."

"It has everything to do with it. I acted improperly. But please don't punish Juliana by sending her away from the only home she has ever known because of my indiscretion."

Gabriel's eyes darkened, his expression turning suddenly

vague. He stared at her for some time, not saying a word, as if he were at war with his own thoughts.

Finally, he spoke. "There is something you need to know," he said quietly then. "The hemlock, the fire; these are not simply coincidental accidents, Eleanor."

What was he implying? She sat at the edge of her seat, and waited for him to continue.

Gabriel got up from his chair and walked to the far corner of the room where he stood before a large, very old-looking trunk that was covered by a faded tapestry. She wondered how she had never noticed the trunk before as she watched him take a key from a chain around his neck and open its lid. He removed something from inside and turned back to face her.

Gabriel said nothing, simply handed her a worn, very old-looking scroll of parchment.

Eleanor took it, unrolling it most carefully. The words written upon it were in Gaelic, the handwriting quite difficult to decipher, and she could only make out some of what it said. Confused, Eleanor looked up at Gabriel.

"I can only make out some of the words such as 'nine hundred years,' and I think it mentions a 'death...' What is this, Gabriel?"

He shook his head. "I forgot you cannot read Gaelic."

"I can a little. I understood something about a curse and St. Columba's staff. This parchment looks very old, as if it were written centuries ago."

"That is because it was."

Gabriel reached for the scroll to take it, as if just by holding it, it would burn her.

He sat in the chair beside her. "Do you remember yesterday morning, when we made the circuit to the Dunevin graveyard?"

She nodded.

"I'm sure it couldn't have escaped your notice that the MacFeagh ancestry have many of them met with early and untimely deaths. It certainly escapes nobody else's notice, least of all mine."

She simply nodded again.

"Undoubtedly you have heard that a good many people believe we, the MacFeaghs, somehow sinisterly do away with our own. As if that even makes sense."

Gabriel glanced at her briefly before continuing. "It is an observable fact that the people of my family die, often and quite young. It is a sequence that has been repeated time and again. It will seem to stop for a while, but inevitably, it happens again. And in a manner of speaking, it was the MacFeaghs who brought it on."

Gabriel then related for Eleanor the story of his unfortunate ancestor and the Jura witch who had saved him, and then set down the curse that would punish him and his kind forever, finishing with the legend of the St. Columba staff that had vanished so many years before. "And since that time, whenever a MacFeagh laird has allowed himself to care for someone close to him, they have died through mysterious circumstances."

"And she left behind this?" Eleanor asked, motioning toward the scroll.

Gabriel nodded. "Since this has been going on for some time now, you can surely understand why people believe I, and my ancestors, are demons."

Eleanor fell silent, thoughtful, ruminating on the incredible tale she'd just been told. Of anyone else, at any other place in the world, she would have immediately thought it a made-up deception, to explain away something much more nefarious.

But not on this isle—and not with this man.

"I was just about to burn that damned thing last night before I discovered the fire in the nursery."

Eleanor looked in his eyes and saw fear there. "And is there some part of you that perhaps believes the fire occurred because of what you had decided, to destroy the scroll? To keep you from doing it somehow?"

Gabriel didn't answer her. He didn't need to.

Eleanor sat face-to-face with the anguish he had lived with throughout his entire life, and could only think of one thing to say in response.

"Then do it, Gabriel. Do just that. Juliana is here. I am here. I promise you we won't be struck down by a sudden bolt of lightning. Burn this horrible piece of history so you never have to read, or fear its vengeful litany again."

She swept up the scroll from his desk and held it out to him. "I will do it with you."

Gabriel looked at Eleanor as if she'd just run mad. But then, after only the barest moment of uncertainty, he took the scroll and walked with her to the hearth.

They stood facing the slumbering fire that burned in the grate. Eleanor watched Gabriel, saw the play of emotions across his face—fear, acceptance, resolution. And then slowly, Gabriel extended his hand and dropped the scroll onto the fire.

After a moment, they saw it catch, waited while it took flame, and continued to stand and watch until nothing remained but smoke and ash.

A calm came over the room, like the most peaceful spring morning. Nothing terrible happened because of what they'd done, there was no supernatural retribution. Instead, there was quiet, and warmth, and a feeling of absolute peace.

"I could tolerate it," Gabriel said softly to the fire, "if it were only myself who had been touched by it. But that damnable curse stole my daughter's mother from her when she needed her most, and with it, it stole her voice. Now it even threatens to steal my daughter from me as well." Gabriel looked back at Eleanor, his eyes filled with despair. "Georgiana's family has recently written," he said, his voice rough with emotion, "threatening to petition the Crown for custody of Juliana if I do not relinquish her to their care. It is not out of any concern for her that they do this, I know. Georgiana left a sizeable inheritance to Juliana that she will be due upon her reaching her majority. I promised Georgiana long before she died that if anything ever happened to her, I would never allow her family to take our daughter. Georgiana's upbringing was one of abuse and she feared every day that Juliana would somehow face the same, almost as if she knew what would someday happen."

"But how can they possibly take her?" Eleanor asked. "You are her father."

"I've been in correspondence with my solicitor who tells me that he doesn't believe the Crown would forsake the rights of a father to his child, but there is the chance that Georgiana's family will accuse me of her murder. With my family's less than sterling history, and with the fact that Juliana will no longer speak, my solicitor cannot guarantee what the outcome would be. They will say I have abused her in some way to keep her from speaking. They will say anything in pursuit of their greed. They could make rigorous attempts to force her to speak out against me. At the very least, a scandal would most certainly come about the likes of which has never been seen against a peer, and it would ruin Juliana's chances for a happy, secure future.

Eleanor shook her head. "It's always scandal. Damnable scandal."

"It was for that reason I hired you to be her governess," he went on, "in hopes that if she could be taught the best social skills, I could somehow stave off Georgiana's family long enough to see Juliana safely married." He scoffed then, "As if the fact that she doesn't ever speak wouldn't be enough to keep any man worthy of her away."

As he'd spoken, pouring out the anguish he'd kept to himself for so many years—too, too many years—Eleanor dawned on something so elementary, so obvious, but something Gabriel somehow refused to realize.

No matter how much he tried to tell himself he didn't, he *did* love his daughter. No man who cared nothing for another would trouble so very much, would carry the staggering burden he had for so long.

She realized, too, that it was for this very reason he had reacted the way he had the night before when she had told him she loved him. It was the words he feared, three simple words. Somehow, it was as if he believed that by speaking those words, it would call the wrath of the past upon him.

Realizing this, Eleanor was suddenly filled with a sense of renewed hope—as well as a perfect and logical solution to it all.

She looked at Gabriel, sitting up in her chair. Facing him openly, she spoke the words that suddenly filled her thoughts. "Then as I see it, you really have only one choice in the matter, Gabriel. You will just have to marry me."

15

*G*abriel looked at Eleanor as if he truly did believe she'd run mad.

"What did you just say?"

"I believe I proposed marriage to you."

Eleanor fell silent, as if to come to terms with what she had just said. And then...

"But if you think about it, really, it is the best solution to your predicament. With a wife, and a mother for Juliana, Georgiana's family wouldn't stand any chance of succeeding with a petition to the Crown. You said they'll argue she needs a mother's influence. Let that be me. You must know how much I care for her. She means the world to me, Gabriel. And you must have seen how she has responded. Somehow, I am able to reach her, even without words."

Gabriel let go a slow breath. "Of course I have, but did you hear nothing of what I just told you? About my family's history, the fact that members of my family have been dying unexpectedly...for centuries?"

Eleanor wasn't daunted. "Yes, Gabriel, I heard every word of it, but I choose not to be dictated to by it. You have lived your life trying to outrun a fiction. You burned that terrible scroll in the hearth. I watched you do it. As far as I'm concerned, this curse, if that is what it was, no longer exists. The more immediate problem is the threat to your daughter and you—" she corrected herself, "—*we* must do whatever is necessary to make certain Juliana doesn't come to harm at the hands of those despicable people. It is what Georgiana would have wanted."

Gabriel fell silent, his expression troubled as he went through his thoughts. As she watched the play of emotions on his face, Eleanor realized there was something else she had to do, something she had forgotten in all her enthusiasm.

She had to tell Gabriel the truth of her illegitimacy.

"Gabriel, there is something more you should know. You just told me something about yourself, about your past, but something over which you had no control, despite the fact that it has affected your life very much. Before you make any decision about what I have proposed, there is something you need to know about me."

Eleanor reached inside the pocket of her gown and withdrew a folded scrap of paper she had tucked away inside. It was the notice she had taken from the inn wall in Oban, the one offering the reward for her return. She had come across it earlier that day when she and Màiri had been gathering up the clothing and other things for washing after the fire. Seeing it, she had quickly hidden it away, determined to dispose of it. She decided now that same notice would best explain what she had to say.

She handed the paper to Gabriel without saying a word.

He took up the page, barely giving it a moment's glance.

"Yes?"

"Aren't you going to read it?"

"I have.

"Gabriel," Eleanor said. "The woman described in that notice...is me."

He just stared at her. Finally, he replied, "And are you proposing I should claim the reward?"

Eleanor didn't know whether she should hope he was jesting or not. Instead, she looked down at her hands, her fingers working tightly, regretting she had ever lied to him at the beginning, leading him to think she was someone she was not. "I just thought you should know that I am not Miss Nell Harte." She looked back at him. "I apologize for the deception, but I..."

Eleanor forgot the rest of her words when she noticed Gabriel suddenly opening his desk drawer, removing something from inside. It was a scrap of paper which he then placed on the desk before her.

She saw immediately that it was a twin to the notice from Oban she had just given him. She looked up at him, stunned.

"How long have you known?"

"Since the day we went to Oban. I saw it posted on the dock."

Weeks had passed since then. "Yet you said nothing all this time. Why?"

"Because I knew you must have had your reasons for wanting to keep the truth of your identity a secret."

"I do—or rather I did. Anymore, I just do not know."

Eleanor suddenly wanted very much to unburden herself, to let go of the anger, the humiliation she had kept locked away for so long now. More than that, she wanted to tell Gabriel the truth.

"Gabriel, I left my family because I had learned that the man who I believed was my father was not, in truth, my father. I had always been told that my father had died shortly before I was born, the victim of some sudden illness. But I discovered in the worst of all ways that this was not true. The man the world knew to be my father, Christopher Wycliffe, had died fighting in a duel against the man who my mother had been unfaithful to him with, a man named William Hartley, Earl of Herrick."

"And?" Gabriel asked, sensing there was more.

Indeed, there was.

"When these men met on the dueling field, my father, the man I believed was my father, anyway—Christopher Wycliffe," she clarified, "was killed. But Lord Herrick, my mother's lover, who had shot him, didn't leave the field that day either. You see, he was also killed—but by my brother, who had picked up my father's pistol and had fired upon him as he was leaving. The only reason I was told any of this was because I was being courted by the heir to Lord Herrick, a man named Richard Hartley."

Gabriel nodded, understanding. "A half-brother you didn't know you had."

She was stunned at how calm and matter-of-fact he was being. "Richard had asked me to marry him, and knowing that I could not do so, my mother and my brother had no choice but to finally tell me the truth. If I had never met Richard, I still would not know that I am quite likely illegitimate."

"Likely, but not certainly."

Gabriel's eyes held hers. In them she saw nothing other than clear, profound compassion. "As far as I'm concerned, Eleanor, you are the same person you have always believed yourself to be. No one can take that away from you. It matters not who sired you."

Eleanor felt a twinge at his words, but said nothing.

"That must have been very difficult for your family. Eleanor, I have heard tell of your brother, Lord Knighton, even in my limited social sphere. I also inquired about him to my solicitor when I first came across that notice. Your brother is, from all accounts, a man of honor and integrity. Since he would have been quite young at the time, I would assume, whatever the circumstances with Lord Herrick were on that dueling field, he reacted out of emotion—shock—and certainly not with any malicious aforethought."

Eleanor nodded. "I know that now. But at the time Christian told all this to me, I was so hurt and felt so utterly betrayed by him and my mother, I couldn't see what this must have been doing to them, the burden they had carried these twenty years past. They lived in fear each day that the truth would somehow be exposed. As you are far too aware, society can be most cruel in matters of scandal. They feared for my future. So that is why I wanted to tell you this before you made any decision about your future and Juliana's. The truth of my parentage, it could all still come to light someday. It would be...," she searched for the right word, "...difficult for a man to consider marriage to a lady everyone suspected had been born the wrong side of the blanket."

"It isn't difficult at all. In fact, it's probably the easiest decision this man could ever make. Gabriel simply looked at her and said, "Lady Eleanor Wycliffe, I have decided to accept your proposal of marriage."

THEY WERE MARRIED ALONG THE WAY TO LONDON, AT A SMALL hamlet outside of Gretna Green at the border, a place called Springfield, nestled on the Scottish side of the River Sark. The inn, and its tiny village, had thrived in the decades since marriage laws in England had changed requiring a publishing of banns and parental consent. After inquiring locally, they were directed to The Queen's Head Inn, a tiny tumble-down cottage nestled at the bottom of Springfield Hill, on one side of the turnpike road.

Gabriel spoke with the innkeeper, a Mrs. Johnstone, a cheery woman who spoke with a hinterland dialect and who had greeted them at the door. She referred them to Mr. Robert Elliott, the local blacksmith *cum* 'parson,' who apparently spent his days sitting in the taproom of the inn, nursing a mug of ale while waiting for just such an occasion.

For the price of two guineas, Mr. Elliott performed the short ceremony right in the public room of the inn, with Mrs. Johnstone and her servant, Sawney, standing by as witnesses. Juliana and Brìghde attended the bride, the two girls their traveling companions after Màiri had privately revealed to Eleanor that Brìghde's mother, Eibhlin, had been despairing the night of the *cuideachd* that her mother, who lived in London and who was slowly dying from an illness, had never seen the granddaughter who was named for her.

Eibhlin was in her eighth month of pregnancy and could not safely make the trip, so Eleanor had offered to take the little girl along with them so that Brìghde could meet her namesake before it was too late, much to Eibhlin's—and Juliana's—obvious joy.

When Mr. Elliott suddenly called for a ring to secure the legalities of the ceremony, Eleanor was startled to see Gabriel produce one from his coat pocket.

"Màiri pressed this upon me before we left Trelay," he said quietly to her. "She said it had blessed her marriage to Torquil for thirty-five years before he passed away, and so it would thus bless ours for at least twice that long."

Eleanor smiled as he slid the plain gold band onto her finger. It was the most touching gift she had ever received, more precious than any jewel or diamond.

After the customary hammer clang to the blacksmith's anvil and a quick mug of ale, requisite, Mrs. Johnstone said, to toast in the new union, the new Lord and Lady Dunevin were off across the border and into England by dusk. By the time they broke their journey at a benighted little village called Kirkby Lonsdale just off the main London road between the Lakes and the Dales of Yorkshire, the two girls were fast asleep on the coach squabs.

In the darkness, they couldn't see much more than sparse candlelight in the small windows of the cottages that lined the winding road to the village's center. The coach halted there and Gabriel alighted to look for the nearest inn. But it was market time in the village, which unfortunately meant that all of the inns in the village were full—except one. A local farmer directed them to a small graystone building on the outskirts of town, called quite simply *The Graystone*, where they came upon the proprietor of the place, named fittingly enough Mr. Gray. He was a man whose appearance very much suited his name.

He had but one room left to let, he told them, and the tariff included clean linen, coals for the fire, and ample servings of Mrs. Gray's own hearty breakfast for them all the next morning. The room was the best of the house, he assured them—complete with a bed that royalty had once slept in.

"'Twas my own uncle Ethelred Gray that served Queen Elizabeth back when she were a young miss, e'en afore she became our greatest queen. 'Twas she that gave him that bed from her own chamber at Hatfield, and it's been in the family ever since. I myself were born in that bed after my mother had labored for forty-two hours." He glanced at Gabriel then, adding on a wink, "We've polished it up a bit since then."

In the face of such an auspicious history, and with no other choice left to them, Gabriel promptly rented the room, and without a moment to spare, for as Mrs. Gray was off preparing the room and stoking the fire, another traveler came in asking for accommodation. Gabriel and Eleanor, and the two sleepy girls, quickly repaired abovestairs, filing down the narrow hall to the room Mr. Gray had directed them to.

Gabriel opened the door on what would have been a quite comfortable chamber—had it not been nearly completely taken up with what was undoubtedly the largest bed Eleanor had ever seen. It was a dark, walnut monstrosity of a thing, carved on every possible space, a four-poster that would have had to have been taken apart in to small pieces to get it through the door—and then reassembled bit-by-bit inside the small room. Even then, that would have been quite a chore. The finial tops grazed the low-beamed ceiling and were thicker than most tree trunks. There was scarcely enough room left in the small chamber to walk a careful path around it.

Eleanor took one look at the place, and immediately began to laugh.

"I'll bed down in the stables with Fergus and the driver," Gabriel said then.

"You'll do no such thing," Eleanor said, stepping to block him from leaving the room. "This bed is big enough for all of us. Faith, I think it is big enough for the entire village, as well." And then she looked at him and said quite matter-of-factly, "I'll not sleep alone on my wedding night, Gabriel."

Even if it was a wedding night that they would spend with two nine-year-olds tucked on the bed between them.

Eleanor directed Juliana onto the middle of the lumpy mattress, then helped Gabriel to divest himself of a clinging Brìghde. She then edged around the room and began getting herself ready for bed while leaving Gabriel to stand by, still as one of the carved posters on the bed.

Gabriel watched as Eleanor pulled the pins from her hair and let it fall down her back, removing her pelisse and draping it neatly at the end of the bed before she kicked off her slippers and set them on the floor beneath.

Then she turned to face her new husband.

"I wonder if you would help me with the buttons on the back of this gown," she asked casually. "I fear I might do myself a harm in these close quarters if I try to unfasten them myself."

Gabriel nodded, swallowing, and stood as she came before him, turning her back to him. He had to push her hair away from her neck to see, sweeping it gently over one shoulder. His pulse bounded at the scent of her. To distract himself, he set to working the buttons, his fingers fumbling nervously as his thoughts ran wild with images of Eleanor stepping out of the gown, turning to face him with open arms. It took him some time to get the buttons unfastened and by the time he'd finished, his breath was coming quickly, and his breeches, his lowland attire, were fitting him much more tightly than they had just moments before.

Eleanor pulled her arms slowly from the narrow sleeves of

her traveling gown and lowered the garment so that she could step out of it. As she moved to lay it on the bed with her pelisse, the light from the candle set on the small side table behind her shone through the gauzy fabric of her shift, outlining her figure to his waiting eyes.

Gabriel sucked in his breath. He wanted nothing more than to pull her against him. He wanted to have her beneath him on that ridiculously large bed.

But for the girls...

Eleanor turned to face him. "Please douse the light when you get into bed," she said with a soft smile.

She turned, climbing onto the great bed, sliding across the mattress to the far side of the two slumbering girls, leaving Gabriel no choice but to take the nearer side.

As he snuffed the candle and lowered onto the mattress, trying not to disturb the sleeping girls, Gabriel could think of nothing except the fact that Eleanor—his wife—was lying so close to him, wearing nothing but her shift.

He then proceeded to spend the next hour counting the oaken beams of the ceiling above them, trying to dispel that same image.

ELEANOR WAS THE FIRST TO AWAKE IN THE MORNING. SHE OPENED her eyes to the soft morning light pouring in through the small window set in the wall above the bed, and the delicious aroma of Mrs. Gray's breakfast cooking in the inn's kitchen below.

Lazily, she extended her arms, feeling refreshed despite that hours of travel the day before...and the hours of travel that awaited. She hadn't slept so well in as long as she could remember and she decided it must have been because of Mr. Gray's incredible bed. Surely a bed so extraordinary would give one an extraordinary night in it. She decided then that if they ever made the trip to London again, they would have to make certain to stop in Kirkby Lonsdale again and ask for just this room.

Eleanor sat up on the mattress, ready to face the day, and promptly stilled at the scene that met her eyes.

Stretched across the mattress beside her lay Gabriel, his face still in sleep. His hair was mussed around his forehead, softening the lines of his face. Juliana's dark head lay tucked up against his shoulder, while one of Brighde's small arms was flung outward in sleep to curve around his neck.

Somehow, in the middle of the night, the girls had squirmed their way around him, likely seeking his warmth. He was totally and utterly surrounded by them, and when Eleanor looked closer, she saw that he was actually smiling in his sleep.

Laying back on the bed, Eleanor curled against the slumbering trio and closed her eyes, drifting back for just a little bit longer on Mr. Gray's Incredible, Extraordinary Bed.

THE PERPETUAL HAZE OF LONDON'S BLEAK COAL SMOKE GREETED them like a murky shroud long before they ever reached the city's sprawling outskirts. Even as far out as Chiswick, the stench of gutter waste, the smell of rotting market produce and fish made itself known. Autumn leaves that had left the trees stark for the coming winter, littered the roadway in front of them, swirling around the coach wheels as they drove on by.

Eleanor could remember how as a child she had always been seized by a juvenile thrill of excitement when approaching the city from the country, leaning out the coach window all along the road from Ealing, waiting to catch that first glimpse of Kensington and Hyde Park Corner, after which she knew they would almost be there.

Home.

The feverish bustle, the mingled crowd—the grating, chirping, humming, clopping, whirring, swishing noise of it all—had simply enchanted her beyond imagination. She remembered how she would picture dashing highwaymen hiding out behind the trees of Knightsbridge, waiting to call out 'stand and deliver' and divest them of their riches, just as she'd imagined the ghost of old Queen Anne herself watching from the top floor window of Kensington Palace.

But as they drove now along the populous Strand, and under Wren's Portland stone Temple Bar, where the heads of traitors had been piked not a century earlier, and where the stone figures of the Charles'—the Ist and the IInd—watched them pass underneath, Eleanor felt none of the charm, none of the pent-up excitement she had in her youth.

Instead, she found herself looking around at all the muck and mess and mire, at the many, many people and the carriages and the houses that blocked out any hint of sunlight, and found she longed instead for a glimpse of a mist-ringed standing stone with a pair of fulmars souring overhead, or Cudu stretched out like a Turkish carpet across the stone floor of the great hall.

Their coach stopped first off Chancery Lane, at the offices of Gabriel's solicitor, a Mr. George Pratt, a stout-looking man with quite the bushiest eyebrows Eleanor had ever seen—more one brow than two—set beneath a thinning pate of grizzled hair. Upon being introduced to them, the native Scot had greeted Eleanor and the two girls most warmly.

"A pleasure it is, Lady Dunevin, Miss Juliana and Miss Brìghde. Welcome to London Town."

He was the first to have referred to Eleanor by her married name and she found the sound of it wonderfully comforting.

She was Lady Eleanor Wycliffe no more.

Mr. Pratt took a moment to discuss a bit of business with Gabriel before he furnished the keys to the Dunevin town house on Upper Brook Street, a place Eleanor knew very well. Just off

Grosvenor Square, it was a quiet residential street lined with neat and fashionable homes, and only a few blocks away from her brother's London residence, Knighton House, at Berkeley Square. She couldn't help but wonder how many times she might have walked past Gabriel's door over the years, if they had ever passed each other in the pleasure gardens, or in the park.

As they made their way to Upper Brook after leaving Mr. Pratt, they actually passed through Berkeley Square, and Eleanor found herself looking for the polished brass door knocker in the shape of a pineapple that hung outside the front door at Knighton House. If it was there, it would indicate to all that the family was in residence, and open to receiving callers.

A moment later, she saw it, and a shiver ran through her as she knew a sudden urge to stop the carriage, go toward that house, and climb those small stone steps to the door.

What would she possibly say?

Gabriel must have noticed Eleanor staring at the red brick façade when the coach was suddenly stopped by an influx of traffic. He leaned toward her and asked, "What is it, Eleanor?"

She looked at him and smiled, pushing away her clouded thoughts. "That is my family's house," she said. motioning. "The window there at the top behind the tree is—*was* my bedchamber. Those flowers in the boxes beneath the lower windows were planted by my mother and me just this spring."

The front door opened then and she gave a little gasp when she saw the familiar form of the Knighton butler, Forbes, brushing a bit of dust from a small rug over the front railing.

Gabriel must have sensed her torment at feeling almost as a stranger before something that once offered her nothing but security. "Do you wish to stop in?"

Eleanor thought a moment, and then shook her head. "No. Not now. Not just yet. I would like to get us settled and come up with some idea of what I shall say first. There is so much for me to talk about with them. I don't really know where to begin."

Gabriel smiled at her, touching a finger under her chin to look into her eyes. "The beginning is usually the best place to start anything, lass."

As the coach finally pulled away, Eleanor thought she caught a glimpse of a figure, a silhouette, passing by one of the lower floor windows. Her heart gave a jump and she watched until she couldn't watch anymore, then said silently to herself...

I have come home, Mother.

16

While their baggage was removed from the carriage inside, Gabriel gave Eleanor a tour of Dunevin House, her new London home. Three bays wide with a garden and stabling at the back, it enjoyed a sunny side of the street, opposite a bustling coffee house. Their neighbors, Gabriel informed her, included the sculptress Anne Damer (when she wasn't at her country house), an Italian aristocrat, and the notorious Edward Ball Hughes, the "Golden Ball," a dandy known throughout town both for his trademark black cravats and the custom chocolate-colored carriage that drove him about.

After their tour, Eleanor set the girls to washing their faces while she carried out her first formal duty as lady of her own household. She met with Mrs. Wickett, the housekeeper who Mr. Pratt had hired, and who, she soon realized, was Màiri's opposite in most every way imaginable.

Tall and lanky of figure, she had a narrow face and a quiet disposition with a very, very polite manner of speaking that while perfectly affable, didn't convey an ounce of warmth or feeling beyond its delivery. Meeting her with her rigid formality only left Eleanor longing more for their home on Trelay.

Eleanor set Mrs. Wickett and the two maids who'd been hired with her to the task of preparing the bedchambers for that night. While they began airing the linen and beating the dust from the carpets, Gabriel, Eleanor, and the girls took a carriage drive down busy Piccadilly. It was a fine day and London had come out to enjoy it. After a time, they left off the carriage and decided to walk along St. James Street and the surrounding area to do some shopping and impromptu sightseeing.

They went along Pall Mall, showing the girls the gardens of St. James and the great spectacle of Carlton House, the London palace of the former Prince Regent. Deserted now since his ascension to the throne earlier that year, the palace's furnishings and trappings were currently being moved to the nearby Buckingham House, where the new king had decided would be his London residence.

The girls were filled with excitement at the sounds and sights that surrounded them. As they circuited to Piccadilly again, Eleanor noticed Gabriel take Juliana's hand to cross the bustling street in front of them. Her heart swelled with emotion for this man, who had avoided his daughter out of fear for so long, but now seemed to want to try to make up for all that lost time in one day.

The change in him was astounding. As they passed by rows of shops, Gabriel talked to Juliana, showing her the sights, and accepting her silence as a thing he should not try to force her to change. Perhaps it had been Brìghde's ready acceptance of Juliana's muteness as simply a part of her, but once Gabriel arrived at that same acceptance, the rest had simply fallen into its proper order all on its own.

They stopped for a while at Hatchard's and purchased a parcel of books, both to augment Juliana's studies as well as to begin Brìghde's. They had decided she would join Juliana and some of the other island children in a new school which Eleanor had proposed to Gabriel during their journey to London. Until they could find a suitable teacher, Eleanor herself would teach the children, beginning lessons in English, writing, reading and simple ciphering, while continuing her own education in Gaelic.

After Hatchard's, they stopped for tea and buns at Mrs. Collins' Tea Shoppe. Eleanor had to allow herself a smile when she spotted a young lady, very much like herself not so long ago, sitting with her mother in her own "coming-out" wardrobe, being reminded of the proper angle of her fingers as she took her tea.

They paid a visit to a tailor on Jermyn Street to purchase some new cravats for Gabriel and bought Màiri an assortment of pretty ribbons from the milliner. While Gabriel went off with Juliana to the stationer's shop to purchase some new writing quills and sealing wax, Eleanor and Brìghde browsed the shop windows on Old Bond Street, commenting on a display of bonnets that were decorated with bunches of fruits.

"I winna know whither t' wear it or eat it," Brìghde proclaimed with the honesty of a child. Eleanor laughed and they continued along.

It was as they were turning the corner where they had planned to meet back with Gabriel and Juliana that Eleanor suddenly heard a voice call out to her from behind.

"Eleanor! I can't believe it...is it really you?"

Eleanor turned and immediately froze when she saw Richard Hartley jogging up the pedestrian walkway toward her.

"Richard..."

He doffed his tall beaver hat when he reached her. Dressed elegantly in a suit of buff and navy blue, his boots were polished to a marvelous sheen, every inch the fashionable buck.

He took up her gloved hand, kissing it warmly.

"I have been going absolutely mad with worry over you," he said. "I wrote to you in Scotland, but then thought perhaps my letter got lost when I didn't receive your reply. Then I wasn't certain if you were still in Scotland, so I wrote to your brother, but he did not reply either. So I decided you must be on your way back here to Town and that I would just come back to await your return. And well, good thing I did for here you are!"

He hadn't let go of her hand, and now covered it with his other one, squeezing affectionately. "Eleanor, I wanted to apologize for leaving you as I had in the middle of the season without much in the way of an explanation. I called at Knighton House and left my card two days ago, but again, no reply. Till now." He beamed. "It is so good to see you again. When did you get back to town? Can I call as soon as possible? There is something I would really like to address with you..."

Eleanor realized then that Richard believed she hadn't received his proposal of marriage. Oh, dear, what could she say? She glanced around, searching for Gabriel on the crowded walkway. "We...we only just arrived back in the city this morning."

"This morning?" He laughed. "And already you're out shopping." He seemed suddenly to notice Brìghde standing at Eleanor's side, gripping Eleanor's other hand and staring at him with her usual open curiosity, her blond head cocked slightly to the side.

"Hello there, little one," Richard said. He finally let go of Eleanor's hand to offer his to the child. "I am Lord Herrick."

She took his hand, bobbed a tiny curtsy. "And I am Brìghde," she replied easily. "Your hat is very tall, sir." She looked up at Eleanor then and whispered, "His boots...they are so shiny I can see myself in them."

"Richard," Eleanor interrupted then, "so do you mean to say you have not spoken with my family?"

"No. I was detained longer than I had expected up in Yorkshire. I've only just gotten back to town myself. Your butler, Forbes, merely took my card when I went. I feared having not received my letters, you may have thought I'd forgotten about you. About us." He paused long enough to realize her tense expression. "Eleanor, is something the matter?"

She was chewing her lip and staring at him with wide eyes, this man who, she realized, could very well be her half-brother. Mentally, she began comparing his features to hers, the shape of his eyes, the slight dimple she'd never noticed at the corner of his mouth, so very similar to her own. How had she not seen it before...or was she now simply imagining it?

Before Eleanor could frame a response, Gabriel and Juliana came around the corner then to join them on the footpath. Juliana, uneasy at the arrival of the sudden stranger, and perhaps sensing the awkwardness of the situation, came immediately to Eleanor's side and tucked her hand in hers. Both girls guarded Eleanor like sentries. Gabriel came to stand close behind her, closing their protective ranks. Though Gabriel spoke not a word, it was obvious their relationship was more than passing acquaintanceship.

A good deal more.

Eleanor watched as in the space of a moment, the expression on Richard's face turned from one of elation at having run across her, to one of confusion, then to one of speechless, overwhelming realization.

"Richard," she said quietly in effort to break the pregnant silence that had descended upon that busy city corner. "Please allow me to introduce you to my husband, Lord Dunevin, and our daughter, Miss Juliana MacFeagh. You have already met her friend, Brìghde. Gabriel, girls, this is a friend of mine." She looked at Richard, her eyes trying to comfort him. "A very good friend. Richard Hartley, the Earl of Herrick."

But Richard was staring at Gabriel, who stood several inches taller and even now drew stares from the other pedestrians passing by. After a moment, he peered at Eleanor again, his eyes now vacant with realized catastrophe.

"You...you are married," Richard stated, as if to confirm the words he'd just been told.

And then, as if shaken by unseen hands, every modicum of

gentility and politeness he'd ever been taught returned to surround him like a many-caped Garrick cloak. He stood straighter, putting on a face of polite indifference, and extended a hand toward Gabriel in greeting. "Lord Dunevin, an honor to make your acquaintance."

Gabriel nodded, shook his hand. "Lord Herrick."

Richard glanced at the two girls then and nodded.

"Yes, well," he said, obviously struggling to come to terms with what stood before him in the midst of such a public arena. "I certainly wish you all the best on your marriage." He then bowed his head to Gabriel, "Lord Dunevin." He looked at Eleanor, his face filled with stark despair against the high points of his fashionable collar. "Lady Dunevin. I can only say I'm sorry my letter didn't make it to you successfully in Scotland. My loss is obviously Lord Dunevin's gain."

And with that, he bowed his head, turned, and started walking away from them down the pedestrian path, his back held straight, his shoulders squared.

He never once looked back.

Eleanor hadn't realized she was still standing there, staring at his retreating figure while people strolled around her, until Gabriel finally spoke.

"Are you all right, lass?"

She looked at him, her heart filled with a terrible remorse. "I...I never expected to see him here. I didn't know what to say to him. I wasn't prepared. Gabriel, he should never have had to find out in that way."

Gabriel nodded in understanding. "There was nothing else you could do."

She fought regretful tears. "But what if he had been my mother? Or Christian? I should never have come out."

Brìghde tugged on Eleanor's sleeve, asking her why that man with the tall hat and shiny boots had made her so sad. Juliana just took a step closer to her side. Suddenly, Eleanor wanted to get off that crowded street corner and back to the sanctuary of Dunevin House as quickly as they could.

Gabriel must have sensed her thoughts for he quickly hailed them a hackney that was parked at the corner. Within minutes they were rolling toward Upper Brooke Street, this time purposefully avoiding a pass through Berkeley Square past Knighton House.

That night, they stayed in for supper, eating a quiet meal which they'd had to send Fergus out to fetch from a nearby public house since Mrs. Wickett and the cook had spent most of the day ordering provisions for the kitchen. After supper, Eleanor saw that Juliana and Brìghde were quickly bathed and dressed in their nightclothes, then tucked them both into bed in a chamber just down the hall from her own.

As she closed the door behind her, Eleanor could hear Brìghde whispering to Juliana in the darkness and knew the two would probably spend half the night standing at the window, watching the carriages roll by under the light of the gas lantern at the street corner. She smiled to herself. It was much the same sort of thing she had done as a child when she had first come to London.

An hour later, Eleanor sat alone in her bedchamber, brushing out her hair at the dressing table. She was lost in thought, replaying her meeting with Richard that day again and again. She had taken a bath to wash away the travel dust and to try to ease the lingering disquietude she felt over it all. She wondered how Richard was doing, if he would ever forgive her, and if he did, what she would say to him when next they met. She felt isolated, untethered somehow. She thought about her own family, and suddenly, she found herself longing to see them.

Several times that evening, she had wanted to do nothing more than go straight over to Berkeley Square, to knock on the door at Knighton House, but she hesitated each time. Her mind was at an utter loss for what she would say. She wondered how her mother, how Christian, would react to her new and unexpected family. Would they like Gabriel? Would they welcome Juliana and her muteness into the exalted and always perfect Westover fold?

Eleanor was still sitting at her dressing table, staring blankly at her reflection in the looking glass when Gabriel knocked softly at her door.

"A footman just brought this to the door for you," he said, handing her a folded and sealed letter.

It was addressed to her as 'Lady Dunevin' and she noticed immediately it bore the Herrick seal.

She looked up at him. "It is from Richard," she said as she broke the seal to open it.

The letter was not, however, from Richard, but instead it was from his mother, the dowager Countess Herrick. In the note, she invited Eleanor to tea the next morning.

'Matters needing to be discussed' was written at the bottom of the page. Eleanor knew immediately what those matters would be.

She handed the letter to Gabriel so he could read it.

"Will you go?" he asked.

Eleanor sighed. "I do not know. I don't want to hurt anyone else."

Gabriel nodded. "Give it some thought first, lass. You needn't decide just now. Sleep on it for the night and you can make your decision in the morning, when things are fresh. If you would like, I would go with you."

She looked at him and smiled, bolstered by his support. "Thank you, Gabriel."

"Good night then, lass." He kissed the top of her head and turned to leave. "Sleep well."

He was almost to the door when she called him back. At the sound of his name, he stilled, stopped at the door. Eleanor stood to face him across the room. For several moments, they just stared at one another. Neither of them had to speak to know what the other was thinking. The past weeks, every moment of that time, had been leading to this night, their delayed wedding night.

And now, the waiting was over.

At the silent invitation in her eyes, Gabriel closed the door. He stood across the room, and Eleanor felt herself blushing at the light of longing she saw in his eyes.

Without another word, Gabriel strode across the carpet. In one swift movement, he swept Eleanor up and into his arms. She gasped, realizing the thrill of it, and locked her hands around his neck as he carried her to the bed.

"Shall I snuff the candles?" she asked.

"Does it need to be dark, lass?"

"Well, I thought...I mean, that is what I heard..."

Gabriel chuckled. "Is that what your schoolgirl friends told you?"

Eleanor thought of her dear friend, Amelia B., and the countless nights they had spent whispering beneath the bedcovers at Miss Effington's school, fantasizing about this very thing.

"It isn't fair, you know," she said to him. "Men are practically born knowing these things. You talk about it as if it were nothing more than...than a horserace. Girls are only left to their imaginations and the small *on-dits* whispered by older sisters and cousins." She pulled a face. "Such as the snuffing of candles."

Gabriel stretched upon the bed beside her. "I imagine you've been told that some lasses prefer the dark so they won't have to look at their husband's faces. They can shut out the miseries of their unhappy marriages, doing their wifely duty while pretending that it is a secret lover in their bed instead of a boorish husband."

Gabriel reached for the candlestick. "So which is it you prefer, lass, your husband, or a secret lover?"

Eleanor looked at him and smiled, taking his hand and

pulling him toward her, saying on a breath before their lips met, "Well, fortunately, I don't have to choose, my lord. I have them both."

Their bodies melded together as Gabriel kissed Eleanor deeply, stealing her breath. He pulled away from her for but a moment, and she watched him in the candlelight as he stripped away his shirt, tossing it behind him.

"Hmm, husband, looking at you I think maybe a candle is a good thing."

He nearly laughed. "Will you think so when I'm standing without a stitch to cover me? Some ladies are shocked at the sight of a man's privy parts."

Eleanor sat up before him and trailed a finger along his arm to his chest. "You do remember that I was a student of anatomy, my lord."

Now he did laugh, deeply. "Ah, lass, you do me in."

Gabriel kissed her again, long and slow, brushing his fingers over her ear and twisting her hair around his fingers. Gently, he tugged on that strand, easing back her head as he moved his mouth over her chin to her neck.

Eleanor sighed softly in response.

Three tiny ribbons tied in perfect bows fixed the top of her night rail closed. Three tiny tugs and they were bows no more. Soon Gabriel was pushing the fabric down over her shoulder, kissing along her collar and sending delightful chills running down her back.

Somehow, Eleanor didn't know how, Gabriel had gotten her night rail down around her waist. He laid her back upon the bed, softly into the nest of pillows, and she watched him again, watched his eyes ignite as he took in the sight of her waiting for him.

"Oh, lass, if I'd had a governess who looked like you when I was a lad, I'd have been much more assiduous in my studies."

"Well, 'tis a good thing you did not," she whispered to him as he ran his hands slowly over her. "Else it might be her here with you now instead of me."

Gabriel pressed his mouth to her, saying, "Oh, no, lass, having you in my bed is the only way it should ever have been—and the only way it shall ever after be."

Eleanor arched, realizing a longing inside of her, a longing that begged to be fulfilled.

Gabriel eased her night rail over her hips. Eleanor felt a delightful shiver run over her and dropped her head back against the pillow, closing her eyes and waiting, waiting, waiting for him.

"You're more beautiful than I ever imagined. All those nights I lay awake in my bed thinking about you. How'd I ever get blessed with such a fine bonny lass?"

She whispered to the night, "It was fated."

How could he, with just one tiny touch, make her feel the way she was? It seemed almost impossible, but the more he touched her, the more she felt, until she wondered that if he should suddenly stop, she would lose something very precious.

Eleanor watched in silence as Gabriel stood from the bed and shed his breeches, never taking his eyes from hers until he was naked and standing before her. His body was all bronze skin, dark hair, and muscle. She fixed her gaze briefly on his sex, standing erect from his groin, then looked into his eyes.

Without a word, he slid beside her on the bed and pulled her against him. She welcomed the heat of him against her.

"It will hurt, yes?" she whispered.

Gabriel looked at her, seemingly startled by her question. "Yes, lass, but only for a moment, I promise you. After that, you shall forget it ever pained you."

"That is what I thought."

"And how d'ya know this, lass?"

"Once, when I was younger, I overheard two older boys bragging to one another about what they had done with the daughter of the local grocer."

"And what had they done?"

"Things. Things that had to do with numbers and how far under her skirts they had gotten, things that sounded far more like sport than anything intimate. Nothing at all like this."

"Aye, well there's a difference between men and boys."

Eleanor smiled at him, and shifted her hips against the heat of his hardness. "Yes, I am aware of that."

Gabriel groaned, buried his face against her neck as he slowly lifted her knees around his hips. He came up on his hands above her, watching her eyes as he pressed himself forward.

"If I pain you too much, just say so and I will stop."

"I don't care about the pain, Gabriel. It is worse to not have you. Make me your wife, completely."

His eyes changed then, bright with desire, and Eleanor held her breath, waiting for what seemed like an eternity until finally he joined them forever.

The pain was instant and sharp and then after a few moments, it was gone almost as quickly as it had come, consigned to fleeting memory. In its place was a warm delicious throbbing, a desperation that cried out for the fulfillment of him. She could hear his breathing ragged against her ear and kissed him gently on the side of his face, whispering his name as he struggled to compose himself.

"It has been a long time for me, lass, so long that I no longer remember anyone else. I fear I may come undone if I hold back from you much longer."

"Then don't," she whispered to him. "Don't hold back."

Gabriel drew a breath sharply and moved, drawing back from her. Eleanor watched his face, fixing her eyes on his as she began to move with him, slowly at first, until he, too, was clinging to her. Each movement filled her, until, finally he broke free, groaning out her name and pulsing deep inside of her.

Gabriel's arms were trembling as he struggled to maintain his rigid posture above her. Eleanor reached up to him, and drew him down to where he was resting his weight fully against her, his head buried against her shoulder, his arms holding her.

Moments later, he lifted his head. He kissed her softly, looked into the depths of her eyes.

"You said something to me, lass, the night of the *cuideachd*. I hadn't expected it, those words. I was startled, uncertain what to say. But I know now. I love you, lass, more than I ever imagined a man could love. I'll not fight it any longer."

And then he kissed her, not deeply, not passionately, but tenderly, with all the promise of the future. Their future.

It was beyond anything she could have ever imagined.

17

*E*leanor stepped down carefully from the hackney coach and onto the curved footpath along Grafton Street to stand before the imposing façade of Number Five, the London home of Louise, the dowager Countess of Herrick.

She thanked the driver, removing two coins from her reticule, and then watched as he clicked to his horses and moved slowly down the lane, vanishing around the next corner. She remained standing on the footpath for several moments, just staring at the façade of the pristine Georgian townhouse tucked in the corner of the lane, whose front windows gleamed like ice in the morning sunlight.

Her hands lay tucked away inside her ermine muff, a new purchase from the shopping excursion the day before, protected from the biting wind that blew its way over the housetops, stirring the fallen leaves across the cobbles at her feet. The sudden change in the weather overnight seemed to echo the dire prospect of her errand. Other pedestrians walked casually past and the clip-clop of horses pulling carriages sounded distantly behind her. Still she stood there, wondering just what this visit would bring.

It was evident Richard had told the dowager about seeing her the day before. Did the countess know the truth about the past, about Eleanor's parentage? Or was she simply seeking to call Eleanor to task for rejecting her son's proposal of marriage so abominably?

Finally, realizing, of course, that she couldn't just continue to stand outside in the biting wind all day, Eleanor climbed the three short steps to the front door, rapped upon it, and waited.

"Yes?"

The Herrick butler stood stalwart as a flagpole before her.

"Good afternoon. I am here to call on Lady Herrick, if you please."

He looked at her speculatively. "And whom shall I say is calling?"

"Eleanor, Lady Dunevin. I believe she is expecting me."

He nodded and opened the door for her to enter. He motioned toward a small carved bench set just inside the door. "You may wait here while I ask if her ladyship is receiving."

The house was warm inside, elegantly furnished, and smelled of fresh flowers and early morning baking. Eleanor took her hands from inside her muff, removed her bonnet, and sat to wait.

She could hear the faint murmur of conversation coming from down the center hall, too muffled, though, to discern any of the words. A clock hanging on the wall beside her chimed the half hour. A chambermaid came down the narrow flight of stairs, bobbing a curtsy with a quick "milady" as she passed on her way to the back of the house. On the street outside, she could hear a bread seller calling out "Hot loaves!"

The butler returned moments later.

"Lady Herrick will receive you in the parlor now, Lady Dunevin. May I take your coat?"

Eleanor handed him her muff and bonnet while she unfastened the buttons at the front of her pelisse, turning when he moved to assist her with it. "Thank you."

"This way, my lady."

He led her down the hallway past several doors and a tall case clock to a room set at the back of the house, away from the noise and diversion of the street. It faced out onto a private walled garden through a large window that afforded a pleasant view. The butler stopped at the door to allow her inside to proceed before announcing her.

"Lady Dunevin, my lady."

The dowager countess sat on a settee facing the door as Eleanor came into the room. Her head was covered by a frilled muslin cap and in her lap she had an embroidery frame on which she'd been stitching a neat row.

Her expression wasn't one that was easily discernible, her mouth set in a line that was neither frown nor smile, her eyes clear and watchful, the same pale gray as her son's.

She nodded wordlessly to the chair nearest by, indicating Eleanor should sit. She asked the butler to fetch the tea tray from the kitchen.

When he'd gone, Eleanor spoke first. "Lady Herrick, it is an honor to make your acquaintance." She sat and folded her hands on her lap. "Thank you for inviting me today."

"Truth be told, I wasn't so certain you'd come."

Eleanor looked at the older woman, immediately sensing a deeply-seated bitterness. "Lady Herrick, please know that I—"

The dowager held up her hand, silencing Eleanor's next words.

"When Richard, my son, first came to tell me he had begun courting someone at the beginning of the season, I was, of course, thrilled as any mother with a son of marriageable age would be. I was excited to meet her, this girl who had so obviously charmed him. The name of Wycliffe, however, was the very last one I would have ever expected to hear."

Eleanor looked down at her hands, humbled by the words this

woman had obviously been waiting quite some time to say. She remained silent.

"It was as if the past twenty years had simply melted away," the dowager went on. "I should have told him the truth about you right then, but I must admit to a certain curiosity about you. I decided to wait until Richard asked to bring you to meet me, thinking that the moment I saw you, faced you, I would surely know...I would surely be able to tell..."

"...if I had been fathered by your husband," Eleanor finished for her.

The dowager looked at her, searching her face, no doubt for some sort of resemblance to the former earl. "I didn't know if you had ever been told the truth. A part of me thought that you had and that you were trifling with Richard in a game meant to reopen old wounds."

"Lady Herrick, I assure you I would never—"

She went on. "Another part of me wondered if you were as much a victim in the events of the past as was my son."

Her voice softened then. "I decided I would wait because I knew if you were truly a product of what took place all those years ago, then Frances would never allow you to go through with a marriage to Richard. I can see now that I was right in that assumption."

Eleanor shook her head. "The truth is I do not know who my father was. I don't suppose I ever will truly know."

Lady Herrick stood suddenly and walked to the window to stare out at the garden beyond. She was quiet for a time, leaving Eleanor to simply sit and wait until she was ready to continue.

"Frances and I were as close as sisters in our youth, you know. We went to school together. We even came out together. We always said we would one day get married to our husbands on the same day at the same church. I always knew that she loved Richard, just as I knew that he loved her. But her family had had other thoughts in mind, particularly when the heir to the Duke of Westover came calling."

She turned to face Eleanor again. "She did try, your mother, in the beginning, to make a life with your father, but when the heart is given elsewhere, marriage can be more confining than the loneliest, most forsaken prison." She shook her head. "I know it all too well."

She returned to her seat. "I knew that William was going to meet your fath—" she stopped herself, correcting, "I knew that William was going to meet Christopher at dawn that morning. I knew Frances well enough to know that she could never deceive Christopher into believing someone else's child was his. I stood at the window that faced out toward the Westover estate all morning, watching for his return. When he didn't appear by the afternoon, I knew what had happened. I didn't find out that Christopher had died in the duel as well until weeks later. I don't know whatever became of my husband."

"Lady Herrick, that morning—"

She shook her head. "No explanations, please. I do not wish to know what happened that morning, Lady Dunevin. It was an inevitability long in the making, a tragic end to a tragic beginning for us all. I left that part of my life behind when I left the country to move permanently to London with my son. I have never gone back and I have no intention of ever revisiting it."

She crossed to a small writing table in the corner and opened a drawer, removing something from inside. She walked over to where Eleanor sat and handed her a small hinged box about the size of a deck of cards. Eleanor opened it to reveal a painted miniature tucked away inside. Its subject was a handsome man of about thirty years in powdered wig and frock. He had kind, smiling eyes.

She looked to Lady Herrick who yet stood before her. "This is—?"

The dowager simply nodded.

Eleanor searched the likeness of William, Lord Herrick, for some connection, some similarity to her own features, the tilt of his brow, the set of his mouth, but found nothing, only unanswered questions.

He had been a handsome man, and it was easy to see why her mother had fallen in love with him. Gently, Eleanor replaced the image in its box and returned it to the countess.

"I am so sorry."

"My only regret is that my son had to be so hurt by all of this. He is devastated. Even now he doesn't understand your reasons for crying off any more than he understands why you married another so quickly. He simply believes you grew tired of waiting for him to return from Yorkshire, that his letters never reached you, that he waited too long, lost his opportunity." She levelled Eleanor a stare. "And I have done everything I can to prolong that belief."

The dowager paused. "I have not told him the truth about his father and I do not intend to. At least not now. Like your brother, Christian, Richard was made to grow up far too quickly after his father's death, assuming the responsibilities of the earldom at too early an age. He idolized his father—he still does to this day—and he has worked very hard to be a son William would have been proud of. I think he has succeeded and I will not take that away from him right now."

She shook her head regretfully. "I know I have no right to ask this of you, but I would be most grateful if you would keep our visit today and the things we have discussed between us. The past is the past, Lady Dunevin. There is nothing we can do to change it now. The day may come when Richard should know the truth, but to tell him now would only be cruel. He has already been brought low after seeing you yesterday. Please do not deliver him another terrible blow so soon."

She looked at Eleanor vacantly. "In the best interests of both yourself and my son, I believe things are better left unsaid. You are very newly married and have no need of any scandal for your new husband."

Eleanor lifted her chin at the dowager's insinuation that she had perhaps married Gabriel quickly and deceptively in effort to protect herself from the scandal of her birth.

"My husband was told the truth about my parentage, my lady. *Before* we were married."

Lady Herrick looked somewhat surprised by her statement. "My apologies, Lady Dunevin. I made an assumption about you based solely upon the suddenness of your marriage. That was unfair. Indeed then, Lord Dunevin must be a very exceptional man."

Eleanor smiled at the mention of Gabriel. "He is. He is unlike any man I have ever met before."

Lady Herrick smiled. "Then allow me to congratulate you, Lady Dunevin, on avoiding the confinement of a loveless marriage. Your affection for your husband is clear to anyone who looks at you."

Eleanor stood, sensing that the time for her to leave had come. "Thank you, Lady Herrick, for taking the time to speak with me so honestly." She extended her hand. "I am in your debt."

"And I am in yours."

They started toward the door.

"I wonder, Lady Dunevin, if I might offer you a word of advice?"

Eleanor nodded.

"Do not judge the actions of your mother or your brother too harshly. They only did what they thought best for you under the most difficult of circumstances. Frances has already been punished enough by all of this to last the length of three lifetimes. Despite what has happened between us, I should hate to see her punished further."

"Thank you, my lady. If she could know of your concern, I am certain my mother would appreciate it."

The countess simply nodded, a wistful light filling her eyes. "But that can never be."

After bidding her good day, Eleanor retrieved her things from the butler who saw to the task of asking the Herrick footman to summon her a hackney home.

As she stood waiting on the footpath, Eleanor's first thought was to return to Dunevin House and sit with Gabriel and the girls for a quiet afternoon. But as she climbed into the carriage and settled upon the squabs, she realized there was another place that she needed to go to first.

"To where, my lady?" asked the driver.

"To Hyde Park, if you please."

FRANCES, MARCHIONESS KNIGHTON, WAS A WOMAN OF MOST scrupulous habit, performing her same rituals each day with but very little deviance.

She awoke at five of the clock each morning to wash her face with lavender soap and cold water before taking a breakfast of toasted bread and tea precisely at six.

She took milk in her tea, not cream, and no sugar, and she preferred strawberry jam on her toast, although she had been known to stray to gooseberry every once in a while as well.

She spent an hour each morning reading quietly in the parlor and, weather permitting, every Thursday morning at ten, before most of London society had even begun to stir, she strolled the three short blocks to the Stanhope Gate that led into Hyde Park.

She sat in the same place each time she went, taking the third bench to the right of the entrance just off the Lover's Walk pathway that was partially hidden behind a rather large sycamore that had sprung from two trunks. There she passed the next hour tossing bread crusts to the birds and squirrels while the city awoke around her and the daylight climbed to the highest part of the sky.

Today the weather was colder than in recent days, the wind carrying with it a brisk bite, so Frances had brought along a lap blanket to cover her legs while she sat. It was a thick woolen covering woven for her by some of the tenant's wives at Skynegal, the Highland estate of her son, Christian, and his wife, Grace. The criss-crossed tartan design was done in muted shades of dark red, green, black and white, and it was fringed along the edges. It was a pretty and quite sturdy piece.

Frances had come to this place whenever she was in London for nearly twenty years. It was a quiet corner of the park away from the most traveled promenades and she always found a sense of peace there, a solace that one could only find when truly at one with nature. The wind soughed softly, the waxwings trilled from the treetops above, but today, she found no peace in this place, no solace, only the continuing troubling thoughts of her missing daughter, Eleanor.

As she watched a small squirrel collecting acorns at her feet, Frances wished she could somehow, someway go back in time to right the wrongs she had committed so many years ago. At the time, she had been so young and so very, very foolish, filled with ideas of romance and fairytale.

The feelings she'd had for William had seemed so eminent, so vital to her existence. She realized now they could never have had a future together; and their love affair had only added fuel to the fire of youthful defiance.

Frances's parents wouldn't have dared to reject the heir to the Duke of Westover no matter how much she might have pleaded with them otherwise. Christopher had known that her heart was given elsewhere, yet he'd truly believed he could make her happy, that someday, after he had showered her with gifts and riches and overbearing affection, she would somehow inexplicably change her feelings for him from friendship to the desperate, obsessive sort of love he felt for her.

But in the end, however, even that friendship had gone, leaving Frances with nothing but the bitter shadow of resentment—for Christopher, for her parents, and for a society that had left her its powerless victim.

It was the children, Christian and Eleanor, who had suffered the effects of her mistakes the most, and no mother with an ounce of compassion in her heart for those whom she had born would wish any such pain upon their innocence. At the age of nine, Christian had gone from good-natured boy to the role of nobleman, a man who'd shouldered a burden from then on that would have crumbled most.

In order to secure Eleanor the protection of the Westover name, Christian had given over his life into the hands of his grandfather, the old duke, allowing that embittered man to dictate his life's path in exchange for his silence about the question of Eleanor's paternity.

Her son had done it to protect his mother, she knew, to keep her from being ostracized as an adulteress, and Frances had only agreed to his understanding with the duke out of fear for the life of her unborn child.

Oh, would that she could erase the memory of that horrible night so long ago, the night she had told her husband she quite possibly was carrying another man's child.

Christopher had sat so silent that night, simply staring at her with an expression unlike any she had ever seen. His eyes had been frighteningly vacant, glazed, somehow unreal. His skin had turned an ashen white.

Frances realized now he had known the truth all along, even before she had told him.

"Who is the father?" Christopher had asked, his voice filled with a fearsome calm.

"I do not know," had been her reply, not because she had

sought to deceive him, but because, in truth, she had continued to do her duty as Christopher's wife whenever he had visited her bedchamber.

"Then I will raise it as my own. This is nothing new. Devonshire houses countless brats whose origin is questionable. Brookridge even paid his wife to take a lover so that he could get himself an heir despite his well-known impotence. I shall just be like one of them, pretending not to know the truth.

"You will not see him again," he'd said then, rising from his chair and crossing the room to his desk. "I'll not tolerate being made a cuckold before all the world."

"Christopher, I promise you it will never happen again..."

"Spare me from any more of your hollow promises, madam. You made another promise not so long ago when you married me before God, vowing to '_honor and keep thee only unto me._' Remember?"

Moments later, Frances had watched him taking out his pistol case. "Christopher, what do you mean to do?"

"I mean to ensure that I am never again made to wonder whether my child is my own."

"But I swear to you—"

"You swear? You swear!"

He took her by the arm, yanking her up from her chair and pulled her hard against him, his face twisting, inches from her own. "What you say no longer matters to me, wife. I am finished with your lies and practiced deception."

It was in that moment Frances knew that the obsessive passion of love Christopher had felt for her before had suddenly and irrevocably changed to the far worse passion of hatred.

Christopher took up his quill and scribbled something upon a parchment, taking his time in dusting it to dry, folding it, sealing it with a dollop of wax into which he pressed his signet ring. He called out the door to the Westover footman who appeared in seconds.

"What are you doing?" Frances asked.

He ignored her and spoke to the footman. "Deliver this posthaste to the estate of Lord Herrick. Make sure to give it to no one but the earl."

The Herrick estate, Hartley Manor, was but two miles to the west of the Westover estate.

Christopher turned to her. "Did you think I planned to do away with you when I took out my pistol case, Frances? Sorry to disappoint you, but it's your lover I intend to kill tomorrow morning."

Frances had grown desperately frightened. "Christopher, please, don't do this."

He opened the case and removed one of the dueling pistols from inside. They had been a gift to him from her father, she remembered then. How utterly ironic. "Spare me your tender concern for your lover, madam."

"It is not William I am concerned about, Christopher. It is you. You are not thinking logically."

"Neither were you when you lifted your skirts and opened your legs to another man."

Frances had flinched as if his sharp words had actually struck her. The memory of them stung even now. "Be reasonable. Please. William is a known excellent shot."

"As should be any man who would sleep with another man's wife while at the same time betraying one he had called friend."

Frances attempted one final appeal. "Christopher, if you care not for me, please don't do this to Louise. She has a young son to raise."

He merely scoffed, beyond any reason by then. "If you had had such a care for the feelings of the woman, for their son, you wouldn't have bedded with her husband. I wonder, does she know the woman she considers her closest friend in life might very well be carrying her husband's child? Tell me, is Herrick at

Hartley Manor right now, like you were earlier tonight, on his knees before her, spilling his guts?"

Frances had simply stared at him.

"It is as I thought. The man is too much of a coward to face up to his transgressions. You had no choice since you carry the result of your adultery in your womb. I am doing Lady Herrick the favor of never having to know the torture of having her heart rent in two as I have."

In the end, Frances had been unable to do anything more than hopelessly watch from the isolation of her bedchamber window as Christopher, his father the duke, and then nine-year-old Christian, whom they had roused from sleep to view this spectacle, to know what his mother had done, disappeared into the darkness of the moors in the early morning hours.

She hadn't moved an inch by mid-morning, when only two of the three who had gone returned, the third draped lifelessly over the back of his horse.

Still, despite the bitter tragedy of that terrible dark time, Frances couldn't truly regret it all, because out of it, out of the anguish and heartache and loss, had come her most precious daughter.

From the night she was brought into the world and delivered into Frances's arms, Eleanor had been nothing less than a blessing. It had been six months since Christopher's death. Enlightened beyond his ten years, Christian had become Frances' immediate champion, doing whatever he could to shield his mother and his newborn baby sister from harm.

He had willingly filled the role of brother, friend and father-figure, and never once had he censured Frances for the events of the past. Eleanor had grown into a bright, affectionate young woman, filled with promise for the future—a bright and shining light in their lives—until all of it came crashing down upon them those few months ago when the truth could no longer remain hidden.

After Christian had revealed the terrible details of the past to her, Eleanor had fled, vanishing into the night. She hadn't been seen since, despite the reward that had been offered for her safe return and inquiries made across the land by both Christian and the old duke, whose guilt over what had happened had brought on a total turn. It was getting now to where Frances despaired of ever seeing her daughter again, of ever holding her in her arms, if only so that she might offer her apologies and beg her forgiveness for the mistakes she had made.

The day was moving on, and a carriage or two had passed by as others started coming into the park, so Frances decided it was time to return to Knighton House. Christian and Grace were to arrive from Skynegal later that afternoon, and their friends, the Duke and Duchess of Devonbrook, who had also just returned to town, would be coming for supper that evening. There was much to do.

Frances stood and folded the blanket she'd brought, tossing the last few crusts of bread to the squirrels at the foot of the tree beside her. But as she turned for the gate that would take her from the park, she caught sight of a figure that was making its way toward her along the tree-lined pathway.

It was a woman, she could see, but her distance was too great for Frances to discern her identity. Still, there was something about her, something familiar in the way in which she walked, something that suddenly reminded her of...

Frances stood still for several moments, just watching, hope rising in her breast with each step the woman took closer.

Oh, could it truly be...?

Tears had already come to her eyes by the time Eleanor reached her. Frances wondered if she were dreaming and in the very same moment, hoped against hope that she was not.

"Hello, Mother."

At the first familiar sound of her daughter's voice, Frances lost the struggle against her emotions. She dropped her blanket heedlessly to her feet and softly sobbed as her beautiful daughter came home into the circle of her open arms.

"Oh, my dearest, dearest daughter," she said, stroking Eleanor's back as she held her tightly to her. "I have missed you so very much."

"And I have missed you."

Frances pulled back only for a moment to look on the face she had nearly given up hope of ever seeing again. Despite that only a few months had passed, Eleanor looked different somehow, mature. Her eyes no longer held that youthful bounding spirit. It pained Frances to know she had done that to her.

Frances shook her head. "Eleanor, I am so, so sorry for hurting you like I did."

"I know, Mother." Eleanor brushed a tear from her mother's cheek. "And I am sorry for leaving as I did without telling anyone where I was going. I just...I needed to get away, to take time to sort through everything."

"Of course you did, dear."

Eleanor looked deeply into Frances's eyes then. "Mother, there is much we need to talk about. Things have changed, in my life, things you need to know about."

Frances's motherly intuition immediately sharpened. "What is it, dear? Is something the matter? Whatever it is, we will sort it out. All that matters is that you are safe and you have come back home to stay."

"Actually, that is the first thing I need to tell you. I haven't come back—to stay, that is."

Frances stared at her. "What do you mean? Dear, I know you are hurt by what you learned, but if we could just talk, if I could just explain—"

"Mother, I am married."

Frances swallowed against her immediate dread. "To Lord Herrick?"

Eleanor shook her head. "No. To someone else."

"No, dear. It cannot be. You did this because you were distraught over what you had learned. You weren't thinking. You were just reacting to your emotions. But it is all right. You are under the age of consent. I am certain we can have this marriage annulled."

"Mother, no. I don't want that." Eleanor looked at her mother deeply. "I love him."

Frances was rendered speechless.

Eleanor went on to explain. "Yes, I was upset after what Christian told me, but that is not why I married Gabriel. I married him because he needs me, and because I need him, too. He knows everything about me, about my past, and he loves me. I truly believe now that all of what happened, happened for a reason because it led me to him."

She motioned toward the bench where Frances had been sitting earlier. "Come, let us sit for a spell like we used to and I will tell you everything that has taken place these months."

And so they did.

Frances sat attentively as Eleanor related everything to her of how she had made her way through the Highlands to Trelay, taking on her role as governess to Juliana, and the tender feelings that grew into love for Gabriel. She even told her about the events of his past and Gabriel's current legal trouble with his former in-laws.

When she finished, Frances took her daughter's hand. "Eleanor, dear, forgive me for asking this, but you say no one knows what became of his first wife. You said twice there were incidents, a fire and some sort of poisonous plant in your dinner? These are not simple coincidences, dear. What if," Frances chose her words carefully, "what if your life is at risk with this man?"

"Mother, Gabriel did not have anything to do with Georgiana's death, or anyone else's for that matter. He was at the castle when she disappeared. Only Juliana was with her and she cannot tell us what happened. He was abroad on the Continent when his brother died, and when the fire broke out in the nursery, he nearly killed himself because he thought I was there. Do not forget either that it was he who stopped me from eating that hemlock." Eleanor softened her tone. "There *is* a logical explanation for what has gone on. I know there is, and I just need to find it."

Frances realized she could not persist with her misgivings. Whatever she may think, Eleanor was no longer the impressionable young girl of her youth. In the space of those few months, she had become a woman grown, with a mind of her own, something Frances and the rest of the family were going to have to learn to trust.

"So for how long will you be in London?"

"Not long at all. Only to see to whatever legalities must be put into place to protect Juliana."

"But dear, you were married at Gretna Green, among strangers. At least allow your mother to give her only daughter a proper wedding surrounded by our friends and family."

Eleanor smiled. "We shall have a wedding, Mother, I promise you. But not here. It will be at Dunevin. And everyone will come."

Frances nodded. "May I at least meet this man who has stolen my daughter's heart? And your new daughter," Frances gasped then, covering her mouth with her hand. "I am a grandmother. Oh, good heavens!"

She hugged Eleanor tightly.

"Tonight," she said then. "You must come to dinner at Knighton House tonight, all of you. Christian and Grace will be arriving later today and they themselves will only be in town briefly. We are having the Devonbrooks over and we all would love very much to meet your new family. Will you come? At eight?"

"All right, Mother." Eleanor smiled at her, nodding her head. "At eight."

18

The hackney coach carrying Eleanor, Gabriel and the two girls arrived on Berkeley Square at precisely five minutes before eight, beneath the light of a full autumn moon that hovered low against the London church spires.

They rolled to a stop at the corner of the square where, shaded by a pair of twin great elms, stood the imposing red brick façade of Knighton House, London home to the Marquesses of Knighton for nearly a century past.

Tall bow windows faced the street and were ablaze with light from inside. From behind the coach window, Eleanor looked up past the lower parlor where she had once spent her mornings reading, up two floors to the window that peered out from her former bedroom. She searched the darkness through the trees, looking...she smiled to herself when she spotted a single lantern lit upon the sill. Her heart swelled with emotion. It was a long-standing tradition among the Wycliffes that anytime a family member returned from a visit elsewhere, they would find that candle burning in their window, a beacon to light their way home.

Gabriel stepped down from the coach first, turning to assist

Eleanor and then the girls down behind her. The girls looked especially pretty this evening, each in new frocks—Juliana in pink, Brìghde in blue—with lace pantalettes peeking out from underneath.

Brìghde, who was more accustomed to woolen skirts and bare feet, was especially proud of her new kid slippers and pristine white stockings. She showed them to everyone they met, even the coachman who'd driven them there.

Earlier that day, Frances had sent over Thérèse, who had been Eleanor's ladies' maid since the beginning of the season earlier that year. The sprightly French maid had wept with joy when first reunited with her mistress, and afterward, promptly set to arranging Eleanor's chestnut hair in a lovely coiffure swept high upon her head with small ringlets dangling down the back of it to her nape.

Afterward, Thérèse had ministered to the girls, curling their hair with fire-heated tongs in corkscrew curls and tying them up high upon their heads with soft satin ribbons, just like Eleanor.

They had been delighted.

Upon seeing them coming down the stairs to leave, Gabriel had declared the two his princesses for the night, a comment which had elicited a squeal from Brìghde—and a bright smile from Juliana.

Gabriel, too, had taken special care with his appearance for the evening and Eleanor was touched by his efforts to make a favorable impression upon her family. His face was cleanly shaven, his hair neatly trimmed, curling just below his high starched collar. The coat he wore was a dark bottle green over black breeches and polished boots. They would love him immediately, Eleanor thought, still amazed every time she saw him since coming to London, how very different he looked from the rugged Scottish laird she had fallen in love with.

Thérèse had brought several of Eleanor's gowns along with her from Knighton House and Eleanor had chosen to wear the pale blue-green silk, a favorite and one that held happy memories for her. It was the same gown she had worn the day Christian and Grace had married.

Charlie, the Knighton footman, was standing ready at his post at the door, and grinned widely as they approached.

"Good evening to you, Lady Eleanor. 'Tis good to see you back." He tipped his tricorn hat to Gabriel and the girls. "My lord and misses."

He opened the front door for them to where the Knighton butler, Forbes, already awaited. The usually staid and formal man couldn't disguise his joy at seeing her again as a smile crossed his face. "Lady Eleanor, welcome home."

"Forbes, 'tis good to see you. Please allow me to introduce my husband, Lord Dunevin, and this is our daughter, Miss Juliana MacFeagh, with her friend, Miss Brìghde Macphee."

Forbes bowed his head respectfully to Gabriel, and nodded to the girls as he secured their cloaks and hats and closed the front door behind them.

"They await you *en masse* in the parlor, my lady," he said as he headed for the back of the house with their cloaks.

The parlor was situated down the central hall and as they approached, Eleanor could hear the murmur of conversation coming from within. She didn't know why she felt so suddenly nervous. This had been her home all her life, and this was her family, but she still felt a flutter of anticipation as they approached the room. She set her hand on Gabriel's arm and took Juliana's hand with the other while Brìghde took her place at Gabriel's other side.

Together, they headed for the door.

Conversation hushed to silence the moment they stepped into view. Everyone was there, her mother, Frances, sister-in-law Grace, the Devonbrooks, even the old duke, who sat in an armchair near the hearth and who Eleanor was more than a little surprised to see. He hadn't been a usual visitor to their home during her upbringing.

Everyone was there, except for her brother, Christian. He was not in the room.

For the smallest of moments, no one spoke, they just looked at one another in a suspended silence, as if no one quite knew what to say first. Fittingly, it was Grace, standing close by the door and who, as hostess now at Knighton House since her marriage, broke the silence.

"Eleanor, welcome home. We are all so happy to see you."

The petite blonde crossed the room and embraced Eleanor warmly, whispering in her ear, "I have missed you so terribly. Christian is dreadfully grumpy when you aren't around."

The Grace Eleanor faced now was a stunningly different woman to the meek young miss who had married her brother in an arranged marriage six months earlier. Grace now exuded a confidence that showed all the way from her elegant blonde coiffure to her perfectly matched slippers and silk gown.

Eleanor smiled in thanks of her effort to ease the tension of the situation. "I missed you as well, Grace."

"And you must be Lord Dunevin," Grace said then, extending her hand to Gabriel in greeting. "I am Grace, Eleanor's sister-in-law. Until you happened along, I was the newest member of the Wycliffe clan. I'm so pleased to welcome you to the family."

Eleanor had briefed Gabriel beforehand on the formalities of each person's noble title, and so Gabriel took Grace's hand, bowing over it gallantly. "Lady Knighton."

After quickly welcoming the two girls, Grace led them forward toward the center of the room. "Won't you come in and meet the rest of the family?"

From that moment on, the room buzzed with conversation. Everyone started talking all at once, pressing forward to welcome Eleanor back into the fold of her family and to meet the mysterious stranger she now called husband.

So many questions. So many embraces.

How had they met?

Where had they married?

Were they planning to remain long in the city?

Eleanor got lost amid the sea of welcoming faces and introductions, until suddenly, she sensed someone standing beside her.

She turned to find her brother waiting.

"Oh, Christian."

"Nell, thank heavens you're home."

Her brother barely managed to utter his favorite pet name for her—the name he had always called her and which she had chosen to use when she had gone to Trelay—before he crushed her against him. She felt her breath catch as he hugged her more tightly than he ever had before. Eleanor could feel him fighting to hold his emotions in check, and she felt regretful for all the worry she had caused him the past months. She felt her own composure slip as her tears fell against the shoulder of his jacket.

He whispered into her ear, "I am so very sorry," and didn't release her for several moments.

Finally, she settled and she smiled brightly at him, taking his hand. "Come, brother, there is someone I wish you to meet."

Eleanor led him to where Gabriel stood with Frances and Juliana. "Christian, I would like to introduce you to my husband, Lord Dunevin of Trelay. Gabriel, this is my big brother, Lord Knighton."

"Christian, if you please," he added and the two men shook hands. While they exchanged polite greetings, Eleanor took a moment to study her brother.

Like Grace, he had changed in the past months. No longer did he appear a man who shouldered the burden of the secret that had utterly altered the course of his life. He looked freer, and happier, actually, as if he had come to terms with himself and the past, allowing him to see the beauty of his wife untainted by the resentment of having been forced to marry her. He even appeared to have begun repairing his relationship with their grandfather, evidenced by the way he had immediately taken Gabriel over to meet the old duke. Eleanor was thrilled to see this most promising change for the better.

Christian then returned to hunker down before Juliana, who immediately stepped closer to the comfort of Eleanor's skirts.

"It is a pleasure to meet you, Miss MacFeagh. That is quite a pretty dress you have." He extended his hand to her. "My name is Christian, and I would like it very much if I could be your uncle."

Juliana looked to Eleanor, who smiled at her and nodded encouragement. After a moment, Juliana slowly lifted her hand from behind the fullness of Eleanor's skirts, and placed it tentatively in Christian's palm.

Christian stood, still holding her hand, and led Juliana and Brìghde over to the small aviary where Frances's pet canary birds were chirping on their perch from all the excitement.

Earlier that day in the park, Eleanor had explained the circumstances behind Juliana's silence to Frances. As she'd listened, Frances had been filled with a grandmother's compassion and had clearly briefed the rest of the family. Eleanor beamed to see how wonderful and welcoming they were with her.

"Well, now that we've all dispensed with the introductions," Grace said from the parlor doorway, "Forbes informs me that our dinner is ready to be served."

The group collectively made their way across the hall to the spacious dining parlor where a formal supper had been laid upon the long mahogany table. The best Knighton silver had been brought out, polished until it gleamed beneath the light of the chandeliers above, and cut crystal goblets had been taken from storage in the pantry. Only the finest for this most special occasion.

Eleanor started toward her usual seat at Christian's left, and noticed Grace had seated Gabriel on her other side with Juliana between them. Catriona disappeared upstairs only to return moments later with their three-year-old son, James. He was a perfect miniature model of her husband, Robert, dressed for dinner in ankle-length trousers, short coat, and shirt ruffles.

She sat James in a Chippendale high stool at the far corner of the table between her chair and her husband's, directly across from Brìghde, who soon had the boy involved in a serious discussion about the curliness of her hair.

The meal progressed happily, through five separate courses, with delicious food, a warm fire, and pleasant conversation. The others all asked about their home on the island, where Trelay was located, what it was like to live there, how long had been their journey from Scotland to the city. Eleanor told them all about their wedding over the anvil at Gretna Green, followed by their stop at Kirkby Lonsdale and Mr. Gray's Incredible Bed. Gabriel and Robert discovered they had both served on some of the same battlefields on the Peninsula, and then the two fell into discussion with Christian about their Scottish tenancies. It was as if the past months melted away, as the family quickly righted itself back on its moorings.

After the meal, everyone withdrew to the parlor for tea, port, or whatever other refreshment was at hand. Brìghde and Juliana took turns playing with young James on the carpet before the fire, making card houses out of Christian's best whist deck that were then toppled when Brìghde pretended to be the Gaelic giant, Benandonner, sweeping her arms outward with a roar.

"Nell," Christian said as he settled onto the settee, port in hand, "how about a bit of music? It's been too long since we've heard you play. And perhaps my lovely wife would accompany you on the pianoforte?"

He took up Grace's hand and kissed it, staring warmly into her eyes.

Eleanor couldn't help but smile, watching the two of them so happy together now that Christian had finally banished his own personal demons from the past.

When he had married Grace earlier that year, they had been strangers at the altar. It was a marriage that had been arranged between their grandfather, the old duke, and Grace's uncle. Their rocky beginning had had to weather some stormy waters. It had taken some time, and a chase that led all the way to the Scottish Highlands, but now it was plain to see that Christian had truly won his wife's heart.

Somehow, too, in all the upheaval and heartache of the past season, the duke and Christian had come to an accord with one another. Throughout her childhood, Eleanor could remember how it had been so bitter between them. Time had been when the two men wouldn't so much as sit in the same room. Now, they spoke cordially to one another, discussing the news of the day, even sharing jest, and seemed well on the road to mending their lifelong difficulties.

1820 was, it seemed, a year of new beginnings for them all.

Grace then stood from the settee, but instead of heading directly for the pianoforte, she stopped a moment in front of where Juliana and Brìghde were sitting. She spoke to them in a quiet whisper that only the three of them could hear.

"Girls, usually when I play, my maid, Liza, sits beside me at the pianoforte and turns the pages for me. But Liza is not here with us in London because she is back in Scotland getting ready to marry a most handsome man named Andrew MacAlister. So I wonder if I might entreat you both to take up Liza's place beside me on the bench tonight?"

Juliana looked at Brìghde and then to Eleanor. Eleanor stood and held out her hand, which, after a moment, Juliana filled with her own. Brìghde and Grace followed suit and together the four walked to where the pianoforte stood.

Gabriel sat back in the far corner, watching as his daughter walked hand-in-hand with his wife across the room. He remembered a time when he had thought getting Juliana to speak again would never happen. But in the time since she had been with them, Eleanor had shown him that Juliana need not be considered odd or even cursed for her silence, that she was just as beautiful a girl as she had always been. Because of it, he had been able to better come to terms with the fact that he might never hear his daughter's laughter or sweet singing again. Now, he found, if that was to be the case, he could accept it.

As Grace set her fingers to the keys and Eleanor took up a flute, a twin to the one she had at Dunevin, Gabriel looked about the room, watching the faces of the others he now called family. That night, these people, all of them, had gone out of their way to make them feel welcome and secure, accepting them into their fold without question, without judgement. Realizing this, it was easy to see now why Eleanor was the extraordinary woman she was.

Gabriel watched her from across the room as she lost herself in the music she played. Eyes closed, she moved her head to the gentle air of the stirring melody. She was a woman who gave everything of herself without a thought of receiving in return, a woman who had the uncanny ability of seeing beyond a person's outward circumstances to the true spirit sometimes locked deep within. She was the woman he loved completely, he, a man who had thought he could love no one.

His feelings for Georgiana had been based on honor, concern, sympathy for the deplorable situation in which she had lived. He'd loved her, yes, but in a way that was so very different to the way he loved Eleanor. With her, Gabriel had found a way to shed the fear that had haunted his life. Eleanor believed in him, and she had made him believe in himself again, so that when he looked into those green eyes, the man he saw reflected there was someone he didn't recognize. If it took the rest of his days, he was going to show her just how deeply, how completely she had touched his life.

Eleanor finished her piece and everyone applauded, calling out for more. She looked briefly at Gabriel before she bent down and whispered something into Juliana's ear. Juliana looked at Eleanor, her eyes filled with hesitation, before finally she nodded and slid from the piano bench to stand beside Eleanor.

And then Eleanor handed Juliana her flute.

No person in that room made a sound as Juliana took a tentative breath and then set the flute to her lips to play. Though not too difficult a tune, it drifted from Juliana's fingers like the trilling of a bird, and Gabriel was spellbound. He remembered the sound of her sweet child's voice once singing that same song from the castle courtyard many years ago. He had believed it was a joy he might never again know.

Until now.

Somehow, without words, without uttering a sound, Juliana had found a way to sing again. Her singsong melody filled his soul and Gabriel felt something deep inside him swell. He closed his eyes and took in the song fully, breathing deeply, .

She finished the piece and even the old duke stood from his chair, calling out "Bravissima!" along with the others. Juliana lowered her eyes and stared shyly at the floor. She didn't see Gabriel crossing the room until he had lowered onto one knee in front of her. Very slowly she lifted her head to meet his gaze.

"That was wonderful, Juliana. Truly."

And then, for the first time in what seemed like forever, father and daughter embraced.

ELEANOR LAY AWAKE ON THE BED, STARING OUT THROUGH THE sheer curtains onto the pale light of the moon shining above the trees. She had tried to fall asleep, turning this way and that on the bed, but could never quite find a place that offered her comfort.

It wasn't the bed, she knew, or the moon shining through her window that was making her feel so restless. It was the thought of that same moon shining down on a castle far from there, on a misty island surrounded by bottomless blue sea.

If she closed her eyes, she could almost see it, the endless sky, the hills that stretched out to the shore, carpeted in every possible shade of blue and purple and green all mixed together. She closed her thoughts to the sound of the carriages driving by outside and searched for Màiri's soft voice humming some old Gaelic ditty in the kitchen. She longed for the scent of fresh bannocks, of evenings sipping tea by the peat fire, of Cudu's wiry hair beneath her fingers, of the gentle distant *baa*ing of the sheep on the machair. She yearned for the sight of her rugged Scotsman standing in kilt and sark.

Much as she had wanted, needed, to come back to London, much as she was so happy to be reunited again with her mother and Christian and the others, Eleanor quite simply wanted to go home.

As if sensing her troubled thoughts, Gabriel turned quietly on the bed beside her. He took her gently against him, wrapping his arms around her from behind.

"You're not resting easy, lass. What troubles you?"

She let go a breath. "I don't feel as I belong here, to this place, any longer, Gabriel. Yes, I grew up here, but it is another place that calls to me now."

He kissed her ear, nuzzling her neck. "I feel it, too, lass. It is like the sky before the storm, refusing to allow any moment of still. I've been thinking of Dunevin, too, longing for it for the first time in my life, but I just did not want to take you from your family so soon after you had returned to them."

Eleanor turned onto her side to peer at Gabriel in the near-darkness. His face was etched in moonlight and filled her heart to bursting.

"They are my family and I love them all, but you and Juliana are my home. You are my life. Please take me home, husband. I do not want to look out on row after row of buildings and smoke. I don't care to hear the brick dust man cursing the butcher at the street corner. I certainly don't want to watch another young girl being scolded for holding her teacup the wrong way. I want to look out and see nothing, nothing at all but the blue..." She looked into his eyes, "...and you...and our children running down the castle hillside."

"Children?" He blinked at her in the darkness.

It was a subject they had never discussed. Before now.

"Yes, Gabriel. I would like to give you a son. Our son."

"Oh, lass..."

Gabriel wreathed his fingers into her hair and took her mouth in a tender kiss that lasted as long as either of them dared not breathe. Beneath the bedclothes, Eleanor hitched her leg gently over his, hooking them limb-to-limb, body-to-body. She could lay like that forever, she thought to herself, warmed by the touch of his skin, the gentleness of his hands, and never ever feel alone or out of place again.

"I have decided something else," she said to him when the kiss had ended, but their mouths were still nearly touching and their breaths mingled between them.

"What is that, lass?"

She slanted him a look. "I've decided I do not much like you in breeches. I prefer the kilt."

Gabriel smiled, then chuckled softly against her, as he slid his hand against her under the bed coverings.

"Well, that is a good thing to know, lass...especially since I'm not wearing any now."

Eleanor fell silent, but only for a moment before she said, "I don't know if I can believe you, sir. I'm afraid I shall have to ask you to prove it."

And prove it he did.

Twice.

19

*E*leanor sat reading quietly by the fire in the front parlor while Juliana and Brìghde were stretched out upon the carpet at her feet, painting across big sheets of paper with watercolors. To look at them, flat on their bellies, feet crossed behind them, one would question why they had any paper at all. There was more paint splashed across their noses, cheeks and fingers than any other place.

As Gabriel had promised, they were to leave the city to return to Scotland and Trelay first thing in the morning. It had been a week since their arrival and so much had happened in that short time, it seemed as if nearly a full month at least must have passed.

Mr. Pratt had met with the solicitor for Georgiana's family earlier that week, and after apprising them of the change in Gabriel's circumstances, they had wisely decided to abandon their pursuit of a petition to the Crown. Their marriage, coupled with the might of the Westover reputation, had been adequate enough persuasion for them. Furthermore, Juliana's legacy from her mother would thereafter be put into a trust so that it could not legally be squandered before she reached her majority.

Afterward, they had visited with Brìghde's grandmother, who

lived alone in a small tumble-down place in Cheapside. Gabriel had hired a physician who upon thorough examination of her, diagnosed that the cause of her illness was due only to the acrid coal smoke that clouded the rooftops of London and was not, as they had first thought, life-threatening. If she moved from the city, he predicted, she would quite certainly make a full recovery. Thus, when they departed for Scotland in the morning, Brìghde's grandmother would be traveling with them back to Trelay.

Christian and Grace had left the day before to return to Skynegal with the promise to ferry down to Dunevin sometime the following month. Catriona and Robert, meanwhile, would be stopping in when they returned to their estate, Rosmorigh, in the Highlands after the Christmas holiday.

For Hogmanay, and to ring in the new year, Eleanor had invited everyone to travel to Trelay when she and Gabriel would be married again, amidst the mist and the green and an altar of ancient standing stones along the castle hillside. This time, they would be surrounded by their families and friends and all the islanders, with the stirring song of Dunevin's resident piper carried on the sea wind.

For now, it was just Eleanor and the girls at the house that afternoon. Gabriel had gone off earlier to retrieve the last of Eleanor's belongings from Knighton House, numerous trunks, boxes, and crates which he was sending on ahead by separate coach and which would be waiting for them when they arrived back on Trelay.

Eleanor had spent that morning penning several pages of chatty correspondence to Amelia B., apprising her of all that had taken place while Mrs. Wickett was busy bustling about—as much as the staid Mrs. Wickett could endeavor to "bustle"— taking care of the details of closing up the townhouse until they might return next season.

Eleanor had just finished reading a chapter in her book, leaving Mr. Darcy thoroughly regretting his behavior toward

Elizabeth Bennett, and thought to ask Mrs. Wickett for a cup of tea, when she happened to catch a glimpse of Brìghde's painting spread out at her feet.

It wasn't so much the colors, but the image that caught her eye, for it was nearly an exact copy to the mural Juliana had painted upon the walls in the Dunevin schoolroom. This time, though, Brìghde was lending a hand to it, and Eleanor watched with curious interest as she would draw a bit, then glance at Juliana as if to ask if it was right.

This went on for several minutes, concentrating on the figures of the two in the water and the one on the hilltop, the bit that Juliana had never been able to finish in the schoolroom because of the fire. It was almost as if, somehow, mysteriously, Juliana had somehow conveyed to Brìghde exactly what to draw —but of course that wasn't possible. She hadn't spoken a single word.

Finally, after few more minutes of this peculiar silent interaction, Eleanor leaned in closer to them to ask, "Brìghde, dear, what are you doing?"

The child swept a stray blonde curl from her eyes, leaving a smear of blue paint across her forehead. "I'm drawin' in *Jwee-lhanna* on top o' this hill. She dinna want to do it herself.'"

Eleanor sat more forward, bending to look at the drawing closely. "How do you know that she doesn't want to do it?"

"Because she told it to me, my lady. That's how."

Eleanor was puzzled. "She told it to you? But what do you mean? How did she do that?"

Brìghde sighed. "She told it to me in her thoughts, my lady. Can you no' hear them? 'Tis clear as the birds singin' outside in the trees, it is."

Eleanor stilled, listening closely, but heard nothing, nothing but the silence.

"Brìghde, do you mean to say you can hear what Juliana is thinking?"

The blonde little girl splashed a bit of paint on the drawing. "Oh, aye."

"Right now, I mean? Right at this moment?"

The child nodded. "Aye."

"But how, Brìghde? How can you hear her thoughts?"

She shrugged. "I dinna know. It just happens, is all. 'Tis been that way since St. Michael's Day."

Eleanor's heart had begun drumming in her chest. "So are you saying Juliana is talking to you? Even now?"

Brìghde looked at Juliana, scrunching her forehead as if she didn't understand something, then smiled softly and nodded. "Aye, but I dinna ken her meaning, my lady. She says she misses her doll. That is why she had me draw it for her here."

Brìghde pointed to one of the two figures in the water.

Eleanor drew a curious breath. For Juliana, she knew that doll signified Georgiana. She looked at the painting again, more closely this time. Why did it suddenly look as if the figures in the drawing were struggling?

"Brìghde, is that meant to be Juliana's mother there?"

Brìghde shook her head. "Oh, no, my lady. The lady Georgiana is here."

She pointed to the rounded head of the seal peeking out from the waters. "You see, when the sea came to take her, the lady Georgiana, she didn't really leave like the man said. She became a seal-woman, a *selkie*, so she could always watch over *Jwee-lhanna*."

Eleanor remembered the day they had taken that first excursion on the isle, how that same small seal had seemed to follow them. But surely not...

Eleanor pointed to the other two figures. "Brìghde, why is Juliana's doll in the water?"

Brìghde glanced at Juliana, they seemed to communicate with just their eyes, and then she answered simply, "She says because the man took her there and gave her to the sea, but he told

Juliana she must never speak of it, not a word to anyone, or else the sea would come to take her da away, too."

A shiver seized Eleanor then at the ominous words, prickling along her neck. And then she realized. Juliana was trying to tell them what had happened that day to her mother, using the doll as a means to keep from going against the warning of whoever it was who had harmed Georgiana.

Eleanor's hands trembled slightly as she reached slowly forward and pointed to the third figure on the drawing, the one in the water with Georgiana, the one Brìghde had called "the man."

"And who is this, Brìghde? Who is 'the man' who took away Juliana's doll?"

Brìghde looked up at Eleanor and said quite matter-of-factly, "Why, he's the ghillie, my lady. The laird's ghillie. He's the one who gave Juliana's doll to the sea."

Fergus.

Eleanor felt as if someone had just pushed her back, stolen her breath. Her eyes fixed upon the painting, studying it to every detail, taking in the scene depicted there. And then suddenly, it all made perfect sense.

It had been Fergus all along.

It had been Fergus who had put the hemlock on her dish on St. Michaelmas Eve, as a warning perhaps to Juliana to continue her silence.

It had been Fergus who had set the fire in the schoolroom when he had seen the scene Juliana was drawing that day, something he had forbidden her to speak.

And it had been Fergus who had killed Georgiana, drowning her in the sea while Juliana watched on from the shore, and then menacing her never to speak of it to another.

It had been Fergus who had stolen Juliana's voice.

But why?

Eleanor got up from the settee and looked to the hallway

outside the door. "Girls, I want you to stay here. I am going to take your picture and put it someplace safe so that we can show it to Lord Dunevin when he gets home. It is so pretty, I know he will want to see it."

Eleanor took the drawing, its paint still damp, and headed from the room, closing the door softly behind her. She glanced about the hallway but saw that no one else was nearby. She hadn't seen Fergus all morning and she wondered if he had perhaps gone with Gabriel in the carriage to help with the trunks. Eleanor quickly retreated to the kitchen.

There she found the housekeeper.

"Mrs. Wickett, have you seen Fergus this morning?"

The woman shook her head over a list of the packing she was going over. "No, my lady, I've not since him supper last night."

Eleanor nodded and thanked her before turning to leave. Her heart was beating so rapidly in her chest, she had to take deep breaths to steady herself. All she could think about at the moment was finding Gabriel.

She heard a door close at the front of the house then, and clutching the girls' drawing, she hastened toward it.

But the hall was dark, vacant when she got there and she noticed that the door to the parlor where she'd left the girls was now ajar. She reasoned that Gabriel must have gone in there looking for her.

She headed for the door. "Gabriel, I—"

But he wasn't there. Instead, Juliana and Brìghde stood in the middle of the room, both peering at her in question.

Eleanor walked into the room. "Girls, did Lord Dunevin just come home? I thought I heard a door."

"Aye, you did hear a door, leddy," came a voice from behind her then. "But it weren't the laird. 'Twas me."

Eleanor turned just as Fergus stepped from behind the shadowed cover of the door. She felt an immediate shiver run over her and realized she still held the drawing in her hand.

Fergus realized it, too.

Eleanor moved instinctively between him and the girls.

"I can see from tha' picture and the look in yer eye that you have ferreted out the truth." He scowled at Juliana. "I tol' the miss she must keep her trap shut else her da would be taken to the sea with her ma."

Eleanor lifted her chin as he all but confirmed what she'd begun to believe about him. "And she did, so frightened, she couldn't even speak at all." Eleanor stepped a bit more between them. "How dare you do that?" she said, her voice quavering with emotion. "How dare you terrorize a child like that all this time, filling her with such terrible fear?"

The man smirked unpleasantly beneath his grizzled beard. "It were a fine clever plan, it were, and it was workin' just fine until *you* came along, askin' all those questions, stickin' your nose in, tryin' so hard to refute my family's curse."

"*Your* family?"

Fergus nodded his head, seemingly proud. "Aye. Did ye no' know I were a Maclean on my mother's side?" His narrow eyes glinted at her. "'Twas my own grandey who told me all about our ancestor witch's curse against the ancient MacFeagh."

Eleanor felt her stomach roil. The man was actually bragging about being a murderer.

"But why, Fergus? Why would you do such terrible things? Gabriel has always treated you kindly, like a member of his own family."

"Family? *Pah!*" Fergus curled his lip in disdain. "I was ne'er more than the ghillie sent off to do this and do tha'. We Macleans were ne'er good enough for the MacFeaghs, even way back to the one MacFeagh what got this all started. A Maclean saved his life, she did, and how did he repay her? By refusing her at every turn. He tricked her and abandoned her, but in the end, we were the stronger for we've had St. Columb's enchanted staff all these years, hidden in a place on that isle that even he dinna know of."

...that even he dinna know of.

They were the very words Seamus Maclean had spoken to Eleanor that day she had gone to his cottage in Oban looking for her shoes.

"It is in *Uamh nan Fhalachasan,* isn't it?" she asked. "'The Cave of the Hidden.'"

Fergus's eyes grew wide on his weathered face. "But how did you—?" And then he realized. "Seamus Maclean, that bloody fool. He told you, din't he?"

He spat in disgust. "It winna matter, though, because you will soon join the first Lady Dunevin." He removed a menacing looking knife from the side of his belt. "Two dead wives and two dead lassies. I'm thinkin' 'tis going to be terrible hard for the Devil of Dunevin to explain that away."

Eleanor caught a movement then, out in the hall, and spotted Gabriel's shadowed figure lingering just outside the door, listening to it all. She tried to keep Fergus talking so that Gabriel would realize the truth.

"But why, Fergus? What did the MacFeaghs ever do to you?"

"When the laird's da, Alexander, died, his son, Malcolm, he thought to replace me. Told me I was too old to be a laird's ghillie anymore, that I no longer fit with the new laird of Dunevin. I couldna let him do that. It would have been a disgrace to me and my family, an affront just like that MacFeagh had done all those years before."

"And so you killed him? You killed Malcolm MacFeagh?"

"Aye, 'twas simple. They all thought it were the supper that did him in." He scoffed then. "They forgot about the secret passageway out of the laird's chamber. All it took were a bit of laudanum slipped into his port and one large pillow."

Eleanor could see Gabriel was still listening at the door. She feared Fergus would notice if the girls saw him there and so held out the painting with a flourish. "But why, then, Georgiana? Why did you kill her?"

"Because 'twas she that figured out 'twas me who'd done in the laird's brother when she stumbled upon me going in to that passageway. She was going to tell the laird. I couldna let her do that. I—"

Fergus noticed Juliana then, noticed her peering anxiously toward the door. He turned just as Gabriel rushed forward, tackling the older man and tumbling with him against the settee.

The knife went flying and the two men struggled against each other and Brìghde started screaming, eyes wide as they grappled on the carpet, scattering the paints and papers and furniture everywhere. Eleanor quickly drew the girls away, ushering them out and into the hallway while calling for Mrs. Wickett to summon help.

By the time Eleanor turned back to the door, Gabriel had overpowered the older man and was holding a panting Fergus up by the throat against the wall.

He spat out through a clenched jaw, "I should kill you now for what you've done to my family."

But then Gabriel glanced toward the door and noticed Eleanor and the girls watching him in horror.

The look in Juliana's eyes, the terror, stopped him from seeing his threat through. Instead, he glared at the ghillie. "I will not subject my daughter to any more of your madness. But rest assured you will very soon pay for your deeds."

Gabriel held the man, confining him to a chair tied with a drapery cord, until Mrs. Wickett, no longer staid, but quite flustered with alarm, returned with the magistrate, Mr. Peel, who was accompanied by two menacing Bow Street runners.

It took some time to explain everything to the authorities. Having listened to the details, with Fergus himself now proudly taking responsibility for the crimes, Mr. Peel assured Gabriel that charges would indeed be pressed, an indictment would surely follow. A trial, the magistrate warned, could take some time, as long as a year or more. Gabriel referred the matter to Mr. Pratt, his solicitor, as he was of no mind to remain in London for that long.

They would all leave in the morning, as planned—without Fergus, would be taking up residence in the stone hall of Newgate Prison to await his fate.

EPILOGUE

He's a fule that weds at Yule;
When the corn's to shear, the bairns' to bear.

— SCOTTISH PROVERB

The seven days between the Yule and the New Year are known throughout the Scottish isles as *Nollaig*, a time when no work should be done, when there is much celebrating and gift-giving, a season that is abundant with festivity and cheer.

There was a race on Yule morn to be the first to open the door for he who 'let in the Yule' would be assured of prosperity for the coming year. Each child waited patiently, sure to receive a Yule penny, or *bawbee*, from their elders. Holly and mistletoe hung from every doorway for it was renowned throughout the isles that the faeries took shelter under their leaves and would protect all who displayed the sacred plant.

A company of young men would go from cottage to cottage each night, chanting Christmas and Yuletide songs so that the people of the house would reward them with bread, butter, crowdie and other treats for the chanters to feast on later.

Leading this motley group of carolers this season was Young Donald MacNeill himself, dressed in a bright coat made up of various tartans and topped off by a floppy hat that looked quite comical. To encourage his audience so that they might reward his company of carolers well, he sang quite loud and quite off-key, causing much laughter and bringing the householder to give him a whole basket full of bannocks just so he'd stop.

On the eve of the New Year, a large candle scented with various herbs and spices was lit in the great hall. It had to be tall enough to burn through the night so that it would ensure good luck and prosperity in the new year. Bonfires and torches burned, children recited Hogmanay rhymes. Clouds were studied in the early evening sky, and if the largest and fleeciest lay to the north, it would surely be a year of plenty for man and beast.

It was a time of true rejoicing, and there were so many reasons for them to celebrate. Thus it was the perfect time for a traditional Hebridean wedding.

Not long after their return from London, Juliana had staggered them all when she came down to breakfast early one morning, took her seat at the table, and as if it were any other day, calmly asked for a bit of salt for her porridge.

Gabriel had dropped his coffee cup.

Màiri had said a prayer of thanks to the saints.

Eleanor had simply smiled for she had always believed that the day would come when Juliana would finally have something to say.

That wonderful day had come shortly after the cobbler, Seamus Maclean, having heard the truth behind the loss of Georgiana and Malcolm MacFeagh—that they had been at the hands of his own cousin—had come to Trelay to extend an olive branch to Gabriel after their past years of discord. He had brought with him a lovely new pair of brogues, wedding brogues made of the finest leather and worked with intricate designs. After gifting them to the Eleanor, he had offered to show Gabriel where to find the legendary 'Cave of the Hidden.'

They went together on a brisk afternoon to the far side of the isle, a place that bore the full brunt of the sea where trees did not grow and where nothing could graze. Sheer rocky cliffs and tooth-like sea stacks made up the landscape, and it was there, tucked at the base of one particularly rugged cliffside, they found the opening to the cave. Inside, nestled against the rock wall and wrapped in a tattered and faded cloth of tartan, they finally found the long lost Maca'phi staff that had been stolen so long ago. It was returned to its rightful place in the old wooden trunk in Gabriel's study at the castle, where it would remain protected, never to be removed again.

From that moment on, it was as if the sun had suddenly dawned on a new and glorious day. And indeed it had.

From that day, Juliana laughed, she sang, and she remarked on most everything she saw, and no one ever complained. There were often times when Eleanor would catch Gabriel just staring at his daughter, listening to her as she told him in her lyric voice some story or described something she'd seen with a smile of utter adoration on his face.

Frances and the old duke arrived from London shortly before the Yule, bringing with them a surprise that had Eleanor fairly blubbering with delight. Her dear friend, Amelia B. had come along with them for the wedding, bringing her entire family in tow, husband and two children, and the friends had sat up all through that first night, tucked away by the fire in Gabriel's study, drinking numerous pots of tea and chattering like they had back when they were schoolgirls.

Christian and Grace arrived from Skynegal on the Yule eve, bringing with them the most blessed news of their expected child some time the following summer. The Devonbrooks, Catriona and Robert, sailed in from Rosmorigh with young James, and brought with them, too, Robert's brother, Noah and his wife Augusta, with their infant daughter, 'Gussie,' who had her mother's black hair and keen eyes, and her father's easy temperament.

Hogmanay morn dawned to a dusting of new snow across the heathery hillside below the castle where, despite the weather, Eleanor still insisted they be wed. As she was readying to make the short walk on Christian's arm, to where the guests were already assembled between a scattering of ancient standing stones that overlooked the bay, she heard a knocking on her chamber door. She opened it onto the unexpected arrival of the old duke.

In his hands, he held a small box wrapped in colorful paper and tied off with a silk ribbon.

"My child, they say it is never too late to make amends. Though I treated you, your mother, and your brother ill for far too long, I hope you will accept this as a first token of my deep regret, of a grandfather's affection, and of my hope for your happy future."

Eleanor opened the box to reveal an elegant necklace, a long chain made of finely woven strands of gold. Hanging from it was a rounded pendant carved in gold and colorfully enameled with the Westover crest.

"There is a tiny button," the duke said, pointing to the pendant's side.

Eleanor found the catch, pushed it, which causing the pendant to spring open. Revealed inside she found an elegant filigree *oignon* timepiece. A moment later, the tiny chinging of chime song began to play from the piece, trilling out the tune of one of her favorite Mozart sonatas.

Eleanor had never seen anything like it before. She looked at the duke with wonder-filled eyes and smiled.

"Thank you, sir. So very much. It is truly lovely." She held it out to him. "I wonder, would you help me to put it on?"

He said then, as he hitched the clasp behind her neck. "It was your father's."

Eleanor turned, struck by his words, and he looked at her with nothing but sincerity in his aged eyes.

"Yes, *your* father, Eleanor. Christopher was a great lover of music, and would be so proud of your talent for the flute. I had this piece made into a pendant so you would always have a remembrance of him near. Even though you never knew him, I assure you he was a good man."

"Of course he was," Eleanor said, blinking away tears as she embraced the duke, her grandfather, for the very first time in her life. "I shall cherish this always."

That day, the sun broke through the scattered winter clouds overhead, and showered the gathering with brilliant beaming light as Eleanor and Gabriel vowed their lives to one another, this a second time, on that ancient hillside among the snow and the stones and with their family and friends around them.

As they looked out across the bay afterward, Eleanor swore she spotted the familiar shape of that same small seal who had followed her and Juliana. She smiled to herself, and silently promised Georgiana that she would love and protect her daughter always.

That night, as the revelry in the great hall stretched on well into the early morning hours, no one noticed when the groom quietly spirited his bride away, stealing up a secluded side staircase that only they knew about.

Gabriel had had craftsmen from as far away as Edinburgh working on the restoration of the castle's top floor for the past months now after the fire, and they had finished the new laird and lady's suite just in time for the wedding night.

As they stood outside the newly varnished door, Gabriel drew Eleanor close and kissed her tenderly, this woman who had so changed his world. He gazed at her, losing himself in the warmth of her green eyes. It was then he suddenly remembered the words that had been written by the Jura witch all those years before:

Only one of pure heart and eye will right the wrongs of the past...

He silently thanked whatever enchantment it had been that had brought this woman, this woman of pure heart and eye, into his life.

"Grace tells me I must carry you over the threshold, or risk dire consequences."

Eleanor was nibbling at his ear, anxious to be alone with him. "Then by all means, my lord, you must."

Gabriel swept her up and into his arms, taking her in a deep and passionate kiss that sent tingles to her toes and made her head giddy with delight.

He kept on kissing her as he nudged the door to open and crossed the room.

He didn't take his mouth from hers until he had laid her on the bed, atop a freshly stuffed goosedown mattress, on their new bed, in their new marriage suite at the very top of the castle.

It took Eleanor but a moment before she suddenly realized...

And when she did, her eyes lit with delight.

"Gabriel! Is this...it cannot be...but it is. It's Mr. Gray's Incredible Bed!"

The four fat carved posters stood like walnut tree trunks surrounding her. Overhead, the intricately carved canopy was draped in newly-woven tartan draperies.

She looked at him, clearly astonished. "However did you—?"

Gabriel grinned. "Oh, it took some doing and a great deal of persistence and persuasion, but in the end, I finally managed to convince our chatty innkeeper friend that we simply could not have our children born in any other bed but this one."

"Oh, Gabriel!" Eleanor threw her arms around him and kissed him all across his face, his neck, his ears. "Thank you! It is the finest wedding present a bride could ever receive."

He added, "I had to promise him and Mrs. Gray that they

could come to Trelay to visit in the summer." He grinned. "Ah, but there is one thing we must see to before we can ever think of having our children in this monstrosity of a thing." He gave her a look then that absolutely curled her toes.

Eleanor beamed, already knowing what he would say. "Oh, and what would that be, husband?"

Gabriel didn't even bother to answer her. Instead, he loosened his marriage cravat, pulled it from his neck, and tossed it to the floor, then joined her on the bed. Then Gabriel drew Eleanor close against him, touching his mouth to hers in a kiss that promised how he would spend the next few hours showing her instead.

AUTHOR'S NOTE

Dear Reader:

I hope you have enjoyed your visit with Gabriel and Eleanor, as well as friends from the previous books in this series as we ventured to the misty western isles of Scotland. Though the isle of Trelay doesn't truly exist, I did base it largely on the two small islands of Colonsay and Oronsay, which lie off the Argyllshire coast, near to the seaside town of Oban, where Gabriel and Eleanor sailed in the earlier chapters of this story.

The castle of Dunevin is also from my imagination, although I did model it on various Highland fortresses I've visited, including Duart Castle on the isle of Mull, and Castle Stalker on Loch Laich in Argyllshire, both tower houses and both very near to where the story of *White Mist* is set.

Clan MacFie is the most common spelling for one of the oldest of the Scottish clans, so ancient, in fact, that its early history is unwritten. It is claimed by some that the clan did spring from either a faerie woman, or a seal woman—a selkie— but it is generally believed that the earliest members of this tribe of dark-haired ancient Scots were the original inhabitants of

Colonsay, which they held until they were dispossessed of it in the seventeenth century.

After that time, the MacFies fell the way of other broken and dispossessed clans, following some of the other, larger clans to the nearby coast and larger isles.

The magic colour staff of the clan that is mentioned in the story is indeed a true legend of the MacFie clan, and was believed to have protected them for hundreds of years before it mysteriously disappeared around the same time the MacFies lost their ruling place over their windswept island. It has never been seen since, but its image is depicted upon several of the carved Celtic tombstones of long-ago MacFie chiefs that can be seen to this day at the sanctuary on the isle of Oronsay, founded, they say, by Saint Columba.

If you have ever visited the Isles and Highlands of Scotland, you must know it is truly a place of mist and magic. The ancient Gaelic language still lingers throughout the isles, and in more recent date, it has even enjoyed a resurgence. History itself whispers across the heathery hillsides like the legendary skirl of the bagpipes, and in some places, you can almost begin to believe time has stood still for hundreds of years.

And, finally, about Mr. Grey's Incredible Bed...

I admit to borrowing this unique piece of history from a story I once read that detailed a large and ornately carved bed that had spent many years in the honeymoon suite of a hotel, only to be retired and discarded to a parking lot. Luckily, a canny-eyed antiques dealer spotted it, and rescued it, only to discover on a hunch, after nine years of careful research that included DNA analysis of the wood and its varnishes, that it is very likely the marriage bed of Henry VII and his wife Elizabeth of York—dating back to the 15th century! I could think of no better place for Gabriel and Eleanor's future children to come into the world, and thought it a much better fate than to be discarded in a carpark.

All my best, J.R.

ABOUT THE AUTHOR

Jaclyn Reding's award-winning, bestselling historical and contemporary romance novels have been translated into nearly a dozen languages. A National Readers' Choice Awards finalist, and Romance Writers of America RITA Award nominee, she is the proud, proud mom of two grown sons, and willing minion to an elderly cairn terrier and a tuxedo cat. Home is with her family in New England, in an antique farmhouse that she suspects is held together purely by old wallpaper and cobwebs. A lifelong equestrian, she spends her free time in the saddle, going over plotlines and character arcs with her confidant and toughest critic, a very opinionated retired racehorse named Brunello.

For more information, visit
www.jaclynreding.com

ALSO BY JACLYN REDING

Daughters of the Duke

The Pretender

The Adventurer

Regency Rakes

White Heather

White Magic

White Knight

White Mist

Coming Soon

The Secret Gift

The Second Chance

Spellstruck

Tempting Fate

Chasing Dreams

Stealing Heaven

Deception's Bride

Milton Keynes UK
Ingram Content Group UK Ltd.
UKHW042256170324
439575UK00004B/265